Kitty Kitty

ALSO BY MICHELE JAFFE

Bad Kitty

Bad Kitty, Volume 1: Catnipped

MICHELE JAFFE

Kitty Kitty

HARPERTEEN
AN IMPRINT OF HARPERCOLLINS*PUBLISHERS*

HarperTeen is an imprint of HarperCollins Publishers.

Kitty Kitty
Copyright © 2008 by Michele Jaffe
All rights reserved. Printed in the United States of America.
No part of this book may be used or reproduced in any manner whatso-
ever without written permission except in the case of brief quotations
embodied in critical articles and reviews. For information address
HarperCollins Children's Books, a division of HarperCollins Publishers,
1350 Avenue of the Americas, New York, NY 10019.
www.harperteen.com

Library of Congress Cataloging-in-Publication Data
Jaffe, Michele.
    Kitty kitty / Michele Jaffe. — 1st ed.
        p.   cm.
    Summary: When seventeen-year-old Jasmine Callihan is whisked off for
an extended visit to Venice, Italy, at the start of her senior year, she tries
her best to stay out of trouble but gets caught up in trying to solve a murder mystery.
    ISBN 978-0-06-078111-8 (trade bdg.)
    ISBN 978-0-06-078114-9 (lib. bdg.)
    [1. Murder—Fiction. 2. Foreign study—Fiction. 3. Fathers and
daughters—Fiction. 4. Racially mixed people—Fiction. 5. Venice
(Italy)—Fiction. 6. Italy—Fiction. 7. Humorous stories. 8. Mystery and
detective stories.] I. Title.
PZ7.J15342Kit 2008   2008000756
[Fic]—dc22   CIP
                                                                     AC

Typography by Andrea Vandergrift
1 2 3 4 5 6 7 8 9 10
❖
First Edition

—— ❧ ——

For Jennifer Sturman,
who is totally twenty-four karat

Dearest (in mostly alphabetical order) Meg Cabot, Holly Edmonds, Susan Ginsburg, Dan Goldner, Sarah Hughes, Elise Howard, Jennifer Langham, Amanda Maciel, Abby McAden, Laura Rosenbury, Jennifer Sturman, Josie & Sebastian Sturman, Eric Wight, Gelateria Nico, Gelateria al Sole, Harry's Dolci, Pizzeria Ae Oche, Bar Bonifacio, Narwhals, Betsey Johnson, Agent Provocateur, Chocolate croissants, Cupcakes, Tacos, Pizza, Caffè latte,

I send you gigathanks from 1 Gratitude Villas, Thanksylvania, Planet of Seriously-I-Could-Not-Have-Done-This-Without-You in the galaxy IOU1.

Airkisses,
Michele

Kitty Kitty

To: Jasmine Callihan <Jasmine.Callihan@westborough.edu>
From: Office of the College Counselor
<James.Lansdowne@westborough.edu>
Subject: RE: Senior Questionnaire
Date: September 8

Dear Miss Callihan,

Thank you for your thoughtful wishes on the beginning of the school year. Although we miss having you here in person, I hope you are enjoying your time in Venice. I remember having tea at the Grissini Palace Hotel with my grandmother when I was just a boy and thinking it was a lovely spot. What an enviable place to call home.

I've thought very seriously about what you said, and no, I do not think it would be better if the Senior Questionnaire asked "How do you imagine your tombstone?" rather than "Where do you see yourself in five years?" Nor do I think you need to worry; I am quite sure that when the time comes, yours will have more to say than "Here lies Jas. She did what she could with her hair."

Most sincerely,
Dr. James Lansdowne
College Counselor
Westborough School for Girls
Los Angeles, CA

To: Jasmine Callihan <Jasmine.Callihan@westborough.edu>
From: Office of the College Counselor
<James.Lansdowne@westborough.edu>
Subject: RE: RE: RE: Senior Questionnaire
Date: September 15

Dear Miss Callihan,

Thank you for asking after my grandmother. She is, in fact, still living but I doubt she is considering a trip to Venice. If she is, I will be sure to warn her that the Grissini Palace Hotel is now "more like a tree than a hotel because it is filled with nuts."

I am sorry that you found our list of Potential Work Environments on the Senior Questionnaire so limiting. Frankly it had not occurred to any of the faculty that we could be alienating a "sizable chunk of our students" by not including "Big Top" and "wherever taxidermists work" on that list.

Thank you for bringing that to our attention.

Sincerely,
Dr. James Lansdowne
College Counselor
Westborough School for Girls
Los Angeles, CA

To: Jasmine Callihan <Jasmine.Callihan@westborough.edu>
From: Office of the College Counselor
<James.Lansdowne@westborough.edu>
Subject: RE: RE: RE: RE: RE: RE: RE: Senior Questionnaire
Date: September 30

Miss Callihan,

Thank you for your suggestion that I call you Jasmine. As you know, it is school policy that all students be referred to by their last names.

While I see that it does strictly conform to the essay topic "Challenges I Have Faced," I am not convinced that writing your college essay in the form of a screenplay entitled *Dadzilla vs. Jas: Bloodfeud! Forever!* strikes exactly the right note. Along the same lines, while explaining that you suspect insanity runs in your family does fall into the "challenge" category, I'm not positive that is something you want to highlight for a college admissions committee.

Yours,
Dr. L

P.S. I am unclear on what you are getting at when you say "Also would time spent in a foreign jail count as an extracurricular activity?" Please elaborate.

To: Jasmine Callihan <Jasmine.Callihan@westborough.edu>
From: Office of the College Counselor
<James.Lansdowne@westborough.edu>
Subject: RE: RE: RE: RE: RE: RE: RE: RE: RE: Senior Questionnaire
Date: October 4

Jasmine—

My weekend is going very well, thanks for asking.

Look, you really have nothing to worry about. Although you feel that you are "slightly dead inside," I am positive that you can write a dynamite essay. You just need to find the right topic. What about some of your Little Life Lessons? You are still keeping up with those, aren't you? You should have added at least sixty-five new ones since you've been gone. Some of the girls have shared theirs with me and they are very provocative. If you'd like to send me some of yours, we can discuss how to go about turning them into an essay. The advice that writers always give is to write what you know. I'm sure if you just put your mind to it and build on an episode or episodes from your real life, you will come up with something outstanding.

Best,
JL

To: Jasmine Callihan <Jasmine.Callihan@westborough.edu>
From: Mary Pease <Mary.Pease@westborough.edu>
Subject: Thank you
Date: October 9

Hi, Jasmine!

It's me, Mary, Dr. Lansdowne's assistant. I just wanted to tell you how much we've all enjoyed your fake college essays. The entire teacher's lounge was in stitches when we read "How Not to Steal a Limo" and "I Met Death in Las Vegas and He Was Wearing a Speedo (and a Turquoise Mesh Shirt)." What an imagination you must have to make all that up! Thanks for the great laughs and good luck with your real essay.

Mary

Chapter One

My best friend, Polly, thinks that people should come with warning labels, like mattresses. If they did, mine would be CRIME SCENE DO NOT CROSS.

Or at least it would have been, once. But not anymore. Not since Jas's European Exile started. For the past six weeks, nothing had happened to me.

Even the horoscope I found while skimming the newspaper to do my current events assignment for Italian class, on the Saturday morning this all started, said:

> "The Gobi Desert is one of the most inhospitable places in the world, and your sign is likewise right now. You feel battered by storms outside your control and beleaguered by a drought of change. Rest, meditate, and conserve your strength until this dry period passes. Any attempt to alter its course could have grave consequences."

Yes. As though having to go to class on Saturday was not bad enough, my horoscope compared my life to the Gobi Desert. And said there was nothing I could do about it. Horrorscope was more like it.

As the full meaning of its words sank in, I realized I had two choices. I could either continue to soldier on, dead inside but wearing the mask while the fates Riverdanced over my whole life's happiness. Or I could take action. Because as far as my eyes could see, there were no Graver Consequences than sitting around as my life ebbed from me a little more every day. My friends, my boyfriend, my whole world was 4,000 miles away, going on without me. If that horoscope told me nothing else, it was that things could not get any worse. (Yes, Fates, I hear you laughing. I know, I'm so, so funny.)

I'd been waiting patiently, but the time for patient waiting was over. It would have been jolly to email a friend for some moral support, but it was 11:00 on Friday night in Los Angeles and all my friends would probably be out doing something really fun. Without me. Plus, ever since my dad saw the bill for the day I spent fourteen hours hitting the GET MAIL button on my email screen praying to see Jack's name pop into my inbox, I wasn't supposed to go online from my room. As was always the way these days, I had to be an Army of One.

I took a big breath and marched next door to my father and Sherri!'s room at the Grissini Palace Hotel (& Insanity

Emporium), full of brave purpose, and knocked. But all the Brave Purpose in the world could not have steeled me against what I faced when the door opened.

My father was standing in the middle of the sitting area wearing a shiny yellow shirt and shiny black bike shorts with yellow piping.

To express the complete dreadfulness of it, you've got to understand that for the entire seventeen years of my life, my father has exclusively worn safari suits. Some people have a signature color, like my superchic friend Polly (pink). Or a signature scent, like my demon cousin the Evil Hench Mistress, Alyson (Bubble Yum). My father had a signature look. That of an explorer of the African out-back.

If there is such a thing as the African outback.

True, he let me iron the sleeves on the safari jacket he wore for his wedding to my stepmother, Sherri!. And while we were in Las Vegas, he nightmarishly substituted khaki shorts for the long pants. But fundamentally, there was always a Ready for Safari feel to his look.

No longer. Unless they'd started holding safaris during the Tour de France.

I would not be lying even a little if I said that I would have taken the Nightmare on Khaki Street ensemble over what I saw before me. Because what I saw before me wasn't just a code red toxic fashion disaster. It was another sign of what I had been trying to deny. My father and his mind had split ways.

I know, I should have seen it earlier. The writing was on the wall forty-four days before, when the happy Isle of Jas (population: me) had been brutally destroyed by the dread beast Dadzilla.

What? You have not heard of Dadzilla? Allow me to introduce you:

Behold!
I am Dadzilla, the
frightening & super evil
monster with big WWWWW
fangs for crunching up the
cherished dreams
of young girls like
my daughter, Jasmine.
Whose are my most favorite and extra
good, washed down with a sip of
her teensy-tiny tears of girlish dismay.
(Tears of dismay are quite delicious.)
I   know multiple sly tricks to coax forth
the   small sweet tears, such as: The Why Not
Ruin Jas's Life one, which, after years of hard toil,
I have finally perfected. BWAHAHAHAHAHA!

Whatever can this mean? Ruin Jas's life? Perfected? I will present Dadzilla's action plan in a single easy-to-read chart:

FRIDAY BEFORE MY SENIOR YEAR OF HIGH SCHOOL STARTS:	Learn that the guy of my dreams, who is a rock star and taller than me (Jack!!!), dreams of me too.
SATURDAY BEFORE SCHOOL STARTS:	More learning about that, plus KISSING!
SUNDAY BEFORE SCHOOL STARTS:	Father announces we are moving to Venice, Italy. In twenty-four hours.

"And pack something warm," Dadzilla adds. "I don't know when we are coming back."

Naturally, I asked what any normal-thinking person would ask: "Are you speaking in code?"

To which he replied: "Why is everything a joke to you, Jasmine?"

A joke. Of course. Because, which is more likely? That a father would pull his daughter out of her respectable high school the day before her senior year was starting, thus guaranteeing that the only college she'll be able to get into is one with "——& Beauty School" in the name? Or that a father is speaking in code because the FBI has the house bugged?

That's right. Someone was suffering from Acute Crazy in the room, but it wasn't me.

I tried to plead with him, but that just made it worse. Not for Dadzilla the quaint arguments of reason and logic. My saying "But I can't drop out of high school" was like a peanut-butter-and-cracker snack pack to him, just making him thirsty for more.

"Nonsense," Dadzilla replied, gnashing his fangs. "You are not dropping out of school. You will just do your work from Italy. Six hours of Italian instruction a day, and for the rest of your classes, it will be like you are being homeschooled."

I was just about to point out that it seemed to me one crucial part of being homeschooled was being AT HOME, when Sherri! came in.

Sherri! is the very best stepmother in the world, and I am not saying that just because her superpower is to be unhateable. For one thing, she is the only person I know who exclusively writes in glitter pen and dots her i's with a heart (or butterfly, depending on her mood). It is also super fun to go shopping with her because she is always being mistaken for the movie stars she body-doubles for (last year, Sherri! won the Golden Breast, Thigh, AND Hand awards for her excellent work, and this year she is up for the Golden Ankle as well).

But more than any of that, or her quiet brilliance at the management of my father, I love her because she's a beacon of hope in my sad world. The fact that—despite being young and gorgeous and able to attract any male of any species in our solar system—she genuinely loves and wants to be with my father shows that we Callihans must have some special superpower that bewitches mates of whom we are completely unworthy. Since this is the only explanation apart from intense mental illness that I could come up with for why my boyfriend, Jack, might like me at all (and say that he wanted to be my boyfriend even though he was the hottest man on the planet and I was, well, me; and moving halfway around the world; and we'd only had two real dates, during which I'd been grounded, so they took place at my house), it was reassuring to see the phenomenon at work in my father and Sherri!'s case.

Also, of all the women my father dated after my mom died when I was six, Sherri! was the only one who talked to me like I was an equal. Which I guess isn't that surprising since she is only eight years older than I am (yes! And with my dad! Callihan Super Attractor Beam is so strong), but it is still notable and has earned her a special plaque-with-silver-flower-holder attached in my Most Favorite People Hall of Fame.

So when she came into my room after my father's life-shattering announcement, I was relieved. Yes, my father had lost his few remaining marbles, but here was Sherri! to help me look through the couch cushions and find them. Perhaps if we acted quickly, Dadzilla could be quelled and returned to his less terrifying supervillain persona, the Thwarter, where he merely tried to thwart my girlish dreams, not snack on them.

Then Sherri! said, "Isn't it thrilling, Jas? I've always wanted to visit Venice and now we're going to live there! And Cedric is going to write the definitive book on the history of soap."

She calls my father "Cedric," I suppose because that is his name, but really that should have been enough to make her run away screaming from the beginning. I had bigger things to think about, though.

"Soap?" I repeated as hope died within me. "Did you say *soap*?"

"Soap," my father confirmed. "Don't pretend I never told you."

Which was an easy command to follow because there was no pretending required. I was one hundred percent sure + shipping & handling that he had never mentioned this burning passion for soap to me. Still, that didn't mean he wasn't in its grip. In addition to being a professor of anthropology, my father is a certified genius, and geniuses are not like normal people. He'd done this whole uproot-our-lives-in-the-pursuit-of-knowledge thing before, four years earlier, so it was possible that soap really was the reason my life and my heart were ripped from me and we were moving to Venice.

But not, I suspected, the whole reason. Because later that night I'd overheard (by accident! I just happened to be leaning out the window at the time!) him saying "I have to be sure

Jas is safe, and I can't do that with her running around Los Angeles." Leading me to conclude that perhaps some part of our fleeing LA like mobsters on the lam had to do with the teensy adventure I'd had in Las Vegas. The one featuring that whole almost-getting-killed thing.

Which, I would like to note in passing, had not been my fault AT ALL. And the police departments of two states had THANKED me. And also, I had not ended up getting killed. But the idea that Vegas might have partially motivated our Venetian holiday did give me an idea: If we had moved because I had gotten into a microdot of trouble, then, by the inverse property, if I showed I could stay out of trouble, we could move back.

Simple, elegant. Practically a mathematical proof is what that solution was.

Okay, yes, I am aware that from time to time in the past I'd been the kind of girl that Trouble hung around seedy cafés waiting for. And that my cousin, the Evil Hench Mistress Alyson, referred to me not without reason as Calamity Callihan. But that was Ye Olde Dayes Jas, a Jas so distant from my new form it was practically the stuff of legends, like unicorns and wereponies. From that moment on, I vowed, I would be Innocent Bystander Jas. The Model Daughter that they modeled Model Daughter porcelain figurines on.

And I knew just how to make myself invisible to Trouble because I knew what had gotten me tangled with Trouble in Vegas. It was all because of my supposed superpower.

Not for me the couture superpower Polly has of being able to outdress anyone and identify every garment, accessory, and nail polish color by designer and season; or Roxy's useful superpower to be able to build things, like the working satellite she once made out of a lemon and a piece of string (as well as her ability to pick anyone's pocket without them knowing it); or Tom's superpower to be the nicest guy in the world and also imitate anyone's voice perfectly; or my boyfriend Jack's superpower to disable people with his Super Smile. Or even Evil Hench Alyson's to turn people into a piece of gum–slash–toilet paper she scraped off her shoe with just one look (or at least make *me* feel like she has). No, none of those groovy powers were mine. My superpower?

Attractive to cats.

Yes. And although this might sound nice (Cats! Furry and cute! Fun!), it's actually a curse. But what it meant was that if there was one single thing I needed to do to avoid Trouble's tractor beam in Venice, it was avoid cats. How hard could that be?

Not hard! So easy! It's not like you run into cats all the time just randomly!

Except in Venice. Or, as I believe it should more accurately be called: The Lost Continent of Kittyopolis. Not only are there more cats in the streets of Venice than anywhere else I'd ever been, but the symbol of the city for, oh, the past nine hundred and three years, has been a winged cat. (Okay, a winged lion. But still.) So if you had been working to erect a Jas-Not-in-Trouble Slalom Course, Venice would be it.

(And that doesn't take into account the fact that the city pretty much oozes Mystery and Wonder which are like mind-altering Slurpees for a girl like me.)

Despite the fact that Venice was like a pitfall party just for me, and I was a broken girl who spent her time walking around with a hole in her chest where her heart should have been, I had surmounted these challenges and managed to steer clear of Trouble and his best friend, Lurking Menace, for six weeks. Having a million hours of Italian classes and all that nice away-from-home-schooling to do helped. I also worked to explore the non-cat beauties of the city. There are things in Venice that would cause people with weak constitutions to pass out and die on the street from beauty overload. Such as the slab of chocolate-hazelnut ice cream, which comes topped with whipped cream, a paper flag, a mylar pom-pom, and a cookie.

Yes. Mylar pom-pom AND cookie.

I know.

And, of course, any remaining free time could be filled by conjuring up images of all the supercute and nice and be-boobed and normal-haired and intensely fascinating girls my UNBELIEVABLY HOT boyfriend was meeting while I was away.

Despite all this Fun-n-Beauty, some part of me could not shake that conventional desire to graduate from high school and attend an institution of higher learning. Even Model

Daughters are allowed to dream, and it was this dream that had carried me to my father's room that morning. Specifically, the dream of being allowed to join my pals in San Francisco for their tour of West Coast colleges, which was happening the next week, and which my father had said he'd "take under consideration."

Here is how dedicated I was to my dream: Instead of screaming in agony and calling the emergency service to come perform an eye-ectomy on me when I saw my father in his bike shorts, I whispered, "Brave Purpose," to myself and said, "Why hello, Lance Armstrong. Have you seen my father anywhere? I have a question for him."

Yes, the high road was what I was taking.

BikeShort Dadzilla said, "What are you talking about? Who is Lance Armstrong?" Which is the kind of thing only a certified genius can get away with saying without being locked up as a certified lunatic. For good measure he added, "If that was a reference to my outfit, I am wearing this because I don't want to go bald."

"Ah," I said, because one should not provoke the insane. "Of course."

Sherri! joined us then, wearing, I am pained to say, a matching black-and-yellow bike outfit. (Although, unlike Somepeoplezilla, she looked fantastic in it.) I guess the whole bald thing left me looking a bit puzzled because she said, "Cedric and I ran into a colleague of his—"

"Norris is a chemist, not a colleague," my father interrupted her to say, further showing off his genius grasp of conversational mores.

"A chemist," Sherri! resumed, "who had a heart attack last year and lost all his hair, which for some reason launched your father on a health kick. Norris said he lost thirty pounds like that"—she snapped—"taking spin classes here in Venice, so we're going to start too."

I am sure I was about to say something extremely witty and clever, but Dadzilla chose that moment to turn around.

If her father in bike shorts is something a girl should never ever have to see, him in them from the back is that times a hundred million. Especially if they happen to have the words SIR LIGHTNING emblazoned across the rear in bright yellow. And double especially if he then does a deep knee bend and says, "I quite like these shorts, Sher. I may start wearing them all the time."

Which is the answer to the question: Which one of the Four Sentences of the Apocalypse is guaranteed to bring on the End Times?

In case anyone ever asks you.

Unaware that he was leading the charge toward Armageddon, Dadzilla was full of sprightliness. From the middle of some kind of stretching exercise, he growled, "What is wrong with you, Jasmine? Are you sick? You're making a face."

By averting my gaze I was able to regain the use of language. "Why, Father, nothing is wrong," I said. "I am not making a face. I am just pleasantly surprised to see you looking so—"

I broke off there, and not only because I had no idea what word could possibly come next. I did it because in the process of Gaze Averting, I'd spotted something reflected in the mirror on the top of Dadzilla's dresser. Something incredible.

I'd only got a quick glance because I didn't want to be obvious, but a glance was enough. Because what I'd seen was a printout with the logo of a travel agency on the top, the name CALLIHAN below it, and below that, a list of flights between Venice and London and somewhere in California. What else could that mean than that he was going to let me go and meet my pals in San Francisco? As a surprise! The best surprise in the entire world!

To say that my heart soared inside me like a super-bionic butterfly would be saying too little. I'd been reading Charles Dickens novels where the heroines are kind to their dear sweet papas, and I felt like one of those girls now, all clingy and brimming with wide-eyed tenderness. In my mind I pictured myself with bouncing curls and tiny bows in my hair and tattered but well-mended pantaloons.

"What did you come to ask me?" Dadzilla demanded then, and not exactly in a tone that a Dickens father would use.

But at that point nothing could dampen my mood.

I laughed sweetly, in the Dickens manner, and said, "Oh, it was nothing, Papa. I just wanted to ask you if there were any little favors I could do for you while I was out today."

The "Papa" might have been a bit much because he narrowed his eyes and said, "What is wrong with you, Jasmine?"

"Can't a daughter be kind to her precious parent?"

"Not if that daughter is you."

"How *molto* amusing you are! I would love to stay and expose myself to more of your wit, wisdom, and sporty style, but I must go be enriched by the Italian language in the classes you kindly arranged for me. You have a nice spin class, and be careful. I wouldn't want anything to happen to you."

He peered at me with his Everywhere Eye for a moment, but my conscience was as clear as 7UP and he found nothing. Finally he said, "Stay out of trouble and we'll see you tonight for dinner. And don't think you'll get out of it by having room service in your room, because you won't. I want to talk to you."

If I'd needed confirmation, I'd just gotten it. Dinner + talk = SURPRISE. More math! "Of course," I cooed, shaking my curls. "It will be a delight to share a simple meal with you."

I hightailed it back to my room, and, once the door was closed, did a very special dance for joy. Not only would I get to go to San Francisco with my pals, but Jack had said that if I made it back for the college trip he'd fly in from Los Angeles for a day or two to see me. San Francisco was like around the corner from him! He could come just for lunch! Where lunch means kissing! And dessert! Where dessert means ice cream! And also kissing!

It was like a bonbon–and–Tater Tot dream, and all I had to do to make it come true was stay out of trouble until dinnertime. Which was nothing compared to all the staying out of trouble I'd done for the past six weeks. Just to be on the safe side I put my lucky Cookie Monster Underoos on over my Wonderbra, and quickly scrolled through the outfits Polly had organized and cataloged on my computer for me to find the one that looked the most suitable for Mayor of Mind-My-Own-Business Island.

As I reached the door to leave, I saw my horoscope sitting on the desk. The Gobi Desert! Grave consequences! Ha ha! How could I have believed for a second something sandwiched between an article about two robbers who dressed as nuns, an open letter from chief of police C. Manzoni about the rubbish problem, and an advertisement for a wig store? What a silly girl I was. With a carefree flourish, I crumpled it up and tossed it in the trash.

Which was unfortunate because as I did that, I threw away the crucial clue I'd need to save at least three lives. One of them my own.

Chapter Two

Of course, I didn't know that. Instead I went prancing off to Italian class, basically to my doom, like a six-foot-tall prancing thing.

It was, as the natives would say, a *bellissimo* morning with the sun sparkling on the water of the canals, and the gondoliers shouting cheerily to one another, and the birds doing little bird dances in the sky, and there was a general feeling of *la dolce vita*. In fact, I was in such a carefree letting-my-hair-down mood I was inspired to compose casual poetry.

I am glad Trouble
is not ice cream because then
I could not have any.

Everyone I passed on my way to the Francesco Petrarca Instituto per le Lingue (or, as I liked to call it, Frank's L'il

Language School) seemed like they were in a *dolce vita* frame of mind too. As I went over the first bridge, I exchanged *ciao ciao*s with the woman from the gelateria I stopped at on Wednesdays, and the tall man with the Great Dane from the pizza restaurant.

When we first got to Venice I thought people just recognized me and said hello out of pity, given that it was pretty clear I was not Venetian. For example, the average Venetian girl is short, cream-colored, and boobed, with hair whose T-shirt slogan would be something like "Ask Me About Being Cute!" (if hair wore T-shirts), while the average Jas is tall, cappuccino-colored, and non-boobed, with hair that would be more appropriately dressed in an "Ask Me About Your Missing Puppy" tee.

But I realized the inhabitants of Venice were just very civilized. Los Angeles people never say hello on the street unless they are planning to make you the star of a crime scene photo. In Venice, even if you only know someone a little, like if you sat next to them once at the gym when Sherri! made you go to "Lo Rubber Fun Workout Relax," and your rubber band suddenly got a mind of its own and flew out of your hand and hit them in the eye and they had to wear an eye patch for two weeks, they say hello to you. Just to make up a random example.

Anyway, "without a care in the world" is likely how any of the people I strolled by (except the woman with the eye patch because she sort of veered away from me quickly and probably didn't get a complete look) would have described my general air of joy-to-all-creatures-great-and-small-ness, and they would have been right. Although my father had brutally ripped me from the bosom of my bosom pals and the lips of my liptastic boyfriend; and brought me to live in a taco-free country where most of the medication was administered using the Up-the-Butt method; and where there was a prime-time program called *Naked News* where the news anchors were indeed naked, which is not something to show to an impressionable teen girl whose boyfriend is both incredibly hot and incredibly far away; despite all of these travails, I was not bitter. If I had been any more full of the milk of human kindness, I would have been a cow.

That feeling kept up as I arrived at Frank's, and even increased when I saw the name card ARABELLA RANDOLPH in front of the seat next to mine. Arabella was my Italian-Class Friend, one of those people you chat with casually in a certain setting but never see otherwise. She was also my only friend in Venice, and she'd been absent all week and I'd totally missed her. We'd initially bonded over our fascination with our teacher, Professore Rossi. Not a crushlike fascination, although Professore Rossi was in his early twenties and not bad-looking. It was more of an "Um, did he really say what I think he said?" kind of thing that was half the result of him speaking in Italian and half the result of him saying things that were slightly unexpected.

Like, Professore Rossi objected to the fact that if you just went by our textbook, you'd think that everyone in Italy was either a butcher, a train conductor, or an aunt. This, he felt, was not representative of the *diversità e ricchezza* (diversity and richness) of the Italian people. He wanted to show us a more accurate picture, so he generously spent his OWN personal free time (emphasis *his*) making up dialogues for us to practice on, such as this one:

RESEARCHER 1: The smaller monkey would be better for this experiment.

RESEARCHER 2: How can you be sure it is properly sedated?

RESEARCHER 1: We will use an injection.

Yes! Because the only thing that might both exemplify diversity and richness AND come in more handy during a trip to Italy than being able to discourse about when Paolo and Francesca did/will/might arrive on the train from Bologna, is being able to direct experiments on lab animals.

You can see why I had to supplement my Italian course work by dedicatedly watching *Il Commissario Rex*, a television show about a German shepherd who works as a police detective, and episodes of *CHiPs* translated into Italian.

(Neither of which, apparently, should be recorded as an

Independent Study Project on my college applications, despite the fact that they clearly reveal the "healthy go-getter attitude" that Dr. Lansdowne says should be represented in that space.)

(Little Life Lesson 1: Life is filled with Deep Mysteries.)

Obviously even the most up-to-date model of Model Daughters would be intrigued by the personal life of someone who thought that monkey sedation was an exemplary discussion topic, so Arabella and I spent most of class passing notes that speculated about how Professor Rossi spent his free time.

As soon as I put out my name card, Arabella slid a note over to me.

Professore seems to be in le totally good mood.

One of the reasons I liked Arabella so much was because she believed that if she took any English word and either added "le" before it or an "o" on the end it became Italian. This made her amusingo with a side salad of Le bOnKeRs. I still couldn't decide whether Arabella's warning label should be CAUTION: UNSTABLE or SPECIAL HANDLING REQUIRED.

Like her outfits. She always wore black motorcycle boots with shiny silver buckles, and today she'd paired them with a green cashmere sweater five sizes too big for her, a leopard-patterned turban, and extra-long false eyelashes. The other regular fixture of her wardrobe was a huge fake (I assumed) diamond brooch that she'd attach somewhere on her person; today she was using it to pin a feather to the turban at a jaunty angle, making her look kind of like the love child of Robin Hood and a maharaja. Which was actually a fairly conservative look for her.

I opened my notebook and wrote back:

Where have you been?

I was sicko. What did I miss?

Professore has a new boyfriend. He spent the night at his house last night.

How do you know?
DID YOU FOLLOW HIM?!?

Ha ha. No, he was wearing the same shirt yesterday but not the leather jacket, and it's not his. See how it's more worn out on the right-hand side? But Professore Rossi is left-handed. Plus, he smells faintly like Calvin Klein's Obsession for Men today, which isn't his regular—

Before I could finish, a shadow fell across my notebook. "Do Signorina Callihan and Signorina Randolph have something to share with the class?" Professore Rossi said, towering over us.

"I was just asking Jasmine how to say 'birth certificate' in Italian," Arabella said, hitting him with Wide Eyes of Innocence.

"*Certificato di nascita,*" he told her. "Will there be anything else?"

"Le not," Arabella said pleasantly.

"*Bene.* Then we may continue without bothering you?"

Ho ho ho! Teachers are so LE FUNNY.

The rest of the lesson zipped by because we were supposed to discuss our life goals, and I earned praise from Professore Rossi by saying I wished to sniff out crime. (Thank you, *Il Commissario Rex*!) I was already thinking of what flavors of gelato I would reward myself with for lunch, when Arabella passed me a final note that said,

Can I talk to you after class?
It's le important.

As we filed out I asked, "What's going on? Are you okay?"

She hesitated for a moment, like she was trying to make up her mind about something. Finally she said, "I have to talk to someone at Prada. Come with me."

Polly would never have forgiven me if I'd gone to Prada— aka LogoLand—so I convinced Arabella to stop for gelato instead. I was kind of distracted while we were ordering because the radio was playing a song where the singer was describing all these guys his girlfriend could be hanging out with, guys with titles and fancy yachts, and how he wished he could just reach out and take her hand and tell her that he might not have a Lamborghini but that those other guys were weenies. I was thinking that not only did I know just how he felt but I could give him a few tips on heartache, when I realized Arabella was talking to me.

She was saying, "You know how today in class you said your goal in life was to fight crime? Is that true?"

"*Sì, signorina.* Why?"

"I lied about my goal. I don't really want to be a lawyer, I just wanted to learn the word. Have you ever seen those kiosks at the mall where they write your name on a grain of rice?"

"Sure."

She looked up at me and her eyes were shining with excitement. "I want to own one. To help people make special memories."

Definitely SPECIAL HANDLING REQUIRED. I wasn't quite sure what to say, but fortunately she wasn't waiting for a response because she plowed ahead, almost desperately. In fact, as she went on about having already started researching it and her search for a feng shui person who could properly orient her kiosk, I had the impression that while she was passionate about rice art, it wasn't what she really wanted to talk about. So when she broke off in the middle of a sentence about micro-pens, I wasn't completely surprised.

But I was surprised by what she said next, which was: "Jas, I think someone is trying to kill me."

Since that's the kind of statement that sets you speeding down the road past the NOW LEAVING MIND-YOUR-OWN-BUSINESS ISLAND! COME AGAIN SOON! sign, it was clear that in my role as a Model Daughter I should pretend to have developed rapid-onset deafness and scurry away. Which is, of course, exactly what I did.

In an alternate universe.

What I did in this universe was say, "What makes you think that?"

"I think there's been someone following me all week. That's why I skipped class. I didn't want to leave my house."

Be a Model Daughter, I commanded myself. *Ask no questions. Batten down your hatches. Where hatches mean Eyes. And also Ears.* "Can you describe the person?" my mouth said. Traitor mouth!

"No, I've never seen anyone."

"Then how do you know you're being followed?" Shut up, traitor mouth!

"A fortune-teller told me I'm in grave danger."

"I think fortune-tellers tell everyone that to get them to

pay them money. Has anything else happened to make you think that?"

"No, but I can feel it. A lurking menace. In the shadows."

Oh, good. Not only was her stalker invisible, he qualified as a member of the Lurking Menace Club. It is so nice to have sane friends. I imagine.

But it was a relief and helped to put an end to the tug-of-war going on between Model Me and Traitor Mouth of a Thousand Unnecessary Questions. Because while having friends who were being targeted by killers was contraindicated by Model Daughters, having friends who were just delusional and possibly paranoid wasn't entirely disallowed. In fact, you could make a case that Model Daughters had a responsibility to the community to be kind to the insane.

"You don't believe me," Arabella said with a wounded puppy expression. "No one believes me. I tried to tell—"

She'd been looking up at me but now she glanced over my shoulder and suddenly her face turned deadly white. Like she'd just seen an ax-wielding murderer. Or a ghost. Or a ghost with an ax.

"What is it? What's wrong?" I asked as I turned to follow her gaze. I was increasingly convinced that whatever was going on with Arabella was in her head, and what I saw—or rather didn't see—just proved it. Behind us were some gondoliers, a guy wearing a dress and wig passing out flyers to a Mozart concert, a nun, a man in a tweed cap, and a woman with massive blond hair talking on a cell phone. No one who would make the Ghouls-n-Villains annual calendar, even in the honorable mention category.

Apparently, she was seeing something different than I was, because as I turned back she said, "It—it's not possible." And then her eyes got huge and she grabbed my arm and shouted, *"RUN!"*

Chapter Three

Allow me to pause here for a moment to say that while it might be unusual for most people to have others shouting "RUN!" at them, it happens to me pretty often. And I've developed a simple set of guidelines for these situations:

Little Life Lesson 2: Don't do it.

Little Life Lesson 3: Ever.

Little Life Lesson 4: Especially if you are trying to be a Model Daughter and the person who yelled it at you is a nineteen-year-old girl dressed like a homeless pixie whose life goal is to Write on Rice and who adds, with a quiver in her voice, "They're going to kill me, too."

They. Are. Going. To. Kill. Me.

TOO.

But sometimes doing What Is Right is not an option, such as when the nineteen-year-old homeless pixie whips out her Incredible Hulk strength and starts dragging you down the tourist-filled street at a rapid pace.

"Where are we going?" I shouted at Arabella as she bounced me off of two tourists.

"It doesn't matter," she said desperately. "We just have to get away from him."

"From who?"

"The man in the straw hat. He's following us!"

I glanced around and saw a straw hat bobbing through the crowd behind us, but no evidence at all that he was on our tail.

"Are you sure?" I asked.

"Watch."

Arabella moved like someone who'd aced Advanced Placement Dodging Through Crowds, which should have made me suspicious, but I didn't have time for that. Without warning, she yanked me around a corner and started running faster. As she wove expertly between the tourists on the crowded street, cleverly using me as a buffer, I stole a look over my shoulder and had to admit she might be right: The straw hat was still behind us. And gaining.

Whizzing past luxury boutiques and tourist landmarks, I realized that this could be an enticing metaphor for my college essays. Like a lesson—*bam*—about not rushing through life—*bash*—because you miss things and—*thud*—can wind up in a lot of pain. Out of nowhere two men carrying a pane of glass appeared, blocking the entire street (for real. A PANE OF GLASS), but instead of, oh, stopping, Arabella ducked down and dragged me under it.

Little Life Lesson 5: When towing a six-foot-tall girl, try to bear in mind that her head clearance is different from yours.

After putting How Low We Could Go to the test, we were confronted by a gaggle of Russian tourists with large rolling bags clogging the entire side of the Bridge of Sighs in front of us, and I knew we'd reached the end. This was it. I had to admit I was kind of relieved. I'd had all the—

Arabella sped up. Before I realized what she had in mind, she was leaping over suitcases like hurdles. From there it was just a simple matter of winding between souvenir kiosks, cafés, and people stopped in the middle of the path to snap memorable vacation photos—*smash!*—into Saint Mark's Square, the biggest piazza in Venice.

Saint Mark's is filled with three things: 1) Tourists 2) Cafés 3) Carts that sell birdseed to tourists so they can feed pigeons out of their hands while they sit at the cafés. I tried to suggest that since there was such a big crowd to le mingle ourselves with we could stop and catch our breath, but Arabella had a different plan. The Tear-Through-the-Middle-of-the-Square-Swinging-Jas-Wildly-into-Objects Plan.

What was pleasant about this was it allowed me to experience several of the rules of physics firsthand. For example, the faster you are going when you bash into a man with a hard-sided briefcase, the more it will hurt (Force = Mass x Acceleration). And that being pulled between two women chatting and carrying large shopping bags will result in them screaming not-very-nice things at you. (For every action there is an equal and opposite reaction.) And my favorite: A Jas in motion—such as one who sidesteps to avoid running into a stroller and instead finds herself tripping over a small dog and launching into the air as though she's a trouble-seeking missile—will stay in motion unless acted on by an equal but opposite force.

Like the little girl I crashed into.

A little girl whose mother had just bought her a bag of birdseed. Which flew into the air, traced a parabola, and cascaded back down (gravity = 9.81 m/s^2), landing on me. Or rather, in my hair.

Where a hundred pigeons suddenly decided to have lunch.

Oh hello, icing the cake of my day badly needed!

The nice thing about having your head dive-bombed by pigeons—besides how lovely comma un it feels—is that you can't see anything. Which, okay, doesn't matter that much when you are busy being the pull toy of Le Crazy Person. But seeing does come in handy when Le Crazy stops without warning and you keep going, crashing into something hard.

Something that says, *"Che diavolo fai? Sei pazza?"*

This does not mean "Ah, just what I wanted today, a very tall girl to fly into my arms!" but is more along the lines of "What the hell are you doing? Are you insane?" Not the kind of thing Model Daughters want to hear, ever.

Especially not what they want to hear when the pigeons take off, and they can see again, and what they see is that they've run right into a police officer. A police officer who looks as angry as he is large. Which is very.

So I said the first thing that I could think of to explain. It turns out, "The smaller monkey is better for that experiment" is not actually a multipurpose phrase.

In fact, some people might even think you were insulting them. Especially if they happened to look a bit like a large ape and had probably been mocked for it during their formative years.

"Who do you call a monkey?" asked Officer Ape—whose name tag read ALLEGRINI—not exactly in a Filled-with-Fun tone.

Little Life Lesson 6: There is no JAS in TROUBLE.

Little Life Lesson 7: But there is a JAS in JAIL SENTENCE FOR INSULTING A POLICE OFFICER.

I did a rapid search of all my extracurricular vocabulary and managed to come up with: "There are no monkeys here. That crazed assassin is after my friend to kill her," while pointing at Straw Hat, who had just entered the square.

I was pretty sure I got all the words right, but Officer Allegrini didn't move.

"He is a bad guy!" I said, waving my arms for emphasis. "A dangerous assassin! He plans to murder my friend."

"Pardon, *signorina*, but please explain," Officer Allegrini said in Italian. "To what friend do you refer?"

That's when I realized there wasn't anything wrong with my Italian. It was my story.

Because Arabella had given me le slip.

Chapter Four

Little Life Lesson 8: If the police already think you are making up a friend, having the person you described as a crazed assassin march right up to you and say *"Bellissima! Eccomi qui!"* (Beautiful lady! Here I am!) will not help your credibility any.

"Arrest him!" I cried. "He is an assassin!"

The straw-hatted assassin laughed as though he was a visitor from the Planet of Hilarity. "But no, I am merely a gondolier," he said.

"He is merely a gondolier," Officer Allegrini repeated like he'd been mind melded.

"Which is an excellent cover for being an assassin," I pointed out.

Straw Hat shook his head and said, "No, I do not think so. First, the gondola is too slow for making a good escape. Second, this cover would work only in Venice. I do not think you could make the living being an only-in-Venice assassin."

Then he smacked himself on the forehead and said, "Pardon me, I am very rude. My name is Massimo, but you may call me Max." After which he bowed, took my hand, and kissed it.

Allowing me to notice:

1) he was speaking English, with only a very faint accent
2) he'd had to bend down to talk to me
3) (down, as in, he was taller than I was)
4) he had longish light brown hair
5) and mysterious smoky blue eyes
6) that made him seem kind of fascinating
7) and could have gotten him a DANGER: HOT SURFACE label
8) BUT HE WAS NOT AS FASCINATING OR HOT AS JACK—
9) (who was possibly at that moment meeting a willowy marine biology major with a double-jointed tongue who once outswam a pack of sharks and an angry dolphin while carrying adorable orphans on her back)
10) —AT ALL.

Possibly not in that order.

As Max stood up he whispered, "Leave the *carabiniere* to me," and winked.

WINKED.

I was so stunned that by the time I reacted he was already talking to Officer Allegrini, saying in Italian, "Thank you very much, my friend. We shall not detain you any longer. This lady has apologized and I have graciously decided not to press charges. Also I will tell my uncle, the *capo* of police, what a good job you have done. Now leave us, we would be alone."

And Officer Allegrini did! After hitting me with a look that said seeing me again wasn't going to top his to-do list, he melted into the crowd like a lozenge. Leaving me completely on my own with someone who, while probably not an assassin, had just chased me halfway around the city.

Who was now smiling at me and saying, "At last, it is just the two of us! I thought he would never leave!"

There were probably three hundred things I should have said but what came out instead was "Your uncle is not the head of the police."

"Do not spoil it for Officer Allegrini! The *carabinieri* may have very sharp outfits, but their brains are not so sharp and they have few pleasures. He thinks he has earned a commendation. You do not wish him to be unhappy, do you?"

I stared at him.

"No, I did not think so. I could tell you have a kind heart from the first time I saw you. Now tell me why you make all this trouble for me."

I blinked at him. "You're the one who chased after us."

"Of course. Because you were running."

"We were running because you were chasing us."

"I chase you because you are running."

"You chased us first."

He shook his head. "I did not chase you. Max does not chase girls. Girls chase Max."

"If you weren't following us, what are you doing here?"

"Aha! I did not say I was not following you."

"But—"

"I did follow you. To give you back this." He reached into his pocket and in the back of my mind it occurred to me that if I were an assassin, this would be exactly the moment when I'd pull out my gun and start shooting.

Instead, what he pulled out were seven euros. "Your friend leaves her change when she buys her gelato," he explained. "Signora Lee cannot leave the stand to bring it to her, so I go after to return it."

"Wait, you were bringing Arabella her change? That's all?"

"Sì," he said. "I try to be the good sam. Especially where the *bellissime* ladies are involved."

It took me a second to figure out he meant Good Samaritan. "That was really nice of you. I'm sure my friend will be grateful."

He frowned. "I doubt it. She is not a gentleman. She leaves you here to face the police all alone, holding the cat bag."

"The what?"

"The bag from which the cat has been let out."

"I don't think that means what you think it means."

"Our first disagreement already! I am glad things are progressing so quickly. And since we are being honest, I will tell you: I do not think this girl is a good friend for you."

Maybe it was just because I wanted to be a Model Daughter and avoid any sightseeing trips to the Temple of Trouble, but I found myself believing he really was a gondolier trying to do a good deed. Which meant he wasn't an assassin, which meant no one was after Arabella, which meant she was insane, yes, but fundamentally safe. I felt so relieved I was almost giddy. "Okay. Well, I'll take that into consideration. I'm sorry if we inconvenienced you, but—"

He cut me off. "Do not worry, I understand this is not your fault. No doubt you ache with the injury you have done me. Fine. It is over. We will never speak of it again. What time shall I call for you on the gondola tonight?"

"What?"

"To make up for having me arrested. I am very upset about it."

"You weren't arrested. You almost had *me* arrested!"

"The smallest of details."

"And you don't look upset."

"Inside," he said, tapping his chest, "I am desolated. Also I am hungry. Ah, this is a better idea. Come and have a pizza with me now."

"I really can't. I have to go back to my hotel."

"Max understands. Say no more."

"What do you understand?"

"You are afraid to be alone with me. Afraid of my charms. I know this is a problem."

"Of course," I agreed. "That's exactly what's going on."

He nodded sympathetically. "It is very common. But do not worry, you will get over it. The only cure is to spend more time with me."

"Or I could spend no time with you. Rip myself away."

"But this will just make your heart bleed and why should you suffer? I cannot allow that."

I decided I'd had my daily dose of Vitamin Lunacy with Arabella and I didn't want to risk an O.D. "That's really nice of you, but I'm afraid I'm not allowed to go out. Ever." I started backing away. "Thank you for returning my friend's money. Ciao."

"So brave!" he said. "And yet, you must be careful. I will keep my eyes open for you, but I am afraid this friend will bring you trouble."

Superfantastico! Now I had relative strangers making dire predictions about my future!

Of course, given the way things had been going, he might be right. Turning to go, I found myself wondering where Arabella had vanished to. And where Max had learned to speak such good English. And if—

Nothing. I was going to wonder nothing. About My Own Business was where I wanted to be Going, and my pigeon-styled hair and I were taking the express train, making no stops, to that destination. Model Daughters who earned their parents' trust and were allowed to meet up with their pals for a college visit (and their boyfriend for kissing) did NOT get chased through the streets by potential assassins, or run into police, or have their hair attacked by birds. I would wipe all of that from my mind and it would be like it never happened. No one, especially no one of the species Dadzilla, would ever know about it.

Only at that moment did I become aware of an American voice speaking very fast behind me. It was the woman with the big blond hair I'd spotted behind Arabella and me earlier, when the Dragging Through Venice marathon began. She was now saying into a cell phone, "Yes, Doug, I'm sure. It was *her*. Being chased by an assassin! At least that's what her friend said. I was following her the whole time. No, she disappeared but the girl who was with her is an American, named—J-A . . . Hang on, I can't see the rest."

Little Life Lesson 9: If you are trying to be a Girl Out of Trouble but you happen to have a name tag for Italian class, be sure to keep it well hidden in your bag.

Little Life Lesson 10: It is also a good idea to have an alias prepared because at the times when you find yourself needing one, chances are you won't really be in a frame of mind to think of something good.

I sped up as soon as I heard what she was saying but she managed to catch up to me. She waved a business card in front of my face and said, "I'm a reporter. You're going to be famous. Tell me how to spell your name. Is it Jane?"

"Yes," I agreed, practically running now. Model Daughters are allergic to fame. "It's Jane."

"Jane what?"

I said, "Jane Doe." And then the monkeys in my head who always like to help me out added, "—nut."

"Jane Doughnut?" the blond reporter lady repeated, giving me a look filled with pity and scorn, which seems like a hard combo especially since we were both nearly sprinting, but she managed it. "What is your name, really?"

"Jane Doughnut," the monkeys affirmed.

She said into the phone, "Jane Doughnut. That is what she says. Yes, I'll see if I can do a bit better."

Which I decided was my cue to disappear. Because although the monkeys were VERY curious about why Arabella was being followed by a reporter, Model Jas perceived that knowing more about it was contraindicated for her continuing longevity.

I'm not proud of what I did next. Lying is not strictly in keeping with the Model Daughter creed, but I was desperate. I glanced over the reporter's shoulder, did a double take, then came to an abrupt halt. "Look!" I said, pointing. "There's my friend!"

"Where?" she asked, following my finger.

"She's taken off her turban but that's her, next to the jewelry store. I'm positive."

I waited until the reporter had taken two steps toward

what I was pretty sure was an old woman with a walker, then turned and fled. Although the Grissini Palace Hotel was just around the corner, I chose a circuitous route back to it just in case I was being followed. After weaving through five squares, crossing eight bridges, ducking into and out of two stores— on purpose! Totally! Not because I was at all distracted wondering why Arabella would have reporters following her, which might have caused me to stop paying attention where I was walking and wind up somewhere I'd never been before and have to ask directions from a hunched-over old woman who made me carry twelve water bottles up to her attic apartment in return—I slowed to a normal walk.

I was safe. Arabella was safe. That whole brush with Trouble was behind me. Over and done with.

Yes, I really believed that. No, that scratch near my eye is not a lobotomy scar.

Chapter Five

According to my translation program, this is the essay I wrote to introduce myself to my Intermediate Italian class during our third week here:

Good day. I am called Jasmine Callihan. I have seventeen years and am born and evolved in Los Angeles. Because cleaning agents are lacking a definitive history, my father, who I call Lo Zilla del Dad, has made the subtle choice to move to Venice in the middle of my life. Despite the factoid that if I had a euro for every time my father has done the weird and wonderful thing of this type I would be able to buy a pony (if it was very small), still I question if there is a dark and majestic reason that we have exited the scene, but Lo Zilla is staying mum. He answers only interrogations such as "I can go to the Internet café for IM with my small friends?" To which, ten times for nine, he says "NOT!" in a monster voice.

But apart from the fact that I must cohabitate with Lo Zilla and my half-mother Sherri!, and in the absence of my friends and my heart, Venice appeals to me a lot. We live in the Grissini Palace Hotel, which is in a palace on the Grand Canal and is crammed with beauty. The building is made in 1586 by an unstable person smarting from thwarted love, and so it surprises not that even today it is chock with unstable people such as: Lo Zilla and Sherri! who are a paragraph of joy in themselves but I will save you that; Colonel Larabee who scribes a book about his life and sometimes could be found talking to the armor suits that make the lobby so homelike; Camilla, the concierge who bursts with information about every guest and is my friend but normal? No. She has a fish named Orlando the Furious who inhabits a bowl on her desk with coins on the bottom because, says Camilla, he will require only metal alloys to live on. And try if you do to give him even the smallest crumb of bread for food because he look zestless, then everyone runs crazy like you are attempting to murder him in his bed! If fishes had themselves beds, I mean to say.

This is where I live. It is incredible that I have not also gone unstable.

I got a B-plus on the essay because although my verb tenses were "reckless," my vocabulary was "surprising and muscular."

I didn't tell Professore Rossi that I learned most of it from my *ChiPs*-watching rather than from class. I didn't want to hurt his feelings.

Despite the fact that the Grissini Palace was like Crazy Zoo, Proudly Displaying All Aspects of Crazy, Twenty-four Hours a Day, I loved it there. As soon as I arrived inside its walls I could tell that something was UP. I was trying to figure out what when I saw Camilla, standing behind her desk, waving me over.

Camilla had a dark brown bob and a round face with wide-spaced blue eyes and looked more like a little porcelain doll than a real person. She was twenty-five and from a distance her face was so sweet you wondered what she was doing working in a place like Crazy Zoo, but when you got up close you could see that there was a hint of the insane around those eyes. Usually she was energetically bouncing from minding one person's business to minding another's, but today she looked almost as zestless as her fish.

Even though my desire to escape the lobby—aka the Place Where Dadzillas Roamed Free—was extreme, she looked so sad that I detoured toward her. "What's wrong?" I asked.

"Oh, Yasmine, it is awful here today. The Save Venice people start to arrive. For the big events this week? And they all want to know where the ice machine is. Why do you Americans love ice so much? Is it because you are hot-blooded?"

"I don't know, it could—"

"*Sì,* I bet that it is," she rushed on, musing to herself. One nice thing about chatting with Camilla was that you didn't have to prepare any material because her superpower was to be able to hold both sides of a conversation by herself, complete with interruptions. "I wonder if I should date an American boy. I did date a Canadian once. Are they different from Americans?"

"I imagine that—"

"This one, he wasn't crazy for the ice. He did like—" She cut herself off there, looking at me as if she'd just noticed my presence. And as if what she were seeing was not exactly a gorgeous dessert tray. Pained is what her expression was.

"I do not mean to be rude, but I am not sure that this hairstyle is the most good for you," she said finally. "It looks like you have been picked at by the birds."

My desire for flight suddenly million-troupled. "Birds. Ha-ha. I was just trying out something new. Well, it looks like I have to—"

"I suggest you do not try this new thing out," she said. "Yes, I tell you as girlfriend to girlfriend, if I were you I would go to your room and fix it before your surprise tonight."

If I'd still had any lingering thoughts about who Arabella was or if she was okay—which I did NOT—this reminder of Things to Come would have erased them. "How do you know about my surprise?"

She snorted. "My job is knowing. Also, this morning after

you go, the Sherri! came to arrange for the airport transfers. You are going to have the colossal fun, no?"

And was clearly about to say a lot more when her phone started ringing. Muttering, "I bet this is another looking for ice," she answered it, and I dashed to the elevator.

As it went up, I started a to-do list in my mind:

Get to room without being seen by Dadzilla.

Do not do anything to antagonize-slash-upset Dadzilla.

Avoid all encounters with the insane (except Dadzilla).

Practice Surprised-n-Grateful expressions for when Dadzilla announces trip.

Pack clothes and presents for pals—(chocolate shaped like a salami for Roxy; pink silk Fortuny scarf and Italian hand sanitizer for Polly; Dylan Dog comic for Tom; light-up gondola for Jack).

Apply pore-shrinking mask.

Go to San Francisco.

¡¡¡¡¡¡¡¡¡¡¡¡¡¡¡¡¡¡KISSING!!!!!!!!!!!!!!

Just thinking about getting to see my tiny pals and Jack made me all giddy, and by the time I reached my room (crossing off the first item! Only six things between me and KISSING) I was refilled with all the *dolce vita* I'd had before my high-speed-chase plus aerial-assault experiences.

Of all the things I loved about the Grissini Palace, the one I loved the very most was my room. Not only did it have an ornate old-fashioned key and a door that locked—which, although I suspected he had a secret key of his own, still placed at least some barrier between Lo Zilla and myself—it was also the most beautiful room I'd ever seen anywhere. My first thought every time I walked in was that Polly would break up with Tom to date my room if she ever laid eyes on it.

It was like a room for a princess, with two beds, both covered with a rose silk spread and a striped pink-and-white silk canopy that attached to a gold crown above each one; a white marble floor with tiny pieces of pink pearl inlaid in a swirly border around the edge; a silk carpet embroidered with bows; a tiny marble balcony; and walls painted to look like pale-green-and-cream-colored marble, except in two places, where there were tiny little dancing dogs chasing butterflies.

For. Real.

The only bad part of my room was that the balcony was on the back side of the hotel, overlooking a little side canal where gondolas were kept overnight and where, on weekends, Venetian teens came to make out. In fact, as I looked down now, even though it was broad daylight, a couple paused to kiss and run their fingers through each other's hair. Right under my balcony. Taunting me.

That is the kind of city Venice is. Although I was deprived of love, love was not deprived of my company. I'm sure it was there all week long, but on the weekends it really made itself felt. Which was why, although it meant at least a day and a half off from school, I usually sort of dreaded them. Because being alone in Venice, which every year is voted "most romantic city in the world," is bad. But being here with MAKING-OUT TEENS UNDER YOUR WINDOW when your boyfriend and his incredibly kissable lips are infinity miles away, possibly meeting a girl who hiked Mt. Everest barefoot and has a sexy scar on her thigh from doing battle with a mammoth that she'd love to show him—that is just cruel.

This afternoon, though, when I looked at the kissing teens, instead of feeling lonely or sad or jealous or depressed or in need of kissing or like my life was an unremitting toothache, I felt happy for them. And grateful, because they reminded me that I should deep-condition my hair.

Six hours fly by when you have packing and pore-shrinking and Surprise-Face practicing to do. I'd just finished my required homeschool half hour of PE (courtesy of my *How 2 Break-dance Like Da Pros* DVD) and was changing into my second-most Trouble-none-of-that-here-esque outfit (Polly Catalog 10b—white-and-brown-striped button-down shirt, purple-and-brown sweater vest, denim skirt, brown cowboy boots with owls embroidered on them, and long amber beaded necklace—because Trouble hates a sweater vest) when the phone rang.

The only person who ever called me was my father, so I put on my most charming voice. "Yes? How may I be of service to you?"

"Jasmine, thank God I got you," said the voice on the other end that clearly did not belong to my father. "It's a matter of life or death."

Chapter Six

"Arabella?" I asked.

"Yes."

"Are you okay? Where are you? Why did you disappear like that today?"

"I had to. It was the only way to escape from him. If he was busy, then he couldn't follow me to Prada."

"But there was nothing to be afraid of, that guy was just trying to—"

"You talked to him? What did he say? Did he say who he was working for?"

"*Working* for? He wasn't working for anyone. He's a gondolier. He was just returning the change that you left at the gelato shop."

"That's a lie," she said.

"But he had the money."

"I didn't leave my change. He just said it to cover up his true motives. That he was following me."

Oh, look who just pulled off the Hint of Insanity High-way at Paranoia Plaza!

"Um, maybe," I said. "Are you sure? Did you recognize him?"

"No, of course not. Why would I?"

"If you didn't recognize him, how do you know he's the one who's been following you?"

"I told you, I never see him, I just know he is there. Wait-ing for me."

"Let me see if I understand. You've never seen anyone. You just sense him."

She made an impatient noise. "Yes. Did you see anyone else? Talk to anyone? Did anyone follow you?"

"A reporter followed me and asked some questions, but I didn't say anything. Why is a reporter following you?"

"What kind of questions? What exactly did she ask you? Things about my family?"

Apparently this was a one-way game of Twenty Questions. "She just asked me my name. Why?"

"What did you say? Did you tell her where I live?"

"I didn't tell her anything—I don't know anything. I don't even know what part of Venice your apartment is in."

"Good. Then they won't be able to get it out of you."

"Who? What are you talking about? What's going on, Arabella?"

"Something deep and dangerous."

"Can you be more specific?"

"I can't talk now. They could be anywhere. Listening. Meet me tonight at Club Centrale at ten P.M. and I'll explain everything."

Of course. Because a secret assignation with a paranoid person convinced that the Someone after her might try to Get Something out of me was just the kind of thing Model Daughters sallied forth to engage in when they were supposed to be tucked into bed.

What Arabella was suggesting was clearly in violation of both my Not Leaving the Hotel and Not Associating with the Insane (except Dadzilla) policies. But I felt guilty completely turning her down. "I can't come out to meet you tonight, but if you want to come here, or tell me what's wrong, maybe I could—"

She lowered her voice to a whisper. "I told you, I can't discuss it now. You have no idea what it's like knowing that anyone could be the ONE." She said it like it was written in all capital letters.

"The ONE what?" I asked.

"The ONE who works for them."

Oh, that ONE. I should have known. "Do you know why they are following you?"

"I think so, but I'm not positive. I asked someone the wrong question. Somewhere down the line I asked the wrong question. I wish I knew which one because then I would *know*."

"Know what?"

"Everything."

My bafflement quota is high but I'd pretty much reached it. "Okay. Um, what about going to the police? They could help you. Retrace your steps, figure out what question you asked where, maybe—"

"The police," she snorted. "Did they help you today? Arrest that man?"

"No, but that was because he was only trying to—"

"Exactly. The fortune-teller told me not to trust the police and she was right. They are probably in on it!"

"Fortune-teller? The one who said you were in danger?"

"Yes. And then the cat, my landlady's cat, looked at me funny. That's a sign! And—"

She broke off and when she came back she said, "I have to go, that's my other line. Don't forget: ten o'clock. I'll be in disguise. You won't recognize me, but I'll recognize you."

And with that sharp turn onto Delusion Drive, she hung up.

While Delusion Drive is very scenic, one visit per day is probably ample, and I'd already had mine when I got to explain to the police that my invisible friend was afraid of being murdered by a gondolier. It was sad that Arabella seemed to have bid sanity farewell, but it was not my problem. I already had plenty of Crazy in my life. Or at least, that's what I tried to tell myself.

I didn't have too much time to dwell on it because at that moment there was a rough pounding on my door followed by my father's voice bellowing, "Jasmine, it is time for dinner. Unlatch this door or I will break it down!"

Hello, Dadzilla! What exuberant charm you have!

On any other night I might have been tempted to see if he really could break down my door or if he was just all chat, because that is the kind of thing a daughter should know about her father, but not on Surprise Night.

Instead, I practiced both the wide-eyed-wonder and hands-clutched-adorably-to-chest one last time, and went out the door with a glad heart and a carefree step.

Never do this.

The dining room of the hotel was more crowded and bustling than usual, and I kept myself busy wondering which of the Save Venice people had disreputable secrets in their pasts. But as soon as I finished ordering pumpkin tortellini in sage and butter sauce (which I highly recommend if you ever find yourself at the Grissini Madhouse), Sherri! got my full attention by saying, "Hurry up, Cedric. It's almost time!"

As though I'd written the script myself, my father said, "Jasmine, we know you've been lonely, and since next week is the week that seniors at your school get off to visit colleges, we thought it would be pleasant for you to have some time with friends." I was just getting ready to clutch my hands and raise eyes filled with loving gratitude when three horrifying things happened:

1) I looked across the room and saw two girls my age, with perfect brown hair and perfect makeup, wearing high-collared lace shirts, pinafore minidresses, Mary Janes, and bonnets enter the dining room.

2) One of them looked at me and started waving.

3) My father went on: "So we invited your aunt, uncle, cousin Alyson, and that nice friend of Alyson's to spend the week with us here in Venice."

Chapter Seven

———— ❦ ————

Actually four horrifying things. As they approached our table, I realized they were also both wearing frilly shorts. And white gloves.

It was almost too much for my brain to take in all at once. As far as I could tell, instead of me going to California to see my pals, my cousin the Evil Hench Mistress Alyson, who was an expert in TortureJasology and should be marked with both PROTECTIVE EYEWEAR REQUIRED and TOXIC MATERIAL labels, had come to Venice with her best fiend. And she was dressed as Little Ho Peep.

It was like shoulder pads under T-shirts, or putting peaches on ice cream—UNSPEAKABLY WRONG. My mind was screaming, *But I was a Model Daughter! I was Trouble-Free Zone! Tiny children could play near me and be safe! And for what? EVIL HENCH TWINS!*

Oh, well. At least now I'll have more time to work on my college essays, I thought.

Or at least, that is what I should have thought. That is what a mature, self-actualized person would have thought. But I wasn't feeling mature or self-actual. I was feeling my heart trying to plummet through my chair, and my throat closing up, and my eyes getting all throbby, and I realized I was about to cry. I know that sounds spoiled. I mean, it's not like I'd lost a limb in a tragic badminton accident defending my country's honor (like the girl Jack might at that moment have been meeting), but I couldn't help it. I'd been so sure I was going to get to go to California. And so excited. And so ready to see my pals. And Jack.

And so ready to not feel lonely all day every day for at least a little while.

We all sat down then and my father proposed a toast and there was much merriment and lighthearted banter and commenting on how good the tortellini were, but it went on without Jas as a participant. I was making a pact with myself never to try to read anything in a mirror again, because clearly the itinerary I'd seen that said CALLIHAN on it had been theirs and not mine.

I tried to console myself by remembering that although officially Veronique was Alyson's Evil Hench Twin, she'd turned out to warrant only a MAY CAUSE DISORIENTATION label and could be nice. Esque. To prove it, she leaned over and gave me a little hug and squealed, "I'm so glad to see you, Jas. You look really good."

Causing me for one misguided moment to think, *Maybe*

this will not be as completely and utterly horrible as I thought.
Which is the kind of thought that might signal a rip in the
universe.

Fortunately, everything was returned to its normal place
when Alyson turned her Hench Gaze in my direction and
said, "God, Calamity, you've been here six weeks and you
still dress like an American. Where did you get that outfit,
Antiques Roadshow Last Year edition?"

Little Life Lesson 11: People in pinafores should not
attempt to crack wise about other non-pinafore-wearing
people's outfits.

"I am sorry, Holly Hobbie. We cannot all be putting the
IT into Italian Fashion the way you and your fancy pants
are." I admit it was not my snappiest comeback, but my eyes
were busy trying to flee into my brain to protect themselves.

Veronique said, "They're called bloomers."

And because there is no snappy comeback for that, I said,
"How was your trip?"

"Totally Visa," Veronique said. "We met this gigacool guy."

One of the nicest things about the Evil Hench Twins is
that they speak their own language, which forces mere mor-
tals like me to ask what they mean, so they can roll their eyes
at us as though we were born with baby-bird brains. "Gigacool?" I asked.

Alyson eye-rolled. "Um, Jas, have you been eating
Cream of Moron soup? Iper-slash-very cool." Another nice
feature of the Evil Hench language is the use of slashes to

link words together for extra emphasis.

"He's totally two commas," Veronique said. "You know, has a bank account with six zeroes behind it," she translated politely.

I nodded like I had any idea what she was talking about. "Where did you unearth-slash-exhume him?"

"We met him waiting for the water taxi at the airport," Veronique explained.

"Um, we?" Alyson asked. "I think I was the one he started talking to."

"Actually, he talked to me first," Veronique corrected.

"Only because you asked him to fix the clasp on your necklace."

"You pretended to have something in your eye."

"I did have something in my eye. That weird mascara you lent me."

I hadn't expected to enjoy my time with the Evil Hench Twins quite so much. I guess twelve hours on an airplane is a long time. I was getting quite interested to see exactly what kind of guy could inspire this level of rivalry after they'd only known him for, as far as I could figure out, about half an hour.

"He thought I was totally Jordache. That means I had the look he wanted to know better. It's vintage," Veronique explained. "Anyway, he said, 'I couldn't help noticing you on the flight from London.' He has the sweetest eyes and when he looks right at you it's like he's—"

"You don't have to write a five-paragraph essay about it," Alyson snarled. "Besides, he was looking at me when he said that."

"He was looking at me too!"

"Maybe he's cross-eyed," I offered. Because it is my way to be the peacemaker.

"Shut up, Jas," my cousin hissed.

A way that is apparently not appreciated by all.

Veronique touched Alyson on the arm and said, "Be nice to Jas, Sapphyre."

Alyson put up a hand. "This is not your battle, Tiger's * Eye."

I paused in the middle of picking up my water glass to look from one to the other of them. "I'm sorry, did you just call each other Sapphire and Tiger's * Eye?"

"Yes," Alyson said. "Sapphyre with a 'Y' and Tiger's * Eye with a star in the middle, but the star is silent. They're our faerie names."

Little Life Lesson 12: Even shortly after watching your fondest dreams be shredded in front of your eyes, you can still burst into uncontrolled laughter.

Little Life Lesson 13: Water propelled out of the mouth by uncontrolled laughter can go really far. And also backward. Which is easy to see if the woman behind you is wearing a white satin dress.

If that happens, however, do not expect the person responsible for making you spit water to apologize or anything. No, she will turn her blamethrower on you and say,

"Can't you go for just one second, Jas, without totally mortifying the whole family?"

And you (meaning me) will say: "Le not."

If you are taking the high road.

But I only partially heard that because I'd turned around to try to dry off the woman Alyson had made me spit on. As I bent down to retrieve the silverware that had flipped off the table when she'd leaped to her feet in horror, Veronique bent down with me and whispered, "I just wanted to tell you I think you are so brave."

"You do?"

"Yeah. The way you're going on like this, despite . . . well, you know."

"What are you talking about?"

"Everything that's going on with you. All alone here, with no friends. It's got to be totally hard. But you're just going along like it's all normal."

I couldn't believe it. Out of everyone, only Veronique seemed to understand what I had been through during the past month and a half. I was genuinely touched. I believe a tear might even have quivered in my eye. I said, "Thank you, Vero—Tiger's * Eye. I'm really . . . that's just really nice."

Veronique nodded, then went on. "Also, I want you to know that I still have my tonsils. And my appendix."

I blinked at her.

"I mean, if you need them. I would totally donate them."

More blinking.

"Well, that's all. I'm so glad you're enjoying your precious time."

"My—what? What are you talking about?"

"Your terminal illness. Sapphyre told me that's why you moved here right when school was starting. Because you're dying and your father didn't want your friends to see you when you were all, like, decrepit. I mean, it's the only thing that makes sense, isn't it?"

"Alyson told you I was dying," I repeated.

"Sapphyre. She told everyone at school. Some of the seventh graders made a supercute card for you. I have it in my room. I was a little scared before we saw you, because Alyson said you'd probably be covered with oozing sores, but you look really normal. What kind of cover-up are you using on them? I bet it's expensive. Not that you're not totally L'Oréal. You know, worth it."

I don't know how long I would have gone on staring at her if Alyson hadn't leaned in to say, "I swear, Jasmine Noelle Callihan, if you continue to embarrass me in front of the Italian people I will personally never forgive you as long as you live."

"That shouldn't be too long since apparently I'm DYING," I told her.

"What are you talking about?" my father demanded. "Who is dying?"

"Oh, nothing," I said, keeping it light. "Just that Alyson went around—"

"Sapphyre. With a Y," my father corrected.

That was it.

I read once in one of Sherri!'s Buddhism books that out of great suffering comes great inspiration, and I believe it, because that's what happened to me. All of a sudden it was as though someone had snapped one of those chemical light sticks inside of me and I saw everything with a new kind of clarity. I'd been going about this all wrong. I knew exactly what I needed to do.

At that moment, BadJas was born.

I pushed my chair away from the table, Badly. "I'm going to my room."

"Before dessert? Are you sick?" Sherri! asked with genuine concern. Which shows what a totally excellent stepmother she is.

But BadJas had no time for pleasantries. BadJas lived a life of emotional independence and scorning. BadJas's warning label read COLD SURFACE.

With a toss of my hair I said, "I'm fine. Don't wait up for me."

"What? What are you talking about, Jasmine?" my father spluttered. "You are not leaving this hotel."

I just kept on walking to the elevator. I was feeling Badder already. Even though my whole life's happiness had been shattered, my resolution to go Bad made me feel a lot better.

And I knew what my first Bad act would be.

Chapter Eight

As soon as I got up to my room I turned on my computer to go online, against my father's direct orders. I admit that this was not likely to win Most Bad Act in a Badathlon, but when you're learning to rebel you must take baby steps.

Waiting for my computer to boot up, I did some Deep Pondering, and the more I Deep Pondered the more our coming to Venice did look suspicious. I suddenly wondered: What if Alyson was right? What if I was terminally ill? I'd suspected all along there was an ulterior motive for our trip to Venice, and WHAT IF THIS WAS IT? In fact, I *had* felt ill at dinner that night, but that could be traced to my Evil Hench allergy. Still—

I only had two emails. One was from someone who wanted to share a secret about improving my love life (get rid of Dadzilla?). The other one said:

To: Jasmine Callihan <Drumgrrrl@hotmail.com>
From: J.R. <JR_211@hotmail.com>
Subject: How is Venice?

It was clever of your father to take you there. I should have guessed.

I'd gotten emails from this mystery person before, and while they were packed full of intrigue, they were low on useful content. But I always found myself writing back, possibly because they often contained strange hints about knowing my mother, and since she died when I was six and my dad won't talk about her, I am a sucker for strange hints. I tried to stay cryptic in my responses, to keep the tone, so I wrote back:

To: J.R. <JR_211@hotmail.com>
From: Jasmine Callihan <Drumgrrrl@hotmail.com>
Subject: Re: How is Venice?

Why should you have guessed my father would take me to Venice?

I'd just hit SEND when my computer binged. Jack was IMing me!!!

NASCARlad: Hey, super girl.
DrumGrrrl: Hi, hot stuff.
NASCARlad: You're the hot stuff. You were engaged in a mad chase

through Venice today! Are you okay?

DrumGrrrl: Wait—how do you know about that?

NASCARlad: Polly called me. I guess she has a Google alert set for anything with the words "blood," "mayhem," and "Venice" so she can keep track of you. And a reporter filed a story an hour ago.

All the Not Wondering I'd been doing about why the reporter had followed Arabella began to creep back in. But then I realized there was a way more important matter to resolve.

DrumGrrrl: How did you know it was me? I used an alias!

NASCARlad: Let's see. The combination between a girl saving someone's life and the alias she comes up with is Jane Doughnut. Of course it was you. No one else would be that cool.

And this is how I know Jack is under some kind of curse. Because normal boys would not think that was cool. They would flee from me like they were wearing rocket socks. But he . . . he didn't. I didn't know why. All I knew was that I really, deeply, and totally missed him and I really, deeply, and totally could have used some of his kissing.

NASCARlad: All the guys in the band are impressed. They want to know what it's like to date a celebrity. You must be having a great day.

DrumGrrrl: Not. But there is one bright spot. I've decided to go Bad.

NASCARlad: What does that mean exactly?

DrumGrrrl: I'm not sure. I need a Bad role model. Can you think of someone Bad?

NASCARlad: ...

DrumGrrrl: Someone with a devil-may-care attitude and a smart sense of fashion?

NASCARlad: Do you mean like Mr. T?

DrumGrrrl: GENIUS! That's it! And it's vintage!

NASCARlad: Why do I feel like I've just done something bad and am about to get into a lot of trouble with Polly?

DrumGrrrl: Not bad, Bad. Rhymes with RAD.

NASCARlad: ... a LOT of trouble.

DrumGrrrl: Ha. Mr. T scoffs at trouble.

NASCARlad: Are you sure this is a good idea? I mean, I really, really wouldn't want anything bad to happen to you. Or anything Bad. I'd miss you too much.

Suddenly all the exhilaration of Badness left me and I felt kind of stupid and weepy. Maybe it was the excitement of the day. Or maybe it was just how much I ached with missing Jack.

NASCARlad: Hey, are you still there?

DrumGrrrl: Yeah I just ... I feel kind of ...

NASCARlad: I hate how far away you are, super girl. I wish I could fly there right now, but we're having a bit of an issue

here. Plus we're about to start shooting the video. The
one of your song.

DrumGrrrl: It's not mine.

NASCARlad: I wrote it for you.

Okay, and that really did make me cry. And I saw how
stupid I was. Not just because I was lucky enough to have the
best boyfriend in the world, but because I was on the verge of
telling him that I loved him even though we'd only had TWO
dates. But really, REALLY good ones.

NASCARlad: Crap, I want to hear more about your Badness but I've
got to run and meet Candy at the studio. I'll IM when I
get back tonight around 1 A.M. your time. Will you be
there?

DrumGrrrl: I'll see if I can fit it into my busy schedule.

NASCARlad: That's what I like to hear. Be careful out there!

DrumGrrrl: Who's Ca—

<NASCARlad logged off>

Candy? Who was Candy? WHO IS NAMED CANDY?
Voluptuous blond women with turquoise eyes and sooty
lashes, who are yogis and have tattoos on their ankles and
neck which, when joined together, make a special picture
they'll be glad to demonstrate for you in the privacy of
their candle-filled boudoir while telling you about the

time they stopped a rhinoceros from charging by smiling at it.

That's who.

And that was who my boyfriend was going to meet.

If ever anyone was in what I learned from studying my SAT vocabulary was a miasma of despair, it was me at that moment.

Little Life Lesson 14: Once you get the candy-inspired phrase "Melts in your mouth, not in your hands" into your head, it is very challenging to get it out.

I was in danger of sinking from Bad to Sad so I asked myself: What Would Mr. T Do?

Mr. T would laugh in the face of boyfriends melting and pals out gallivanting, I decided. He would Put Glumness Aside and pull himself up by his Badstraps. Therefore, so would BadJas.

And she'd do it all wearing her white leather pants. And a fitted white wool jacket with epaulets.

Once I was dressed with Baditude I had to take Bad Action. I heard my father's voice in my head when I had left the hotel dining room saying, *You are not leaving this hotel, Jasmine.*

To which, following the WWMrTD code, I replied (in my head), *I pity the fool who tries to stop me.*

As if to prove that the path of Badness was the lucky one for me, Polly, Roxy, and Tom logged on just before I shut down my computer.

<PrincessP logged on>
<SheRox logged on>
<MrT logged on>

PrincessP: Jas! Are you okay?

SheRox: Had any good DOUGHNUTS lately?

DrumGrrrl: Hello, my charming pals! I'm fine. But I'm no longer Jas. From now on I am BadJas. And I have a plan. And a slogan.

PrincessP: What are you talking about?

SheRox: What's your slogan?

DrumGrrrl: WWMrTD. What Would Mr. T Do. It's vintage.

PrincessP: No, it's not.

MrT: I like it.

SheRox: Does that mean you're getting a Mohawk?

DrumGrrrl: Perhaps.

PrincessP: Don't encourage her, Roxy. Jasmine, precious, remember when you had your last plan? The one which almost got us killed in Vegas?

DrumGrrrl: I believe you mean the plan I had that got us all safely home in Vegas.

SheRox: But we were all there to help you then. Now you are on your own.

DrumGrrrl: I have the Hench Twins.

PrincessP: I just got chills down my spine.

SheRox: I got chills and my hands began to shake.

DrumGrrrl: Listen, it's brilliant. Since being a Model Daughter didn't get me anywhere, my new plan is to get into as much trouble as possible and show my father that Venice cannot hold me. Forcing him to send me home.

PrincessP: Ah. I see that we are using the alternate universe definition of "plan" meaning "a massively horrible idea."

DrumGrrl: I thought you would like it! You're always encouraging me to take an interest in things.

PrincessP: Things. Like, you know, paint by numbers. Or shadow puppets.

SheRox: Shadow puppetry would be a very unique thing to have as an extracurricular for college applications.

PrincessP: But you won't get to fill out any college applications if you keep hanging around with your new friend Arabella.

DrumGrrrl: Really? You interest me strangely. What is she famous for, anyway?

PrincessP: She was recently photographed wearing a unitard. A stirrup pant unitard. Do you understand what I am telling you, Jasmine?

DrumGrrrl: That I shouldn't take fashion tips from her?

PrincessP: That she is unstable.

DrumGrrrl: Have no fear. BadJas doesn't get involved in others' affairs. I am going to be Cool and Aloof. My new warning label is REQUIRES DEFROSTING.

PrincessP: I think it should be OBJECTS IN MIRROR MAY BE

SMALLER THAN THEY APPEAR. At least while you are wearing your Wonderbra. Which I know you are.

DrumGrrrl: Your powers of perception delight me, CONTENTS UNDER PRESSURE.

SheRox: Hey, what's my warning label? I want it to be something good, like VAPORIZES ON CONTACT.

DrumGrrrl: Perhaps CONTAINS NUTS?

MrT: Heh, good one, Jas. What's mine?

DrumGrrrl: You don't need one, Tom. Anyone who can have Roxy for a twin sister and Polly for a girlfriend and not turn to a life of crime deserves a medal, not a warning label.

SheRox: Alas, BadJas, you are mistaken. Tom's label should be MAY CAUSE EXTREME NAUSEA. The way he looks at Polly? It's just wrong. That kind of devotion should be limited to items with the words "chocolate covered" in their names.

PrincessP: Can we put that discussion on layaway and focus here? I'm serious, Jas. Arabella is bad news.

DrumGrrrl: What has she done, apart from commit crimes against fashion?

PrincessP: Well, everyone who's ever been close to her ends up dead.

DrumGrrrl: That's not true. She talked about a brother in Italian class once.

PrincessP: But her mother and her last boyfriend are. And I think one of her best friends lost a limb.

SheRox: According to the article you gave me, Polly, her friend only lost mobility in half of her face—

PrincessP: Same thing practically.

SheRox: —as a result of a freak electrolysis accident.

MrT: And her boyfriend committed suicide. It's not like being with her killed him.

DrumGrrrl: Poor Arabella.

PrincessP: And poor anyone-she-gets-close-to. If she had a celebrity scent it would be called TROUBLE.

DrumGrrrl: Wow.

PrincessP: I knew that would impress you.

DrumGrrrl: Actually I was thinking that "If She Had a Celebrity Scent It'd Be Trouble," would be an ace title for a song. I bet there could be a long drum solo.

SheRox: I hope you will be able to play it with your one arm.

PrincessP: THAT IS NOT FUNNY! LIMB LOSS IS NO JOKE!

DrumGrrrl: Of course it isn't, P. Now I would love to stay and chat, but I told Arabella I would meet her at 10 and it's almost time, so I should dash.

PrincessP: Ha ha.

DrumGrrrl: Don't wait up.

PrincessP: You're not going to meet Arabella, Jas.

PrincessP: Jas?

PrincessP: Hello? What happened to REQUIRES DEFROSTING?

PrincessP: I KNOW YOU'RE KIDDING, JASMINE.

But I wasn't.

<DrumGrrrl logged out>[1]

What I'd realized was that if even a tiny dollop of what Polly said was true, there could be nothing Badder than going to meet Arabella. I was pretty sure that the Someone she thought was threatening her would turn out to be as innocent as the gondolier earlier—whose lips I had totally stopped thinking about (THANK YOU, MAKING-OUT TEENS)—but she still seemed like a good person to stick around if you were looking for Action. Or rather, BADction. Especially BADction that was so bad it got you in the papers.

I'd just touched up my lip gloss in case any reporters were loitering around, when someone pounded on my door and said, "Open up or I'll kill you, Jas."

Only one kind of creature has such a winning way about itself, so I wasn't surprised to see the Evil Henches through the peephole. However they'd totally lied because opening the

---

[1] Tom: That can't be good.

Roxy: Are you okay, Polly? You look kind of funny.

Polly: Oh, no, I'm fine. Jas is just marching about a foreign country with the spokesmodel for Freak Accidents & Other Dangers Inc. Why should I look funny?

Roxy: I really admire the way you can speak even while gritting your teeth.

Polly: I like to multitask.

Tom: Um, does anyone besides me think we should Do Something about Jas? And fast?

Roxy: Actually, I have an idea. But it's going to require Polly to face one of her worst fears.

Polly: Which one? Not chronic halitosis?

Roxy: No, worse.

Polly: Wearing a mismatched bra and panties? Getting jam on my sleeve? Wait—not Sour Patch Kids?

Roxy: Worse.

Polly: You don't mean—you CAN'T mean—No!!!!!!

Roxy: Yes. Um, Tom, I think you should put your arms out. It looks like Polly's about to—nice catch.

door was what almost killed me. With the agony of trying not to burst into laughter when I saw what they were wearing.

Alyson was sporting brown fur boots, a brown fur micro-skirt, brown fur vest, and brown fur hat with earflaps, and carrying a brown fur muff. Veronique was ensconced in a nearly identical ensemble, except in gray fur.

"I told your dad I'd check on you," Alyson sneered.

"And we wanted to give you this." Veronique extracted from her muff a piece of construction paper with a gold rock glued to it. "It's the card the seventh graders made you. The crystal is supposed to help with your healing. It's really important to be in touch with the vibrations of the universe."

"I feel better already," I told her. "But you didn't have to skin some Ewoks and get all dressed up just to give me this."

"Oh, we didn't. Sapphyre and I are going to meet Reggie at a club called Centrale. Do you think you could give us directions?"

My interest was piqued. "Reggie? Is he the two-comma kid?" When Veronique nodded, I said, "I'll do better than give you directions. I'll take you myself! I happen to be going there too." I hadn't planned on having companions on my journey, but we Bad are always happy to bestow the pleasure of our company upon others, especially others who want nothing to do with us.

Alyson shook her head. "Um, that was 'we,' meaning the two of us"—gesturing at the two people wearing fashions from a galaxy far, far away—"not 'we' meaning 'And friend.'"

I gave her one of the wide-eyed looks of gratitude and sur-prise I'd been practicing. "You consider me a friend? I'm so touched!"

She was too speechless to even make the "in the head-slash-brain" comment that under normal circumstances would have oozed out without her even thinking, but Veronique pulled it together enough to ask, "Are you sure it's good for you? To come out with us?"

"Tiger's∗Eye, it's so like you to think of my well-being, but don't worry, my social standing can take being seen with Alyson—"

"Sapphyre."

"—even if she is dressed like an extra from *Star Wars on Ice*."

"What are *you* wearing?" Alyson demanded. "You look like you're ready to attend a comic-book convention as Catwoman, version two-point-loser. Are those leather pants? I can't believe Polly would let you have white leather pants."

"She isn't aware of them, but I'm sure she'll learn to love them as I do. But tell me, how do you know about comic-book conventions? You seem to be very knowledgeable. Do you have a secret life, cuz?"

Veronique gave an audible gasp but whether it was because of what I said or because of the elbow that Alyson planted in her ribs, I wasn't sure. All I knew was that this was turning into the Best. Night. Ever. WWMrTD was definitely an excellent life motto.

Things just kept improving.

We went Badly out via the back stairs of the hotel, and wended our way toward Centrale. Veronique had just explained that their faerie names were part of a larger program of spiritual awakening adopted from *Spirituality for Dummies,* which included talking to the spirits of the departed, when I noticed a spotlight with a large group of people crowded around it on the edge of a canal. Correction: a large group of people, most of whom were in police uniforms.

For six weeks a sight like this would have been a dagger in my eye. I would have forced myself to look and then skulk away, never wondering why there were members of both the police and the coast guard there, or what they were doing with the crane mounted on the back of the ambulance boat.

But not BadJas.

Little Life Lesson 15: Bad loves a crime scene.

Without my even having to suggest it, my feet drifted in that direction until I was standing at the edge of the group. The light was focused on an object, and as I peered over the heads of shorter people, I saw that the object was a body. A body wearing black leggings, a black sweater, and black motorcycle boots with shiny silver buckles.

Arabella's body.

Chapter Nine

As I watched, they pulled a sheet over Arabella's head.

My heart started to pound and my knees got weak and I felt tears pricking at my eyes. I couldn't believe it. Arabella *dead*? Oh. My. God.

For a moment my brain went completely silent trying to take it all in. Then I blurted in Italian, "This is my fault, officers. I want to make a statement."

Or that's what I meant to say.

What I actually said was "I'm the guilty one, Fuzz. I want to confess." Which, while close, is not exactly the same thing in several crucial ways.

Little Life Lesson 16: Announcing you want to confess to a murder is an excellent way to go from Invisible to It Girl when surrounded by a group of police officers.

Little Life Lesson 17: Referring to the police as "Fuzz" also does wonders for your popularity.

What I meant was that I felt *responsible*. That if I'd taken

Arabella seriously from the start and gone to the police or been more encouraging or something, none of this would have happened. But as a meaty hand closed around my upper arm, I had time to think that watching *CHiPs,* while very educational, might not be the best way to master the subtleties of a foreign language.

Still, it was enough for me to understand it when the voice attached to the arm said, "You again," and I looked up and saw I was staring into the eyes of Officer Allegrini. Whose gaze wasn't quite an application for the leadership council of the I-Heart-Jas fan club. In fact his expression was a bit on the ferocious side.

A woman in a suit said, "Take her in for questioning," and before I knew it I was being dragged away from the crime scene to Points Unknown.

Little Life Lesson 18: If you are ever in a Bad situation, you can always count on the support and understanding of your loved ones.

I'm not sure if there's a *How to Behave When Your Friend or Relative Gets Arrested for Dummies* book, but if there is I don't think Alyson read it closely. Unless it advises running alongside the person in question as she is dragged away, hissing, "This is uncalled for-slash-ridiculous-slash-lame, even for you, Jas. Wait until your father finds out."

I should have been cheered by her words. I mean, if it came down to Los Angeles, where I had never once been arrested (that he knew about), or Venice, where it appeared I was going to be held for murder, surely even Lo Zilla would see Los Angeles as a safer locale. Except I had a suspicion that being arrested wouldn't simply get me transferred back to LA, it would get me chained forever to a post in a locked room atop a special turret my father would have constructed for this sole purpose. No, from my perspective, things were looking a little bleak.

Because I am blessed, the Evil Hench One wasn't done showing her Support & Understanding. "If you think we're going to hang around waiting for you, you're wrong," she said.

"Did you know that your eyes glow red in this light?" I asked her.

"It's not that we don't care, it's just that we're already late to meet Reggie," Veronique explained over her shoulder as she followed Alyson.

I said, "Have a great time! If you hear from the dead, call me!" and if Officer Allegrini hadn't chosen that moment to drag-slash-lead me away I would unquestionably have added that they were heading in the complete wrong direction.

Depending on your definition of "un."

The San Marco precinct headquarters, which is where Officer Allegrini took me, looked a lot like police stations in America (hypothetically), except that instead of a Mr. Coffee they had an Espressione! machine on which you could push a button and get an espresso or caffè latte for a euro. Where by "you" I mean, "all those people who were not handcuffed to Officer Allegrini's desk."

I guess that's what I got for confessing to murder, but it was kind of frustrating because everyone in the place was running around chicken-minus-head style, and I couldn't do anything. Or understand what they were saying, because they talked too fast. Except for Officer Allegrini, who seemed to be telling anyone who would listen that I had, in his words, "a brain like a squash," which I think was his polite way of saying I was mentally disabled.

Sitting in a police station when no one is talking to you turns out to be much more boring than you would think. On TV, there are brawls and stuff, but in reality, at least in Italy, it just involved me at a desk watching people—and hours—go by. I was left alone with my thoughts, which were pretty much:

Whether Alyson and Veronique ever found Centrale
Whether I actually cared
What I would say if they asked me the name of my
    parent or guardian to contact
Why they hadn't yet
How I'd only been joking when I asked Dr. Lansdowne
    if going to jail was good for extracurriculars
How you should never joke about things like that
Melts in your mouth, not in your hands
How long it would take me to learn how to perform

"The Rose" in sign language

How Mr. T managed to spend so much time in
leather pants

Oh yeah, and WHAT HAD HAPPENED TO
ARABELLA?!?

As entertaining as these thoughts—now with bonus reel
images of Jack and Candy eating chocolate crème puffs
together in a candlelit bathtub—were, they only occupied me
for about thirty-eight seconds. I tried to think of other things
to do, but practicing my moonwalking didn't seem very
appealing (HELLO LEATHER PANTS) or possible (AND
HELLO TO YOU AS WELL HANDCUFFS) so I turned to
studying my surroundings.

Which roughly equaled Officer Allegrini's desk. This
proved more interesting than it at first seemed, because in
addition to a pack of Brooklyn chewing gum, there were
some case files on it. Since he seemed to have disappeared and
since I was being unjustly held and also because I had just
remembered that I was trying to be Bad and therefore would
not exactly be cooperating and rolling over like a trained dolphin, I decided to do something Bad and started flipping
through them. I know! How Bad is that? Reading classified
police documents! Really, really Bad!

I hadn't just thrown caution to the wind. I'd hoisted it up
like a flag and set fire to it.

My secret fantasy was that they would be about Arabella, but of course they weren't. Venice isn't exactly the Wild Wild West, so most of the reports were of incidents in which tourists got lost and fell into canals. The most interesting files I read were about an eight-year-old who was suspected in more than a hundred thefts but kept eluding the police, and a robbery that happened in broad daylight with no signs of forced entry and in which all that was stolen were teapots. This allowed me to add some choice phrases to my vocabulary like "pickpocket," "bag snatcher," and "inside job," but even the pursuit of knowledge could not hold my interest forever. I'd just decided that getting to go home, even if it meant someone calling Dadzilla, was better than becoming one with Officer Allegrini's furniture, when I realized someone was talking to me in English.

It was the plainclothes detective lady I'd seen next to Arabella's body, and she was asking, "What do you mean when you say you killed this girl? Do you mean that you actually murder her?"

Finally a chance to explain myself! And in my native tongue! The Fates, for once, were smiling upon me.

Little Life Lesson 19: Ha ha ha with a side of ha-sauce.

"No," I said, "I meant that she'd told me she was in danger but I thought she was just being paranoid. And maybe if I'd taken her seriously, she wouldn't be dead."

"*Bene.* It is as I thought." She turned to Officer Allegrini and said something too fast for me to understand, but it made him unlock my cuffs. Turning back to me, she said, "You are free to go."

Although this was an exciting development and I do have a fairly trustworthy air about me, it seemed a bit abrupt. "Just like that?" I asked. "Don't you have any other questions?"

She was already walking but paused to say: "No."

"Does that mean you know who killed her?"

She nodded. "No one. She killed herself. Suicide."

I think part of me had known that was coming and had been trying to deny it. Because what if my not believing Arabella earlier, and hedging on the phone, had been the things that pushed her over the edge? "You're sure?" I asked.

"*Sì*. A girl wearing all black with a large diamond pin is seen leaving her apartment at nine-oh-five. She often wears this pin, yes?"

"Yes, always," I said.

"Exactly. So we know it is her. At nine fifteen the same girl is seen on the bridge. One or two minutes later there is a splash. And then at nine thirty-three the body is found. There can be no question. The *medico-legale*—the medical examiner you say?—confirms there was water in her lungs. She died from drowning."

I sat up abruptly. How had I missed this before? "No way," I said. "She died too early."

"I know it is always hard when someone so young—"

"No, I mean, she thought she was going to meet me at ten.

If she was going to kill herself, it would have been after that, if I didn't arrive. Don't you see? She wouldn't have lost hope until after ten. Someone must have pushed her."

"No, Signorina Callihan, no one pushed her. Three witnesses saw only one person on the bridge. And then no people. And then the body in the canal. Also, there is no sign of a struggle and no one heard a struggle. She committed suicide. You must believe me."

But I couldn't. "Someone must have done something to her," I said. "There has to be another explanation. This just doesn't make any sense."

"No, there is no logic with the suicide."

"No, but—"

"You yourself thought she was crazy, no? Didn't you tell my officers this today? That she thought an assassin was after her but he turned out to be a gondolier?"

"Yes . . ."

"*Bene,* you were right. No one was after her. But the voice in her head, they were too much." She came closer and put a hand on my shoulder. "She was *instabile.* Unstable. There was nothing anyone could do."

But Arabella hadn't been crazy. Someone really had been after her. I was positive now. And not just because I didn't want to feel responsible for her killing herself. "It's all wrong," I tried again. "I swear to you, she didn't commit suicide. Not before ten."

"You have proof of this?"

"No, I just *know* it," I told her, and even as I said it, I heard how the words sounded. Like I was le bOnKeRs.

Like I was Arabella.

But it didn't matter because I was talking to empty air. The detective had already walked away.

I turned to Officer Allegrini, who was sitting at his desk. I had to make one last attempt. "You're wrong, man," I said in *CHiPs*-talian.

"We in the Venice police are not in the habit of asking the opinion of schoolgirls," he said in regular Italian without looking up.

Maybe it was his tone that brought out the extraBadness in me. Or maybe it was because my leather pants were cutting off oxygen to my brain.

Whatever caused it, I couldn't stop myself. I hit him with some more *ChiPs*-talian, saying, "You're wrong about the teapot-snatch job too, my main man. That wasn't no inside job. You should be looking for a left-handed guy with a limp who's trying to quit the cigarettes. Feel my vibe?"

Out of the corner of my eye I saw that the female plain-clothes detective had circled back, and was now looking at me with tears in her eyes. And I am sure the noise she was making only sounded like repressed hysterical laughter but was really some kind of Italian version of awe.

And she wasn't the only one. Officer Allegrini was staring at me wordlessly, no doubt stunned by my deduction and my incorporation of my new vocabulary words—*snatch* AND *inside job.* Double bonus score! Indeed, judging by the several appealing colors of red his face was turning, I think he was really moved.

But then I noticed how he was clenching his fists, and I decided maybe it was me who should be really moved. Like toward the door. "I've got to hit the pavement, guy," I said, standing up, "but you'll see. I'm right about this and I'm right about Arabella."

I was halfway across the room when he yelled, "You read the files on my desk? She read the files on my desk! You had better pray that I never set eyes on you again, Signorina Callihan!"

Little Life Lesson 20: Some people are very rude about taking help from others.

His boisterous bon voyage followed me out of the station and into the foggy Venetian night. My heart was racing with the thrill of my exit, but halfway back to the hotel it had slowed, and I suddenly felt drained of energy. Along with the will to live, the ability to function any longer without food, and the desire to ever wear leather pants again.

Mostly what I kept thinking was: This was my fault. If only I'd been less worried about being a Model Daughter and more worried about believing Arabella, if only I'd helped her, maybe then she wouldn't be dead.

I was convinced she hadn't committed suicide. Even if she were going to kill herself, she wouldn't have done it fifteen minutes before we were supposed to meet. And that wasn't the only thing wrong.

But knowing something is wrong, and knowing what it is, are like Ugg boots and Cuteness: unrelated. I had no idea who would want to kill her, or why, or how they could have done it. I was the only person who thought she'd been murdered, which meant I was the only one looking for her killer. And not only did I have no leads, I didn't even know where she lived. All I needed was one piece of evidence to show the police, one thing to convince them. But I didn't have le clue where to start looking.

Not that it would matter, I realized. The fact that I had not been arrested but merely spent part of the night at the police department would not, I felt, do anything to calm the Dadzilla Wrathphoon that was headed for the Isle of Jas as soon as I encountered him the next morning. Or sooner, since, as I reached the door of the hotel, someone cleared his throat in the alley next to me and stepped out of the fog.

But it wasn't Dadzilla. It was a little boy in an Ali G–style tracksuit four sizes too big for him.

"Missy Callihan?" he said. "It is you, pretty lady?"

"*Sì.*"

He shoved an envelope into my hand. "This is for you, then."

The envelope was lumpy and had an address, CANNAREGIO, 5524, embossed on the flap. On the other side, my name and Grissini Palace Hotel were written in big swirly writing.

Writing I recognized as Arabella's.

"Where did you get this?"

"The lady gives it to me and says if she doesn't arrive to take it back, I should come here and deliver it to you personally. I've been waiting for hours. Good-bye."

"Wait, I—" I started to say, but the boy had completely vanished.

There was nothing else to do. I opened the letter.

Chapter Ten

I don't know what I was expecting. Something profound, maybe a little moving, with a precious object accompanying it.

The letter said:

> Dear Jasmine,
> In case I have to depart abruptly,
> please look after my goldfish.
> Kissos,
> Arabella

And the object? An I-Heart-Hotcakes keychain with seven keys on it.

!

Although the letter only contained sixteen short words and they were all in English, I had a hard time understanding it. I read it over three times, looking for some sign that it was in code. This allowed me to discover that GOLDFISH is an anagram for both DISH GOLF and FIG HOLDS, but that didn't exactly enrich my comprehension.

Please. Look. After. My. Goldfish.

It was practically a haiku! Which is, of course, everything you want in a note from a dead person! If your address is 1 Opposite Road, Backwardsville, Planet of Not.

It was only two in the morning but my day was already going from strength to strength. If I'd been hoping for le clue decisive that Arabella had been murdered that I could show to the police, I was out of luck. They would laugh like tiny hyenas in my face.

Here were the facts:

1) Arabella had, in fact, departed abruptly.
2) Her goldfish would, therefore, need looking after.
3) Once I encountered Typhoonzilla and he learned how I'd spent the past few hours, I would no longer be allowed to leave the hotel.
4) Ever.
5) The last thing in the world I wanted to do right then was walk across Venice in my leather pants.
6) I had no choice.

I was starting to see what Polly meant about Arabella's signature scent being TROUBLE.

The thing is, Venice is a small city, but it was laid out by someone who hated their friends and never wanted them to be able to visit. To get to Arabella's, I would need to consult a map. Since there weren't any map stores conveniently open at two A.M., the best place to find one was in my room upstairs. Which meant sneaking in without alerting Lo Zilla. And then sneaking out again.

Awesomeo!

(Although it did mean I could change my pants.)

The sneaking-in portion of the program went pretty well. I got through the lobby and up to my room and inside it without alerting anyone. I'd just pulled the map out of my desk, when there was a thrashing noise outside my door. Dadzilla's loving voice cooed, "What's going on in there? Open up!"

Not only did it say that, but I saw the key on my side start to turn in the lock as he used a key on his side. I'd been right—he totally did have a secret key!

But this wasn't the moment for Patting Myself on the Back. It was the moment for Leaping into Bed and Pulling the Covers up Over My Clothes. By the time he opened the door, I was fully covered and doing a brilliant imitation of someone who'd just been roused from the slumber of the Model.

"Santa? Is that you? Did you bring me a pony?" I said, pretending to be in the middle of an ace dream.

"Stop being ridiculous," Dadzilla said, not in an ace-dreamy way at all. "It is me, your father. Who is Santa?"

I know it was two in the morning and he's a genius, but really. "Santa Claus is the man who delivers presents to children at Christmas," I told him. "Always wears red? White beard? Jolly?"

"Don't be fresh."

I could have assured him that I was feeling ANYTHING but fresh. Fresh and white leather pants are not two great tastes that go great together. Instead I said, "What brings you to my room at this hour?"

"I thought I heard the door open. I wanted to make sure there were no intruders."

"None except for you."

"This is not something to joke about."

"I completely agree. Are you hearing other noises as well? Voices in your head?"

"Be quiet, Jasmine." He then turned to scan my room with Everywhere Eye. As he did that, I realized the note from Arabella was lying on my desk next to the map.

Gulp.

I had to coax him out of there. "Is there anything else I can do for you?" I asked pleasantly. "Any small service? Perhaps some witty conversation to help you relax?"

That did the trick. "Go back to sleep, Jasmine," he rumbled. Giving me one last scowl for good measure, he backed out of the room.

Although it stings to have your conversational abilities

scorned, I couldn't really focus on the pain, due to the fact that my heart was beating so hard it was about to burst through my Wonderbra (yes, that hard). I closed my eyes and did some deep breathing to encourage it to slow back down to normal. Then I did a little more deep breathing because I was tasting the sweet, sweet air of freedom.

Little Life Lesson 21: If you are in the middle of crime fighting but have had a particularly harrowing day, avoid breathing deeply the sweet, sweet air of freedom.

Little Life Lesson 22: Especially while closing your eyes.

Little Life Lesson 23: And lying in bed.

The next thing I was aware of was a weird cramp in my leg from having fallen asleep in my cowboy boots. I raised my eyelids and saw that it was light outside, and the clock on my nightstand read 6:32.

Then I heard the noises. Getting up–type noises. Coming through the wall of my room that adjoined Dadzilla and Sherri!'s.

If I was going to get to Arabella's apartment, I'd have to do it before Dadzilla was in his full upright-and-unlocked position. Which meant right that second. Which meant no changing out of leather pants.

Le sigho.

I grabbed the map and took off.

It was *molto* more foggy outside now than it had been the night before so spotting the street names, when they were posted, was a super-fun game of hide-and-seek, minus the super fun part. Even with the map, it took me almost an hour and a long discussion with a garbage man to find Arabella's address. Cannaregio 5524 turned out to be next door to Cannaregio 2230 and across a canal from Cannaregio 618. Naturally.

Little Life Lesson 24: Garbage men = urban heroes.

It was an ancient-looking corner building with the front facing the *fondamenta* that ran along one canal and the side rising directly up from the water of another canal. A marble balcony jutted out from the second floor of the facade with a statue of cupid precariously perched on the corner. Sitting next to it was a black cat who stopped cleaning itself as I came closer. It was a perfectly nice-looking cat, shiny with a fancy collar, and yet something about the way it was watching me through the mist could have been used as a teaching aid for the words SINISTER INTENT in a language textbook. I hoped this was not the funny look Arabella had been talking about.

Beneath the marble balcony was a massive wooden entrance door with flaking green paint. There was a row of six brass buzzers next to it that could have used some polishing, and the one next to apartment 2 had the initials AR in swirly writing taped above it.

The biggest key on I-Heart-Hotcakes worked the lock on the entrance door. Behind it was a crumbly stone courtyard with a water gate opening onto the canal at the left. The sound of the water lapping outside gave the space a kind of tranquil feeling that my accidentally letting Big Door slam behind me didn't really add to. But no one threw open their shutters to see what was going on, so I crept up the marble staircase with the lions' heads carved into it which wound along the right side of the house, to the second level where I could see the number 2 on a door without anyone seeing me.

Or so I thought.

Chapter Eleven

I'd sort of figured Arabella just sent me her whole keychain without bothering to weed out the ones I'd need, but when I got to her door I saw that actually there was a reason for all the keys, or at least most of them. There were five locks on the door, four of them shiny and new. In case I'd needed more proof she was terrified for her life. Or, anything to add to the knot of guilt for not believing her growing in the pit of my stomach.

My first thought when I opened the door was, if eyeballs could talk, mine would be squealing, "WOW!" Also, "HELLLLLLLLLLLP US!" My second thought was that I really hoped she'd rented the place furnished and hadn't done it herself because otherwise I would be required to believe she was completely insane and capable of anything. It looked like what I imagined a Keebler Elf brothel would look like (not that I've spent a lot of time imagining that).

There was only one room, which appeared to function

as a living room–dining room–bedroom–kitchen. It had dark wood walls and a dark wood-beamed ceiling but every object that could have a red-and-black-lace ruffle did, from the vent over the stove to the curtains, dining-room chair cushions, side tables, kitchen sink, soap dispenser, coffee table, coffee pot, garbage cans, massive armoire, sofa, and candy dish. Any parts of the room not suitable for Ruffling were filled with porcelain statues of pugs wearing red ribbons around their necks in a variety of appealing poses like "sitting," "begging," and "sitting and begging." There was one supremely awful one on the (ruffled) desk next to her cell phone and laptop with a plaque below it that I think said THE RUNT, but I could only give it a quick look before my eyeballs started to twitch uncontrollably. All the furniture except the armoire were smaller than normal, which would have been fine for Arabella because she was pixie size, but it made me feel like a visitor from Planet Gigantor.

Beyond the main room was the bathroom. It was covered— walls, floor, and ceiling—in tiles with red roses printed on them, which went nicely with the black-and-pink-lace skirts on the toilet, bathtub, and soap dish.

The place was a little dusty but, apart from a pillow and comforter stacked next to the couch, tidy. At least as tidy as an apartment stuffed with Pugs-n-Ruffles could be. I was surprised because with her crazy fashion sense and swirly writing, Arabella didn't seem like the a-clean-house-is-a-happy-house type. It was definitely not the apartment of someone whose signature scent would be called TROUBLE (unless that was followed by "WITH HER VISION"). But from the fake eyelashes carefully lined up on the vanity table to the boxes of stationery neatly stacked on the dining room table, order prevailed. Everything seemed to have its place and be in it.

Except the one thing I had come for: There was no goldfish. Not even a sign of a goldfish. No fish food, no indentation left by a (possibly ruffled) goldfish bowl. Nothing to suggest that the Elf House of Pleasure had ever harbored any water-dwelling animal in its walls. So it had to be some less obvious, more figurative form of goldfish.

I decided I would work methodically around the apartment searching for it. I started in the kitchen, checking through all the drawers (no fish), the cabinets (no fish), the garbage can (two used tea bags, three squeezed lemons, an empty Sweet'N Low envelope, but no fish), and the refrigerator (box of milk, distinctly non-fishy). I thought I might have hit on something in a drawer filled with odds and ends in the kitchen but although it held a bag of change, a ten-year-old Venice phone book, and a tide chart from six months earlier, there was nothing fish or fish related.

Moving to the bathroom, I examined the bathtub (no fish soap or fish-shaped tub stopper), the shower curtain (slightly ripped in the corner but not in a fish shape), beneath all the ruffles (no fish, although I did find a bright blue shirt button), and the garbage (empty). The ruffle around the bathtub was slightly damp, and for a second that made my heartbeat pick up—Who showered before they committed suicide?—but I could already hear the lady detective telling me nicely but firmly that you couldn't use logic when people killed themselves.

Along the side wall there was a dressing table with jewelry on it (no fish). There was a square that was less dusty than the area surrounding it, showing that something had been there and been moved, but it was too small to have been a fishbowl.

The only thing in the laundry hamper was a pair of argyle socks. Fishy in their own way—argyle, Arabella? Really?—but not fish.

As I looked in vain for anything with a fishy cast, I registered other things. Like how in the sink in the kitchen area there was just one glass and one bowl and one spoon. One napkin in a gold (non-fish-patterned) napkin ring on the counter. I'd always assumed Arabella had tons of her own friends outside of class, but now I began to wonder. Maybe she had been as lonely as I was.

There was only a single shelf of books, most of which looked like they'd come with the apartment because they were all in Italian and mainly travel guides to places with deserts (ergo: no fish). The only ones in English were three paperback mystery novels and *Grieving for Dummies*. I spotted something sticking out of that one and got excited in case it was a picture of a fish or marking a passage about "Grieving for Your Lost Fish." Le not.

The bookmark was a photo of Arabella and three people:

a dashing-looking gray-haired man, a bitter-looking scruffy guy, and a very put-together dark-haired woman in her twenties. It looked like it had been taken during a party and everyone except the young guy seemed to be having fun. The section it was marking was titled "After a Parent Dies." Parts of it were underlined, but what struck me most was that from the way the pages were warped it looked like someone had been crying when they read it.

It talked about how there's a period after a parent dies when you try making a lot of deals with God, even if you don't believe in God, begging for a sign or gesture, anything, that shows you they are still near you. That it's a phase to believe that every shadow in the night is the parent's ghost, or every flicker you see out of the corner of your eye is your late parent, watching you, missing you, wanting to be close to you to make sure you are okay.

But the book was wrong, because it wasn't only a phase, at least not for me. My mom died when I was six, which was a long time ago, and I still sometimes did those things. Even though I knew it was irrational, I still woke up in the middle of the night hoping to catch a ghost hand caressing my cheek, still felt jealous when I heard people talking about being haunted by ghosts. Because if they could be, why wasn't I? Where was my mom? Didn't she love me enough to haunt me?

I stood for a long time staring at the wavy pages and imagining Arabella alone in her apartment, reading and sobbing and missing her parent so, so much. I must have been allergic to something on the bookshelf because my eyes got a little teary then and I had to wipe my nose on my sleeve.

As I did that, I had the strangest feeling of being watched, and looking at the window, I saw the black cat sitting there, staring at me, with huge green eyes. This wasn't surprising given my superpower, but it was a little disconcerting. It tilted its head to one side, like it was curious about me, then got interested in something outside and jumped away. When it left I noticed that although the windowsill was dusty on the sides it was clean on the middle and I wondered if Arabella had sat there playing with the cat.

I went to slide the book back onto the shelf and something fell out of it, a pamphlet entitled "MAKING MEMORIES: HOW YOU CAN BECOME PART OF THE 'YOUR NAME ON RICE' FAMILY, AMERICA'S #1 GRAIN-BASED SOUVENIR!"

Okay, who would kill someone whose life fantasy was to have a kiosk at the mall and make the "gift they'll never re-gift"?

Themselves, a voice in my head that sounded a lot like Alyson's suggested. *Seriously, with life dreams like that, why not just end it all? Have you considered that perhaps the reason you have no evidence she was murdered and the police don't think she was murdered was because she* wasn't *murdered?* Happy Friendly Hench Voice said. *Why do you think you're so smart? It's after 8 A.M., which means you've been here almost an hour and you've found what? Oh, that's right, NOTHING. Not even the goldfish.*

HELLO WORDS OF ENCOURAGEMENT WHEN I NEED YOU MOST! It is always cheering to know that you can count on your own head to be supportive.

But the truth was, Evil Hench Voice was kind of right. I was fighting the good fight against Creeping Doubt, but as I turned to tackle her desk I would have given anything for some confirmation, some sign, that I was on the right track about Arabella's death.

Right when I thought that, her cell phone started to vibrate.

Le Creepy, *adj.* 1. having a dead person's phone ring immediately after you've pretty much begged the heavens for a clue. 2. having that happen at 8:10 A.M. on a Sunday.

It rang again. I stared at it. It rang a third time.

Picking it up carefully by the edges, I flipped it open. "Hello?"

There was a slight pause on the other end, like someone was surprised and then a woman's voice said in English, "Hello? Is that you, Bella? It's Beatrice. Look, I'm sorry to call so early but I know you're always up and—"

I cut her off. "I'm afraid this isn't Arabella." And, with a sinking feeling, I realized this probably wasn't my clue.

The voice said, "Not Arabella? Oh. I see. I'm sorry. May I please speak to her, then?"

"She can't come to the phone right now. Would you like to leave a message?"

"Who am I talking to?" the woman asked.

"Who am *I* talking to?" I asked back.

There was another pause and then the woman said in a professional tone, "This is Miss Portinari, Arabella's father's secretary. Would you please ask Arabella to phone me at her earliest convenience? She has the number."

"I'm afraid—" I started to say, but she'd hung up.

Only after the call was over did I realize how weird it was that Arabella's phone was even there. I mean, like any person who had a cell phone (NOT THAT I WOULD KNOW, THANK YOU, DADZILLA), she always carried it with her. The fact that she'd left it behind when she went out that night disturbed me because it suggested that she'd known she wasn't coming back. Like she would have if she'd planned to commit suici—

The sound of heavy footsteps stopping outside Arabella's apartment interrupted these cheery thoughts. They were followed by the jingling of keys and one of the locks on the door started to turn.

Although I had a totally legitimate reason for being there, something in my head told me to hide! Fast! Pocketing the phone and the photo from the book, I considered both the Elf couch and the Elf desk, but there was really only one place big enough to hold me.

Little Life Lesson 25: Being tall can be an occupational hazard while detecting.

To leap to the armoire and wrench open one of the double

doors was but the work of a moment. I just had time to nestle myself between a green fur vest and a zebra trench coat and catch a black wig that fell off the shelf before the last of Arabella's locks unlatched to admit a woman who, judging from the number of ruffles swathing her, was probably the owner of the apartment.

Followed by a more-rumpled-but-not-any-less-mean-looking-for-it Officer Allegrini.

Which is the only reason I didn't scream when something shifted in the darkness behind me and said in a male voice, "Stay quiet and you won't get hurt."

Chapter Twelve

Little Life Lesson 26: If you are really interested in making sure someone stays quiet, sneaking up on them in what appeared to be a perfectly innocent armoire and making threats is not the ideal method.

Little Life Lesson 27: Following that up with "Can you control your hair? I want to see too" is also not recommended.

For some reason this comment soothed me slightly, though. It didn't seem like the kind of thing a Really Bad Guy would say. Which was good, because armoires are not exactly luxury suites and I was smashed against him. From this I could gather that he was about my height (he'd been spying on me the whole time!) and very fit (he'd seen me get all teary reading *Grieving for Dummies*!) and about my age (what kind of creepy person spies on you?) and wearing well-washed jeans (had I picked my nose? Please do not let me have picked my nose) and had really big—

Anyway, all of that would have been very distracting. But

instead, I focused on Paying Attention to Other Things. Like how all the ruffles on the couch were pointing toward the window as though they'd been brushed in that direction. And what Officer Allegrini and the landlady were saying.

They were both talking really fast but as far as I could make out, their conversation went like this:

LANDLADY: This is a grandiose tragedy! She is one who always paid her rent on time.

OFFICER ALLEGRINI: *(Flipping through notebooks on the dining table.)* Grunt.

LANDLADY: Such a nice tiny animal was she!

OFFICER ALLEGRINI: *(Opening boxes of stationery and rifling through them.)* Grunt.

LANDLADY: Yes, I knew it from the commencement who she is even though she used a pretend name. I am very leggy like that.

OFFICER ALLEGRINI: *(Bending to look under the sofa.)* Grunt.

LANDLADY: I don't reveal to her that I know. I keep the secrets like a store vault. In my opinion, if she is wishing to be false named, I will let her. I know of this for I once dated a very famous star of the cinema. Of course, I cannot tell you who.

OFFICER ALLEGRINI: *(Glaring at objects on the dressing table.)* Grunt.

LANDLADY: Even yesterday a reporter comes
    around asking about her but I play the stupid.
OFFICER ALLEGRINI: *(Dragging dressing table*
    away from the wall to look behind it.) Loud grunt.

I liked Officer Allegrini's terse style. It suited him. Also, it was pitched to more or less exactly my Italian comprehension level.

While they'd been talking I'd been getting to know my new neighbor better. There aren't that many different positions two people in an armoire who are both trying to see through the same thin crack can occupy, but we'd tried them all and finally settled into one that had me slightly bent at the knees so his chin rested just above my ear and my shoulder pressed against his chest. Just the kind of cozy posture you hope to assume with a complete stranger.

LANDLADY: What a firm, manly grip you have.
OFFICER ALLEGRINI: *(Loping toward the bathroom.)*
    Grunt.

What I hadn't noticed was that they'd left the door of the apartment open and the black cat had wandered in. Naturally the first thing it did was stalk up to the armoire and stare at the gap I was looking through.

Then it started to meow.

This was bad. I tried to develop a superpower in cat mind

control but since I'd never had much success with that on humans, I wasn't very hopeful. I felt the body behind me take a sharp breath and stiffen. Both of our hearts were pounding fast. We swallowed hard at the same time.

Luckily Officer Allegrini chose that moment to grasp the bathroom doorknob in his Firm Manly Grip. Apparently his Firm Manliness was too much for the knob because it came off in his hand.

He looked from the knob to the landlady in horror. She hadn't seen, so he shifted his weight to hide the fact that he was trying to screw the knob back on.

That's when the cat struck. For no apparent reason other than I LOVE YOU KITTIES, it went to Officer Allegrini and started trying to crawl up his leg. He was standing on one foot trying to shake it off, while desperately working to reattach the knob behind him. It looked like he was doing a crazy dance, or someone had slipped beetles down his back.

Little Life Lesson 28: If you plan to lose control of your ability not to crack up, try not to be stuck in an armoire that is already stuffed to the gills with someone else.

I nearly choked from laughing, and The Body behind me was squirming in a dangerous way. The landlady was busy monologuing in her own world, saying:

LANDLADY: Yes, I am the protectatrix of my tenants.
Of course, this one, she is more than a tenant

to me, you understand. In fact, she says to me
just in a week—

OFFICER ALLEGRINI: *(Shoving doorknob back on.)*
Grunt.

ARMOIRE: *Creak.*

LANDLADY: What was that?

OFFICER ALLEGRINI: *(Back pressing against door
where knob has fallen off again.)* Nothing. You said?

LANDLADY: Ah, yes. She says "Gloria"—that is my
name, Gloria *(giving Officer Allegrini a wink)*—
"Gloria," she tells me, "you are like a sister to me."

Two grunts, one from Officer Allegrini as he finally got the
knob to stay on, and one from The Body behind me. The
cat had lost interest and wandered out of the apartment.

LANDLADY: She was very silent, so much by herself.
Not that I spy, of course. But no matter how
many times I tell her she leaves the shutters open
and I cannot bother but to see. Always I tell her
that all of Cannaregio can see her changing the
clothes but she does not care. I see her yesterday
night and I think to myself, I will have to say
words to her again.

OFFICER ALLEGRINI: *(Heading toward Arabella's
desk.)* Grunt.

LANDLADY: Just look at this dust on the windowsill!

The strangers, they do not understand about shutters. She uses the curtains instead. And you see—this one is missing its rope. Who will pay to replace this, I ask you?

OFFICER ALLEGRINI: *(Picking up garbage can and dumping it on top of the desk.)* Grunt.

All the garbage had in it was a crumpled piece of stationery and a Q-tip. These items seemed to excite him until he uncrumpled the paper and saw it was blank. He used a word I didn't know but which I am pretty sure is not considered Nice, then moved on to inspect the other objects on the desk, pulling everything out of the drawers and spilling out the pencil cup. But nothing seemed to satisfy his thirst for knowledge.

LANDLADY: Of course, I wonder if I should blame myself for this. But it is not what she would have wanted. Still, suicide. So much tragic that she is dead.

As she said that, all hilarity ceased. The Body behind me sagged. There was a gasp and I heard a voice whisper, "Dead?" incredulously and a little too loudly. Fortunately this was covered by Officer Allegrini's response:

OFFICER ALLEGRINI: *(In the middle of the room,*

standing with hands on his hips, glaring around
petulantly.) Grunt.

LANDLADY: Did you find the suicide note you are
looking for?

OFFICER ALLEGRINI: No.

LANDLADY: I'm sure if it were here, you would
have. You are very good at your job I am betting
(batting eyelashes).

Officer Allegrini made one last grunt and started moving
toward the door.

That's when I saw it. Sitting and gleaming on the desk
next to "The Runt." A four-inch-tall blown-glass statue of
a cat.

With a blown-glass goldfish inside its stomach.

It must have been wrapped in paper and stashed in a back
corner, but Officer Allegrini in his zeal had opened it and left
it sitting there on the paper in disgust. And I kind of couldn't
blame him. The cat's head was slightly crooked, one paw was
smaller than the other, and I was pretty sure it was leering
at me.

It was definitely not the most beautiful clue in the world,
but it was mine, and I couldn't wait to get my hands on it.
I used my last remaining mental strength to send the tele-
pathic *CHiPs*-talian message "Scram immediately!" to LAND-
LADY and OFFICER ALLEGRINI, and after about three
trillion years (or two minutes) they got it.

(Exit LANDLADY and OFFICER ALLEGRINI offstage.)

As soon as they'd closed the door behind them, I pushed out of the armoire, assumed my most menacing WWMrTD pose, and turned to face my Armoire Mate.

Chapter Thirteen

I'd been prepared to hit him with "I pity the fool who was spying on me from the armoire" but that seemed kind of harsh when I saw him. My first quick glance showed me a familiar-looking guy a little older than me with reddish-brown hair, a spattering of freckles, and caramel-colored eyes, like what you'd get if you mated a Chuck Taylors/Ben Sherman sweater/worn-in Levi's jeans–wearer with a golden retriever. He was standing in the armoire, gripping the sides, hard.

He said into space, "Bella dead? Committed suicide? No. Oh, God, no. I knew this would happen."

I wanted to know a lot of things, like how he knew it would happen and why he'd been hiding in the armoire to begin with and, oh, who he was, but instead I went into the bathroom and got the (ruffled) tissue box. When I came back he'd sagged and was sitting on the bottom of the armoire between a pair of gold boots and a frog stuffed animal.

He seemed to be losing the fight to hold back tears, but when I offered a Kleenex he shook his head, using his sleeve to wipe his eyes. "I'm good," he said. "Thank you—"

"Jasmine. Jas," I said.

"Thanks, Jas. I'm Bobby."

We shook hands.

After that it was a tad awkward, me standing, him sitting there with his eyes glued to the floor breathing kind of raggedly, neither of us talking. But it gave me a chance to figure out why he looked so familiar—he was Mr. Bitter from the picture I'd found in Arabella's book. Only now he didn't look bitter, he looked sad. And younger.

When his breathing started sounding normal I asked, "So, how did you know Arabella?"

A strange expression flickered in his eyes. "She is—was—my sister."

Oh, hello.

Of course he could have been lying. I mean, that's just the thing you'd say if you were found inside the armoire of a dead girl and wanted to seem unsuspicious, right? I remembered the essay Arabella had mentioned her brother in. It was called something like "Le summer vacation nightmareo." I scoured my mind for details—there was something about le boato and something about fishing gone le horribly wrong and her brother—

"Your boat got a leak and you had to plug it with your Joe DiMaggio baseball card," I blurted.

He stared at me. "Actually it was Pete Rose. But how did you know about it?"

It had been a fairly weak test, but he passed. "Your sister wrote about it in Italian class."

"She did an essay about that? Man, that trip was the worst. Right after our mom died. Arabella somehow got it into her head that we'd starve to death. So we used mini-marshmallows to fish. No surprise we didn't catch anything. When the boat sprang that leak, she completely lost it."

"In Arabella's version you were superheroic, leaping out of the boat to pull it to shore and her to safety. She even compared you to Aquaman."

"Yeah, not so much with the swimming-to-shore heroics. God, she had an imagination." The side of his mouth started to curve into a smile, then got tugged back. "She was a really good little sister."

"I bet."

"Quirky, though. I used to tease her like crazy about her weird habits."

"You mean like how she used a different color pen for each day of the week?"

He chuckled. "I'd forgotten about that. But, yeah. Did you know about the orange juice? How she had to have three ice cubes in it every morning or she'd get bad news?"

"No, she didn't tell me that. But she did explain you always had to make sure to eat your food in even numbered bites or you'd get indigestion."

"When we were growing up, all the knife blades in the house had to point to the right or someone would be mean to her. And she bent the corner of every piece of paper she wrote on because otherwise she thought the message would be misunderstood."

"I saw her do that, but I hadn't realized what it was about!"

"She was a kook, my sister. But I loved her."

After that, things got silent. Dead silent. I decided to try some conversational CPR. "So you came to Venice to visit her? From America?"

"No, I'm spending the year at Oxford. Got to Venice last night. I had a date but I decided to bag it, came here instead."

"Was she here when you got here?"

"No, I let myself in. She'd sent me a set of keys a few months ago. I crashed on the sofa to wait and—" He stopped himself. It was like he suddenly became another person, his expression going wary and a little mean. He got up and took a step away from the armoire toward me. "Who did you say you were again? And what are you doing here? And why should I be answering any of your questions?"

"Arabella was a friend of mine. From Italian class. She asked me to come."

He was standing about a foot from me now with his arms crossed. "Oh, really? Did she also ask you to snoop around? And answer her phone?"

I had not been snooping! I was an invited guest! I scoffed at such innuendo. "Excuse me, but which of us was spying on people from the armoire?"

"Yeah, that would be both of us."

Screeeeeech went the brakes on my Scoffcedes. "That was— never mind. I was here because of this." I pulled the note from my pocket and handed it to him.

He read it, flipped it over, read it again, then kind of squinted at me. "So this is what you were looking for? Her goldfish?"

I nodded. "And I found it."

"Where? She doesn't have a fish."

"There," I said, pointing to the glass sculpture on the desk.

He looked at me scornfully. "You expect me to believe that? Tell your boss this was the weakest excuse ever. I know you didn't get any photos, that's why I was watching from the armoire, but if anything private about my sister comes out in whatever rag you're working for—"

"Is there some medication you should be taking?" I asked him. "Do I seriously look like a reporter to you?"

"No, you're right. You look like one of those parasites who pretended to be her friend because of who our father was."

"Why, thank you, MAY BE JERKY."

"What did you just call me?"

"Nothing. Refresh my memory of who your father was so I can remember why I was using his daughter."

"Nice try."

"I'm serious, I have no idea."

"Arabella Neal? You have no idea?"

"Her last name was Randolph."

That stumped him for a second. "I guess that's right. She was using Mom's name here. But that doesn't mean she didn't tell you. You've heard of Ned Neal?"

"The globe-trotting tycoon? Who started the space airline?"

"You got it. Billionaire. Businessman. Bastard. That's our dad." He was starting to resemble the photo more. "Nothing anyone did was ever good enough for him. Except Arabella. She was his perfect princess. Probably why she couldn't deal with his death."

I remembered reading articles about that: Ned Neal, brilliant entrepreneur, found dead in his palace in Venice. It had happened a few months before we got there, in early summer. "It was a heart attack, right?"

"Arabella didn't think so. She decided he'd been murdered. Because it was so hard to believe that a fifty-five-year-old who worked twenty hours a day would have a massive coronary."

"Couldn't he have been killed? I mean, it wasn't impossible."

"Yep, pretty much. He was locked up all alone in his office, like always, when it happened. They had to bash the door down to even find the body. But Arabella kept coming up with absurd theories about how it could have happened, anyway."

"Like what?"

"Snakes through the air vent. Someone using a vacuum to suck all the air out of the room so he suffocated. Poisonous spiders. And we'd hire all these experts to look into them, and at the end we'd be back where we started. At a heart attack." He was clenching and unclenching his fists as he spoke. "For what? At the end of it he was still dead and gone. And now so is she." He shook his head as if he could shake away the thought and said, "I should probably call Beatrice."

"Is that the woman I talked to on the phone? She said she was your father's secretary, but if he's dead—"

"She's more like the glue that's been holding us all together for the last year. She and Bella were especially close. She'll be devastated that my sister committed suicide."

"She didn't."

"What?"

"I don't believe she committed suicide."

A muscle worked in his jaw. "No, of course not. You wouldn't."

"What does that mean?"

"That you're like Arabella. She wouldn't have trusted you if you weren't. And that means you'll have some elaborate theory to explain it."

"I don't. But it just doesn't make sense."

"Yeah, see, actually, it does. The reason I came to Venice? Bella called me and told me she finally figured out how Dad was offed, and I had to get here right away."

"Really? She said she knew who did it? Did she tell you anything else?"

"Only that it would le blow my mindo."

"That sounds like her. But why does that make you think she killed herself?"

"Every time she was wrong about this she'd get really depressed. Suicide-watch depressed. And I'm sure this was just another one of those. Another mess-up. And she got depressed again. Only this time she let it carry her away." He took a deep breath. "Besides, who would want to kill her? She was harmless."

I thought about that. "I'm not so sure." A snippet from my phone conversation with her the night before came back to me then, her saying, *I asked someone the wrong question. . . . I wish I knew which one. . . .*

My heart started to pound, fast. "What if you're wrong and it went the other way?" I started walking around the room. "What if she actually did figure out who your father's murderer was and she let it slip, so they killed her to keep her quiet?"

"You sound just like her. That's exactly the kind of crazy stupid thing she would say."

I stopped walking. "But it's true. Maybe one of Arabella's theories was right. Maybe this murderer is smart and creative and managed to hide his crimes by making them look impossible."

"How would you go about investigating that?"

"I don't know. Arabella said she was going to Prada. I'd probably start there. Then maybe—"

"You just won't stop, will you?" he said tightly.

"Don't you want to know the truth?"

"The truth? I know the truth." He took a step toward me. I took a step back. "The truth is that my dad died of a heart attack, and Arabella killed herself because she couldn't accept it." He took another step toward me. I took another step back. "Because she kept looking for answers where there weren't any questions." He stepped forward. I stepped back. "And you're doing the same thing."

My back hit the wall. He was standing only inches from me and I could see the anger and the pain in his eyes. I said, "I don't think—"

"That's right. Don't think. Don't ask. No more questions. Why can't you just stop asking questions and accept things and be happy? Why couldn't you just listen to me?"

It was me he had pinned against the wall, but it wasn't me he was seeing. It was Arabella. The sister he thought he'd failed to protect.

"Bobby, there was nothing you could have done."

He pulled away like I'd burned him. "Get out of here."

I was so shocked I couldn't move.

"Go. Leave."

"But—"

"You want to know who killed her? I did. Me."

"Don't be ridiculo—"

"I should have stopped her before she tried another one of her theories. Stopped her before it failed. And I didn't. So I'm your murderer."

Maybe it was the leather pants. I have no idea where the words came from but it was like all the pent-up anger I felt at Dadzilla for moving us to Venice, and the Evil Hench Twins for being evil, and myself for not listening to Arabella, and Officer Allegrini for not listening to me, and even Jack for going off with Candy, which I'd been repressing, came spilling out of me. "I think you want to believe she killed herself because then you can hang around here and feel bad. Like a failure. Fulfilling everything your dad ever said. But I'm not going to help you. I have a cunning murderer to find."

"I told you to go."

"I am." I pushed off of the wall. "My last name is Callihan and I'm staying at the Grissini Palace Hotel. Call me when you stop feeling sorry for yourself."

My hands shook as I wrapped the cat sculpture in the paper and went to the door. I stopped there. "Did you eat or drink anything while you were here?"

He stared at me. "No, why?"

"You didn't touch that glass in the sink? And no one but you has been here?"

He shook his head.

"I'm going to take it."

He followed me to the sink as I slipped it into a plastic bag. "I don't see what—"

"It's for my crazy stupid investigation, to get Arabella's prints," I told him, and walked out.

My legs were still wobbly as I went down the stairs. I'd

never done that, lost my temper, with anyone. I really was becoming BadJas. And I wasn't sure I liked it.

The fog was still thick on the street when I got outside. I had an idea how to get home but it was hard to see more than a few feet in any direction. This was probably a bonus for anyone else around because I was pretty sure that if they'd seen me in broad daylight after the night I'd had they would have had to be admitted to a psych ward for post-traumatic stress disorder, but it wasn't that fantastico for me. I was distracted, pausing at each bridge to see if it was the one I'd crossed on my way there, backtracking once—so at first I didn't hear it. Them. I stopped abruptly.

And so did whoever was following me.

I looked behind me but I couldn't see anything except fog. My heart started to pound against my ribs and I began climbing over bridges, turning down *calles,* not paying attention to where I was going.

The footsteps, quiet, almost shuffling, stayed behind me. I'd take two steps and they'd take two steps. I'd go three and they'd go three. Their pace matched mine, as though they were waiting to see what I did, where I'd go.

I started running.

The sound of my cowboy boots echoed off the walls of the narrow *calle* and were matched by another set, pounding toward me. I made a right, then a left, another right. The footsteps followed, dogging me, always there, coming closer.

And then they weren't. Abruptly, they'd disappeared.

I slowed down, walking on my tiptoes to make sure I could hear.

Nothing.

I took a few steps to be sure. A few more. Silence.

I was alone. I'd done it. Eluded them. I leaned against the wall to catch my breath.

I took a mental memo to avoid wearing cowboy boots in the future if I thought I was going to be followed. They made entirely too much—

Out of the corner of my eye I saw something shiny flash. There was a thud, followed by a shooting pain in my head, and the ground came rushing toward my face. I thought, *Polly will never forgive me for dying in this outfit.* And everything went black.

Chapter Fourteen

———— ❦ ————

I know it's wrong to say, but I was sort of disappointed in Heaven when I got there. Based on several things my aunt Winnie had told me after my mom died—especially the words "most beautiful sight you can imagine"—I'd pictured it as kind of like a huge taco stand, but it turned out to be less All-You-Can-Eat-Fiesta and more gray stone walls. And lots of grabby people. One of whom was now saying, "Miss Callihan? Can you hear me?"

I sat up slightly to see who was speaking and that's when a family of chipmunk clog dancers started rehearsing *Stomp! The Musical!* in my head.

I lay back down and closed my eyes.

"Miss Callihan, are you all right?"

"Yes, yes, fine, it's just the chipmunks," I said.

"The what?"

"Clog dancing," I added by way of explanation.

"Miss Callihan, can you open your eyes?"

I opened my eyes and found myself staring into twin pools of fascinating and mysterious gray.[2] They belonged to Max, the smoldering gondolier from the day before.[3]

I got cautiously up on one elbow. The chipmunks mounted a small protest but nothing as vehement as before. "How did you know my name?" I asked, my fingers quivering to touch the stubble that graced his square-cut, manly jaw.[4]

Max turned behind him and, in his rich melodious voice, said something in Italian along the lines of "She'll be fine, there is no concussion," then turned back to me. Beneath his steely exterior, his eyes smoldered with concern.[5] Smoldering, he reached out with a gentle yet filled-with-smoldering-ness

[2] Jas: Who said that?

[3] Jas: Who said THAT? Hello? I do not think things like that.

[4] Jas: WHAT IS GOING ON HERE?
  BadJas: Thought things needed le spicing up.
  Jas: This isn't spice. This is . . . hey, how did you get to be separate? I thought I was BadJas.
  BadJas: You were doing a lame-o job, so when we got knocked out, I decided to creep past your inhibitions and strike out on my own.
  Jas: You can't do that!
  BadJas: Oh, no? Watch closely.

[5] Jas: You already said "smoldered" before. You can't use the same word twice like that.
  BadJas: Le not?
  Jas: No, it's really bad style.
  BadJas: I believe you mean BadStyle. Plus, you can't deny that Max is totally bow-chica-wow-wow.
  Jas: Yes, I can.
  BadJas: Not to me. I know what's going on in the back of your mind.
  Jas: Really? What am I thinking now?
  BadJas: That Max is so hot he should come with his own misters.
  Jas: No, I am thinking that I am trying to find a murderer.
  BadJas: Fine. If you want to deny your True Thoughts, I'll stop. I don't want to upset you.
  Jas: Thank you.
  BadJas: (Much.)

touch to brush a lock of hair from my forehead and said smolderingly,[6] "Your wallet is on the street next to you with your identity card in it. Apparently the brigand did not have time to steal its contents. Or your phone." He handed both to me.

"Brigand?" I said, slowly sitting upright.

"The thief who attacks you."

I felt the side pocket of my jacket. It was unzipped, like someone had reached into it, but with my fingertips I could make out the lump of the glass sculpture wrapped in paper there, and the photo I'd taken from Arabella's beneath it. I breathed a sigh of relief.

"Something is missing?"

"No," I said. "Nothing is missing."

"He must have been frightened off."

And then I remembered: Right before I passed out, a voice whispering, "Leave them alone."

This wasn't a brigand at all. Whoever did this wasn't interested in stealing anything. They were interested in scaring me. Making me stop asking questions. Which meant someone was hiding something. Like that Arabella's death hadn't been suicide. She'd been murdered.

This was it, IT, the proof I'd been waiting for. Not proof

---

[6] Jas: I surrender.

BadJas: You do? Why?

Jas: Because this is stupid. We shouldn't be at odds, we should be working together.
          You can be in charge. I'll just lay low.

BadJas: For real?

Jas: Sure. I was being too bossy. Come here and we'll hug.

BadJas: That's really — hey, what are you doing with the duct tap —

Jas: You. Can. Not. Use. The. Word. Smolder. Three. Times. In. One. Sentence.

BadJas: *Smurflflkkekreer!*

that you could touch or use or show the police or do anything helpful with, but still, proof.

!

Little Life Lesson 29: If you ever find yourself glad that someone has followed and then attacked you, immediately reassess your life goals.

I looked at Max. "What were you doing here?"

"I am on my way to work on the gondola and I hear a sound, then I see a girl in a heap on the ground. Naturally, I stop. Max does not leave girls lying in heaps on the ground."

"Did you see anyone else? The person who hit me?"

"No. When I arrive, there is just you, and soon a crowd of well-wishers. But I tell them to go. You do not need to be ogled."

I tried to get up all at once, which didn't please the chipmunks, so Max helped me to my feet. That's when I saw the glass I'd taken from Arabella's to lift her fingerprints. Or rather the pieces of the glass. It looked like I'd fallen on it.

I started moving the glass bits into a pile with my boot.

"What are you doing?"

"I want to take this"—I gestured at the pieces of glass— "back to my hotel with me."

"Of course I do not mean to question your taste, but are you sure this is the souvenir of Venice you desire? We are a city known for our glass, but this is not perhaps the finest example."

"I don't want it as a souvenir."

"No? Then perhaps you do this from motives of tidiness. This is very noble but do not worry, there are people in Venice we pay to do this."

"It's not trash, it's evidence. Do you see a paper bag or anything we can put it in?"

"Evidence," Max repeated skeptically, but he went away and came back a minute later with a brown paper bag. "This is suitable? Now what do we do?"

"We scoop up everything that was around where I was lying on the ground, especially the glass," I explained. "But try to only touch it on the edges, not on the flat surfaces."

Max jumped back from the piece of glass he was about to pick up. "Sorry, I am not aware of how we treat evidence."

His concern touched me to the very core of my being. That and the way his broad shoulders filled out the zip-necked sweater he was wearing over a sky-blue button-down shirt. A spark like faeries kissing passed between our fingers when they touched.[7] I said, "That's okay, I'll take your prints later to eliminate them."[8]

---

[7] Jas: Ack! No! Faeries kissing?
BadJas: LE BWAHAHAHA!
Jas: Look, can we call a truce? Just for right now?
BadJas: Will you lift your moratorium on smoldering?
Jas: Yes.
BadJas: Done.

[8] BadJas: And the top prize in the Suck Romantic Tension from the Room sweepstakes goes to . . . YOU!
Jas: There shouldn't be any romantic tension. We have a boyfriend.
BadJas: Who is back in LA, frolicking with women named after toothsome treats.
Jas: *La la lalala la, I cannot hear that—*
BadJas: Do you really think you'd be half so interested in this investigation if you didn't think that Jack—
Jas: *—la la la la la LA, no one is saying anything!*
BadJas: I am not going to stop stating Deep Truths just because you are humming the Smurf song.
Jas: What about show tunes? Ha! I see you quivering!

We worked together like that to gather the larger pieces of glass as well as the other bits-o-debris lying around—some plastic wrap, the corner of a candy wrapper, a pebble—then he helped me sweep the smaller ones into the bag with his foot.

"Wait," Max said. "There is more." And he came and very gently picked several pieces of paper and a peanut shell out of my hair.

Our faces, our bodies, were so close that the tension smoldered between us. It was like every bad teen pop song ever made was playing in the background. I couldn't keep my eyes off his full, soft-looking, begging-to-be-kissed lips, and as he put a finger under my chin and tilted my face up to his, his hooded eyes smoldered with invitation. He said, "I am glad you are not hurt, Miss Callihan."

Our lips were just millimeters apart.

I yawned.

BECAUSE YES THAT IS HOW I ROLL. LIKE A SUAVE THING. In fact, address all further correspondence to me at my new address: 1 Suave Hall, Suave Court, Suavieland, Planet of She's-So-Smooth-I-Can't-Believe-She's-Not-Butter.

I couldn't help it! I'd barely gotten any sleep (not counting time spent being knocked unconscious). Plus I'd skipped dessert the night before so I was *starving*.

Max took a step backward and said, "You will allow me to give you a ride on the gondola to your hotel?"

"No, it's okay, I can—"

"It is perplexing, this business of you denying yourself the pleasure of my company. Is it again because you do not trust yourself in the proximity to my charms? I will turn down their volume."

"I just—"

"Ah, look, the police are arriving. Perhaps you wish to chat with them? I will say only in passing that my gondola is in the opposite direction from where they arrive."

And since another run-in with the police was on the list of Things Jas Needs beneath both Limb Loss and Smaller Boobs, I said, "A ride on the gondola would be great," and followed him onto his boat.

Chapter Fifteen

I'd only been in one gondola before, and that was at the Venetian Hotel in Vegas, so I hadn't realized how nice the real ones were. Max's had sky-blue-and-gold brocade seats with blue silk tassels on them, and a little glass vase with a single yellow rose in it coming off the side. A panel in front of me was hand-painted with a scene of a gondolier wooing a maiden out the window of her palazzo.

I glanced at my watch as I settled in and saw that it was ten fifteen in the morning. That meant two fifteen A.M. in Los Angeles. Suddenly I missed my pals more than ever. I'd been in a lot of Interesting Situations before, but never one where someone I knew was murdered. And I'd always had my friends around to help. But right now they were probably somewhere making up crazy dance moves or eating pizza or watching old alien invasion movies or dressing up in crazy costumes.[9]

---

[9] BadJas: Except Jack who was probably still splashing around in the candlelit bathtub.
   Jas: LE SHUT UP!

For some reason that made me think of Arabella, which made me le sigh.

Max said, "You know what makes Venice unique? It is the silence. On the water, you can go anywhere in silence. She is like the circulation system of the city."

"Ah."

"It is very nice to be out on the water in the gondola, no?"

He was right. The fog was starting to clear and you could see sunlight sparkling on the canal. "Yes," I said.

"And yet you do not seem to be enjoying either it or my most fascinating conversation, which has entranced hundreds of tourists."

"Sorry. It's just that my friend, the one from yesterday in San Marco?"

"*Sì?*"

"She's dead."

His expression of surprise would have been comical if he hadn't almost tipped the boat over. "Dead?"

"Late. Gone. Passed on."

"But, no!" he said. "That is not possible. I mean, she was so full of life—and running—yesterday. What happened?"

"The police say she killed herself."

He stopped rowing completely then and stared at me. After a while he said, "I am sorry to hear this. It is very hard when someone you know does this. Ar—Are they sure?"

"They are. I'm not convinced. I think she was murdered."

"Why?"

"It just doesn't make any sense."

He took a deep breath. "I understand. But the suicide never makes sense. Not for the people who stay behind. You have a reason for thinking she is murdered?"

"She knew something was going to happen to her. She sent me a letter with instructions to pick this up from her apartment." I unwrapped the cat statue and held it up.

He winced. "Please, I am begging you, put that away. I believe it is trying to steal my soul."

I laughed despite myself. "It is pretty hideous."

"That is the understatement *grandissimo*. You are sure she liked you? I do not give this to even my number-one enemy. You have considered that perhaps your friend was crazy? I do not say this to insult her, it is just a fact."

I stared at it. "It's got to be a clue."

"Yes, a clue that she is not to be trusted."

"I guess I'll have to find out where she got it. Maybe that'll tell me something."

"My advice is to take the whole thing and throw it away and never think of it anymore."

"No, I'm going to take it back to my room."

"I would not. It will cause you nightmares. And your head is still fragile. If you must, I recommend keeping it wrapped up. You could start now."

I smoothed out the paper, wrapped it up, and put it back in my pocket.

We went on in silence for a while. I asked, "Why do you speak such good English?"

"Now I know you flatter me. Once my English is good. Now it is mere. My mother is American and when I am younger I spend a year at school in America. But we had a parting of the ways."

"What do you mean?"

"They desired to have Max in their classes. This is understandable, of course. But Max desired not to be in the classes. So we compromised and I left."

"Where does your mother live?"

"One hopes in heaven now. Before that, in Virginia."

"I'm sorry. I didn't mean to bring up a difficult subject."

"There should be no secrets between us. And now let us speak of you. For example, how is it that Venice finds itself lucky enough to be host to such a treasure as yourself?"

"My father is writing a book about the history of soap."

"Your father is a soap maker?"

"He's an anthropology professor. Soap is just his most recent fascination."

"I can see why. It is very fascinating."

"Not to me."

"In my observation I think you prefer less cleanliness and more disorder."

"It would appear that way."

"And your father, what does he think of this?"

"He's not a fan. In fact, I have a feeling that as soon as we get back to the hotel he is going to lock me up forever and never let me back out."

"But then how will you have lunch with me today? No. Something must be done about this."

Whatever it was had to be done soon, because we were pulling up to the Grissini Palace boat dock then. The windows of the dining room overlooked it and I could see that all the tables were full, but none of them were full of Dadzilla. Which meant there was a chance I could sneak back in without him—

"Is this gentleman who comes with gnashing teeth your father?" Max bent down to ask me.

"Yeah." I stood up and braced for Dadzillapact.

He stomped toward us. "Jasmine Noelle Callihan, do you have any idea how big a heap of trouble you are in?" He was looking very DO NOT PLAY ON OR AROUND.

So, of course, the monkeys said, "Somewhere between a Mt. Kilimanjaro– and a Mt. Everest–sized heap of trouble?"

"This is no joke."

"Mt. Kilimanjaro and Mt. Everest are no joke."

Max stepped forward then. "Do I have the privilege to address the famous Professore Callihan? It is an honor to meet you, sir. I am, naturally, an admirer."

Dadzilla directed his Eyes of Searing Anger at him. "Who the devil are you?"

Max said to me, "You see, already he takes a warm interest in me," then turned back to my father and launched into a history of himself, starting with his second birthday party, which had a cowboys-and-Indians theme.

"I don't want to hear about your blasted birthday party," my father said, cutting him off, Zilla-style. "What are you doing with my daughter?"

"She does not tell you? Ah, naturally she wanted it to be a surprise. Is that not right, Jasmine Noelle?"

I stared at him. He nodded encouragingly. "That's right," I agreed.

"What surprise?" Lo Zilla growled.

"It is like this. Jasmine and I meet as one does here in Venice, in the manner of destiny. We chat. She tells me of your burning passion for soap. I say to her, I know the foremost expert on soap. If you come for a row on the gondola with me in the morning, I will arrange for your father to meet my uncle, Lazlo Matrucci."

My father's eyes got huge, but then he said, "Lazlo Matrucci is dead."

"No. He just pretends for the income tax. Would you like to meet him? Yes? Good. You have an appointment today at noon." Max took a notebook out of his pocket, wrote something, and handed the paper to my father. "Here is his address."

My father stared at him, speechless. Speechless! My father!

Little Life Lesson 30: Always carry a camera because you never know when you might want to record a historic moment.

Lo Zilla held up the paper. "This is really where he lives?"

"Yes. He will be expecting you."

Ever a paragon of manners, my father turned, shouted, "Sherri! You won't believe this!" and toddled off.

I was momentarily stunned by this example of Dadzilla management. Max had gifts. Thinking-on-his-feet-type gifts. "That was impressive. I'm sorry about my father's manners. But, thank you. Is that man really your uncle?"

Max beamed at me. "My motives are completely selfish. Now that your father will be busy in the middle of the day, you can have lunch with me. If you are worried you will be bored, let me mention that I am a very accomplished juggler."

I laughed. "I really don't—"

"Before you answer, consider the menu. We will begin with a simple antipasto, perhaps some mozzarella with tomatoes fresh from the vine, sprinkled with *basilico* and drizzled with bright green olive oil. Then tagliatelle folded with prosciutto and cream, put under the broiler until it is golden on the top. That is followed by a steak so tender you could cut it with a fork, seasoned in the Florentine manner, with the tiny potatoes, roasted alongside. And then we finish with a *scroppino*. You do not know what that is? You make it by taking a little lemon gelato in a glass, then adding a touch of cream and—"

He stopped talking because I was kissing him. "That's it!" I said. "That's the answer!"

He gazed at me, blinking fast. "Does this mean you will come to lunch?"

I felt a huge surge of elation wash over me, like when you walk into a bakery and there are dozens of gorgeous cakes in front of you. Like I was the happiest-slash-luckiest girl in the world. I climbed out of the gondola with my sack of glass, said, "I don't know. Maybe. Right now I have to go. Thank you!" and ran into the lobby.

I was so happy to see Camilla at her post behind the concierge desk I almost kissed her too. "I need a candle and some matches."

"Where have you been, Jasmine? They tear up the hotel looking for you!"

"It's a long story. But it doesn't matter. Can you get me a candle and some matches?"

"I suppose, but—"

A pink birthday candle and a box of matches slid down the counter toward me, and a voice said, "Here. I hope you're planning to use them to burn those pants."

I turned around. And screamed.

Chapter Sixteen

IT WAS POLLY, ROXY, AND TOM! POLLY, ROXY, AND TOM WERE IN VENICE! TOM, POLLY, ROXY—

My brain couldn't take it in.

Okay, yes, I cried.

I hope you don't have any idea what it is like to be by yourself for six weeks followed by being with Evil Henches with faerie names for four hours, during which your only friend in Venice was murdered and you spent the night in a police station wearing leather pants and were attacked and had part of your brain start thinking like the heroine in a romance novel, but if you do you can perhaps imagine how I felt seeing my pals.

Even if they were all, inexplicably, wearing water wings.

This was better than a huge bakery. It was like if the Surgeon General declared that you should eat five to nine servings of pastries a day and never look at another vegetable, unless it was on pizza or a taco.

"I'm so happy to see you!" I said, hugging them.[10]

They didn't say anything, naturally being too overcome with emotion. When we got to my room, I ducked into the bathroom to change into a leisure outfit of Polly's selection—burgundy leggings, a long-sleeved dark yellow dress, and my cowboy boots with the rainbows on them—so I would be more comfortable while we caught up.[11]

I was all ready to settle in for a nice cozy chat but as soon as I came out of the bathroom, Roxy and Polly shuffled in there with Polly's carry-on bag and closed the door.[12]

"What are they do—" I started to say, but Tom interrupted me.

"So, Menudo's getting back together," he said.

I stared at him. "I beg your pardon?"

"You know Menudo? The band that gave us Ricky Martin? We flew over with them. Their manager is friends with the

[10] Polly: I'm not speaking to you until you take off those pants. And neither are Roxy or Tom.
   Roxy: I don't think—
   Polly: I have the leftover doughnut holes from the plane in my bag.
   Roxy: Lips zipped.

[11] BadJas: I pity the fool who takes my white leather pants away.
   Polly: What? Who said that?
   Jas: That's BadJas. She says things I'm thinking but don't want to be. And she might be right, P. I've been asked out twice since putting on my leather pants.
   Polly: Give me the guy's name so I can contact his parole officer.
   Jas: Ha ha. I'm not ever getting these pants back, am I?
   Polly: Of course you are, precious. You'll be able to console yourself at my funeral with the fact that you may have lost a friend but you've regained your leather pants. You see, I am doing you an Act of Kindness.

[12] Polly: Tom, you keep her busy while we get ready.
   Tom: How?
   Roxy: Talk amiably of this and that.
   Tom: This and that?
   Polly: Topics of general interest. You know, like music. We just need a few minutes to prepare.
   Tom: Music. Got it.

King and Queen." The Cadillac King and Queen were Roxy and Tom's parents, ex-telenovela stars, now owners of the largest Cadillac dealership west of the Mississippi. "They were coming to do some special show so we hitched a ride on their private plane. I'm not sure they're going to stay together, though, they fought the whole way over."

"Wait," I said, raising my voice so I could be heard in the bathroom. "You came on an airplane with MENUDO? A group that wore Lycra before the Power Rangers made it cool? And you, Polly Prentis, are le busting my chopos over one tiny pair of leather pants?"

"They don't wear Lycra anymore," Polly answered through the door.

"Not since Polly spent nine hours on the plane redesigning their costumes," Tom added.

"What are Polly and Roxy doing in there?" I asked.[13]

Tom said, "What's interesting is Menudo isn't just a band, it's a food, too."

I shut him down with a Steely Gaze. "What. Is. Going. On?"

Although Tom could come labeled with both CAUTION: HOT SURFACE and MAY CAUSE TOOTH DECAY because of his good looks and sweetness, my favorite thing about him is that he can't lie. At all.[14]

---

[13] Tom: This isn't working. She's not distracted.
   Polly: You're doing great! Keep it up!
   Roxy: Try mentioning food. Jas likes food.
   Tom: Food. Okay. Good idea.

[14] Tom: Food didn't work! Now what?
   Polly: Play on her heartstrings.
   Tom: I'll try, but can you hurry it up?
   Roxy: It takes time to build mind-control glasses! Go get her heartstrings and play upon them as on a lute.

"Do you know what a lute looks like?" he asked.

I stared at him.

"Do you think it's more like a piano or more like a violin?"

"I think it's more like a TELL ME WHY YOU'RE HERE RIGHT NOW OR I WILL REMIND POLLY OF HOW YOU USED TO WEAR PLEATED PANTS."

"That was once! One time! When I was seven! Eleven years ago! And my mom made me."

"Do you really think that would make a difference to Miss Prentis?"

He took a deep breath. "Okay, the truth is, we missed you."

I put my hands on my hips with the first two fingers pointing down and wiggled them, the (new) Universal Symbol of Pleated Pants©.

"And we decided you needed us more than we needed a college tour," he rushed on. "I mean, first there was the whole BadJas-slash-taking-Mr. T-as-your personal-savior thing." He shot an apprehensive glance at the bathroom door and lowered his voice to say, "Not that I think that's a bad idea."

"Thank you. And?"

"When you disappeared from email, it was clear that something dire was happening, so—" As he talked, Tom had wandered over to the bed. "What's in the brown paper bag?"

"It's evidence. Don't change the subject."

"Evidence? It looks like broken glass."

"It is. A glass that was broken when I was knocked out this

morning by being hit over the head with an object or objects unknown," I said casually.

He looked at me but said to the bathroom door, "Did you hear that? Someone hit Jas over the head to knock her out."

"That explains her hair," Polly said through the door. And then it opened, and she and Roxy stepped into the room.

At least I think it was Polly and Roxy. It was hard to tell since they were both wearing Teenage Mutant Ninja Turtle masks. They were still sporting their water wings, but had now further accessorized with tool belts. Polly's had duct tape, nail scissors, a rolled-up magazine, a rolled-up sheath of paper-clipped computer printouts, and hand sanitizer in it. Roxy's had pliers, an odd-looking pair of tweezers, a snack-pack-sized bag of Teddy Grahams, and a Pez dispenser. Roxy was also holding a notebook and a pair of safety goggles with spirograph patterns and little flashing lights glued on the lenses.

Oh, hello, Insanity Avenue. It's been so long since I've strolled down your wide and attractive sidewalks. "I don't think the Teenage Mutant Ninja Turtles wear dresses," I pointed out to Polly. "Or floaties."

But the Turtle Formerly Known as Polly was not interested in such cinema verité–type details. "Pull the curtains," she said ominously to Tom as she and Roxy advanced on me. "This is more serious than we thought."

"What are you doing?" I asked, backing away from them.

Polly took the duct tape off her tool belt. Roxy, aka

Donatello, held out the goggles and said, "We are commencing Operation Extricate Jas. Put these on."

"Extricate me from what? What are the Teddy Grahams for?"

"To keep up our strength during the arduous ordeal."

Little Life Lesson 31: "To keep up our strength during the arduous ordeal" is never the right answer to the question "What are the Teddy Grahams for?"

She went on, "Now put on your mind-control goggles so we can access your delta waves."

Little Life Lesson 32: "Now put on your mind-control goggles so we can access your delta waves" is never the right answer to anything.

"What if I like my delta waves the way they are?"

"Don't be balky, Jas," Polly said, twirling the duct tape on her finger.

I took the goggles. "Can't you at least tell me what you have planned?"

Roxy opened the notebook and started reading: "Operation Extricate Jas, Step 1: Convince Jas of the perils of associating with Arabella Neal by telling her about—"

"You don't have to do that," I interrupted.

"Yes, we do," Roxy corrected. "That's the only operational objective we have so far. Well, except Polly's private mission with your Wonderbras."

"Well, then, your operation is over. Arabella Neal is dead."

Polly dropped the tape. "What? When?"

"Last night. The police think it was suicide. But I—"

"Let me guess," Polly said, pushing her mask up on her head, "you are convinced it's murder and you want to prove it and find out who killed her and why."

"How did you know?"

"I spent my youth playing Crime Scene Barbies with you, Jas."

"I could be wrong."

Polly shook her head. "You've been wrong about clothes. And you've been very wrong about guys—"

"Very, very wrong," Roxy agreed. "And you were wrong that time you said we'd pass another In-N-Out burger so we didn't have to stop at the first one but there wasn't another one for two hundred miles and I almost wasted away through Vitamin Burger withdrawals."

"—but you've never been wrong about a crime before. If you say she was murdered, we think she was murdered. What happened?"

So I told them about the whole thing, from the chase earlier in the afternoon through seeing Arabella's body, searching for the goldfish, being in the armoire with Bobby, getting knocked out, and getting an idea in the gondola, only leaving out the part where I kissed irrepressibly hot Max.[15] It was very cathartic and when I was done Polly

---

[15] Polly: Did you just describe Max as "irrepressibly hot"?

Jas: No, that wasn't me, it was BadJas.

Polly: It sounded like you. Are things okay with you and Jack? He left a message on my cell phone that he was worried and really needed to talk to you about something.

Jas: Things are fine! We're like two great tastes that go great together! We're—

Polly: We shall speak of this anon.

Jas: Or anot.

said, "Let's see it. The clue."

Then she said, "Ack, put it away, put it away!"

"You don't like the leetle kitty?" I asked, holding it in front of her eyes.

Roxy said, "It's not, by any chance, made of candy, is it?"

"No, and please don't use that word around me."

Polly had her hand over her eyes now, shielding them. "If you give me the paper, I'll wrap it back up. Jas, please. I think it burns with an inner demonic light. What are you doing, anyway?"

When it had become clear that my friends no longer intended to do an intervention involving my delta waves and duct tape, I'd gotten up and started collecting my tools. As I talked, I'd melted the bottom of the candle and attached it to the ashtray that had come with my room.

"I hope whatever you're doing involves steak done in the Florentine style," Roxy said. "I'm starving."

"What I realized in the gondola was that maybe the clue wasn't the glass art," I explained.

Polly sprang to attention. "Does that mean we can shatter it into a thousand small and unrecognizable pieces? Because I feel a strong urge to do that."

"So if it's not that *objet d'art*," Tom asked, "what is it?"

"The paper it was wrapped in. See how the corner is folded? Arabella always did that when she wrote on something. Her brother said it was some belief she had about the message getting lost if she didn't." My friends were looking at me like I'd just graduated from Loony Academy, the School that Madness Built. "What?"

"Jas, sweetie, that paper is blank. There is no message on it," Roxy told me gently.

"Not yet," I said, putting on my MysticalJas voice. "But watch closely and before your eyes, I'll summon a message from the other side."

At that moment, there was a knock at the door.

Chapter Seventeen

The knock was followed by a voice saying, "Calamity, open up. We know you're in there."

"Hark! A message from the other side!" Polly commented as Tom went to let the Evil Henches in.

"Tommmmy!" Veronique and Alyson shrieked in unison, throwing themselves on him.

They were dressed like backup dancers for a band called 1980s Genies from Hell, if there ever was such a band, in outfits that involved billowy black pants, long-sleeved midriff-bearing shirts, suede ankle boots, black fedoras, and belly chains.

Le yes. Belly chains. With dangly charms on them.[16]

---

16 Polly: Tell me this is all a horrible, horrible dream. Do you see that? You don't, right? I'm having
 a psychotic episode, but that is okay because when I wake up there will be no poofy pants,
 no ankle boots, and no belly chains with fedoras.

 Jas: You're not having a psychotic episode.

 Polly: DON'T SAY THAT!

 Roxy: What's going on?

 Jas: Polly's not psychotic.

 Roxy: Are you sure? Her eyes are kind of rolling around in a weird way.

 Polly: Puffy pants with ankle boots! Hold me!

 Jas: Their outfits are totally Jordache. The look that everyone wants to know better.

 Polly: I want my mom!

 Tom: Can I get some help over here? Anyone?

Because of the way they were clinging to Tom I'd only had a partial view, but I got a complete eyeful as Alyson turned to me and said, "Why didn't you tell us the dead girl was Arabella Neal? We thought it was just some regular nobody, not a Brand Name."

What a kind-slash-humanitarian approach to life! "I'm sorry, I assumed the spirits would inform you. If I'd realized—"

"Shut up, Jas."

Because I am a people pleaser, I obliged her. Also I had work to do. Leaving Roxy to disentangle the Wu-Genie Clan from Tom, and Polly searching through her bag for her BluBlocker glasses, I lit the candle and held the paper over it.

Nothing happened.

When Max was talking in the gondola, I'd remembered the squeezed lemons and the Q-tip at Arabella's and decided that she'd written a secret message in lemon juice for me on the wrapping of the Kitty that would show up when exposed to heat. But as Nothing continued to be the only thing Happening, I thought maybe I'd been wrong. Maybe there was no secret message.

Although I had never practiced Hope-Slowly-Giving-Way-to-Misery-&-Despair as an expression in the mirror, I was pretty sure I was nailing it right then. Because if there was no message that meant the cat was it.

Which meant: Despair.

Also: Doom.

"Try the other side of the paper," Roxy suggested. "The

side you're holding has tape running down it and that keeps the words from showing up."

I moved the paper around.

Still nothing.

"Calamity, if you're done trying to burn the hotel down, maybe we could all, like, go do something. You know, something that doesn't suck."

"Thank you for your support, Genie Sapphyre—"[17]

"It's just Sapphyre," she corrected me.

"—but no one asked you to come and hang out here."

"You always act like you put the U in SUPER, but I bet that Tiger's＊Eye and I[18] can figure out what happened to Arabella before you can."

"How?"

"By summoning helpful spirits through an open, optimistic mind."

"We do it by tuning into the vibrations of the universe," Veronique elaborated.

"Excellent. Go ahead and get started. Here." I handed her the paper the cat had come wrapped in. "See if you and Sapphyre can get the spirits to write on this."[19]

[17] Roxy: Did you just call her "Sapphire"?
Jas: No, of course not. It's Sapphyre. With a Y.

[18] Roxy: And she just called Veronique Tiger's Eye?
Jas: No, silly, Tiger's＊Eye. With a star in the middle, but the star is silent.

[19] Roxy: What is the meaning of this?! Sapphyre. Tiger's＊Eye. I demand to know.
Jas: Those are their faerie names.
Roxy: HA HA HA—wait, you're not kidding, are you?
Jas: Le not.
Roxy: What's your faerie name?
Jas: Jas. The disdain is silent.
Roxy: Mine is going to be KettleKörn. With two capital K's and an umlaut. But the umlaut is silent.
Jas: Naturall—

Roxy grabbed my arm. "Look!"

I'd been right after all! There was a message written in lemon juice! The first word to appear was NONE. Then XPLAN. It took a while, but after about three minutes we had it. It read:

FTHR POISN
THRU HAND
BAUR BX 34
WIL XPLAN.
TRST NONE!
FIND M!

"See, Jas," Alyson said. "All it took was a little positive thinking."

I said, "." Really, it was the only thing to say.

Q-tips aren't exactly fine-point rollerballs, so the short message pretty much filled up the entire paper from edge to taped edge, even in that breezy telegraph style.

"What does it mean?" Polly asked. "I mean, I get 'Trust No One,' because that's upbeat and cheery, but what about the rest?"

"I don't know who M is, but I'm pretty sure this means her father was poisoned through his hand, and the proof of it is in safety deposit box thirty-four at the Bauer Hotel," I said, and I think my voice might have shaken with excitement. Because here, finally, were clues in the offering!

"Is it close to pizza?" ~~Roxy~~ KettleKörn said.

"But Ned Neal died of a heart attack while locked in his office," Polly objected. "I have an article about it, right here."

"Not according to Arabella. She thought he was murdered."

"Oh. Oh, no."

"We could discuss this so much more comfortably with pizza," Roxy said conversationally.

"Oh, yes," I told Polly. "And now we've got some evidence. Let's—Roxy, what are you doing?"

"What, me? It's an interpretive dance. I call it 'Feed Me Pizza or Risk Something Really Bad Happening.'"

"Wait, are you saying you're hungry?"

"Do not taunt me."

"After we pick up the box, I'll take you to a place where they have one hundred and forty-two kinds of pizza."

Roxy's eyes got huge. "Did you say one hundred and forty-two?"

"Yes. And often Italian people order French fries as an appetizer while they are waiting for pizza."

"I LOVE YOU, ITALY!"

With that established, we set out for the Bauer.[20]

---

[20] Jas: Polly, what are you doing?

Polly: Just trying to get you into your water wings, precious.

Jas: I don't think so.

Polly: Look, they even match your outfit.

Jas: N and also O.

Roxy: Polly says we have to wear them at all times while we're in Venice to reduce the risk of drowning.

Jas: I don't think you can reduce a risk that is technically zero.

Polly: How did Arabella Neal die?

Jas: She drow—

Polly: I restius my casius. Put. Them. On.

Jas: Mr. T would pity the fool who tried to make him wear floaties.

Roxy: Mr. T never met Polly.

Tom: Resistance is futile, Jas. Trust me.

Little Life Lesson 33: If you ever want to meet the security staff at a fancy hotel, just march into the lobby with a posse that includes four people in customized floaties and two members of the Jackson 5 Genie Tour, who are vibrating, and announce that you want to get into a safety deposit box that doesn't exist.

Little Life Lesson 34: Starting the whole conversation off with, "Hey, man, how's tricks?" because you're too excited to remember how to say "Good day, how are you?" properly also helps.

Although she was very precise in her home life, Arabella was a bit neglectful of details in her correspondence. Like it turned out, when we got to the Bauer,[21] there was no box 34. There was a box 34A, a box 34B, and a box 34C, but for some reason the desk clerk was reluctant to tell us which one was Arabella's or allow us to try the seventh key on her I-Heart-Hotcakes keychain on all of them just for kicks.

Roxy's suggestion that we try the mind-control glasses on him was unanimously vetoed. Leaving the Evil Henches in the lobby to terrify the guests and beseech the spirits for the answer, the rest of us went outside so Tom could use his Imitate Anyone over the Phone superpower to place a call in what he guessed was Ned Neal's banker's voice asking the manager to extend any and all courtesies to Arabella's friends. I'm not sure if it was the call or the fact that he wanted to get Alyson and Veronique to stop chanting in his reception

[21] Roxy: Passing three pizza places.

area, but although the manager did not look like he wished to throw festive dinner parties in our honor, he did agree to grant one of us access to Arabella's box, 34C.

When you get a mysterious note in invisible ink from a girl who was murdered, telling you that the explanation of another murder is in a safety deposit box, you probably would expect to discover maybe a gun or a bloody knife or at the very least a long document detailing everything that you could take to the police to close the case.

Or, you could find what I did.

Chapter Eighteen

———— ❧ ————

"Okay, let's go over this again, just to be sure," Polly said, reading off the monogrammed notepad she'd been writing on. "One white vinyl little girl's jewelry box with a ballerina on top that plays a hideous song when you wind it up, containing one pink pencil eraser, one package of light blue silk embroidery thread and needle, one black plastic pen with a gold symbol of some kind on it, one small screwdriver, a magnet from Ho Ho's Pancake Shack, five old newspaper articles in Italian, and two scraps of blank white paper with"—she glanced down the table at me to where I was holding the second piece over a lit match; I shook my head—"no hidden messages on them."

I blew out the match. "That's it."

We were settled around a big wood table at Ae Oche, my favorite pizza restaurant in Venice due to its having so many kinds of pizza and every one of them delicious.

Despite the fact that the decor—something they called Old Country Club style, by which I think they meant Crazy Granny's Attic because I've never been to a country club with dusty license plates, oil cans, broken lacrosse sticks, and stuffed squirrels hanging on the walls—offered plenty to talk about, no one spoke. It's a cruel world when Hopeful Anticipation leads only to promotional magnets for Ho Ho's Pancake Shack (Route 1, Mayfair, Virginia. Turn left at the Clown!).

Finally Polly pulled a stack of computer printouts from her bag. "Here's what we know about Ned Neal's death. It's not much, because for the past few years he'd been a bit of a recluse and jealously guarded his privacy. Apparently he was found on the floor of his office in front of his desk early in the morning. When he didn't show up for breakfast as usual, the housekeeper alerted his secretary, who alerted the handyman. They all lived in the house. The office door had to be broken down to get in because it was locked from the inside. He'd died between eight P.M. and nine P.M. the night before, which was the staff's night off, so he was home alone. Security cameras on both the street entrance and the water entrance of his house showed no one arriving or departing during that time. So if we assume he was poisoned, whatever did it had to have been in the office with him."

"What about a pen?" Tom asked. "That makes sense with

the whole 'poisoned through hand' thing, right?"

Roxy, whose superpower is to be able to make a weapons system out of benign household objects, started to reach for the pen from the box to examine it but I stopped her, and said to Polly, "Eye shadow, blush brush, Scotch tape, pink index card."

"What color shadow?"

"The white. It'll show up best."

She pulled each item out of her bag, and I got to work. Balancing the pen on its tip, I started dusting at the end, but Absence of Friendly Prints was the only thing waiting for me there.

I turned to Alyson and held out my hand. "Gum."

"Calamity, I'm not a set of dominos," she announced.

I stared at her for a second. "Did you think you were?"

"Duh, you were treating me like dominos. You know, ordering me around? God, have you been sipping Fool-Aid?"

"I totally would have been, but the guy at the store told me you bought it all out," I said brightly. "Anyway, I'd love to chitchat like this with you more another time, but right now may I please have a piece of your gum?"

"No."

"Are you sure? Because if you don't give me one I'll tell your dad you snuck out last night to meet a guy." I said it entirely because it was the kind of thing she always said to me, but the effect was magico.

Alyson blanched. She blanched! Like a, um, blanching thing.[22]

If I hadn't been wearing floaties (THANK YOU POLLY), I totally would have patted myself on the back.

"We didn't meet a guy," Veronique said, ruining the mood. "Reggie didn't show up."

Before I could enjoy the double whammy wonder of Almondyson being scared AND a guy standing her up—not that I would have! Because I am not a cold snake with icy pops where my heart should be! And also my rib cage!—Alyson hastened to add, "He didn't just not show up, he totally called. He had some family thing."

Sigh. It had been so sweet while it lasted. But now was not the time for Le Basking in Others' Misery (not that there ever is a time for that, of course). Now was the time for Le Busting a Moveo. So I said, "Look, I just need a tiny piece of gum. It can even be one you've chewed, okay?"

"When she finishes dusting for prints, we could try the pen for vibrations," Veronique pointed out.

Alyson pulled a mini-wad about the size of my pinkie off the mega-wad in her mouth and dropped it on my bread plate. I smiled winningly at her—

"Stop making faces at me, Jas."

—and used the gum to stand the pen up so I could dust the main part of it for prints.

[22] Tom: Try "almond." Almonds are blanched.
    Jas: Thanks!

I started near the tip and worked my way down. There were none at the tip, where people usually hold pens, but there were three partial prints near the end. I used the Scotch tape to lift them and pasted them onto the cards.

"Based on the locations, with one underneath and two on top, I'd say it looks like a thumb, index, and pointer finger."

"What does that tell us?" Tom asked excitedly.

"That someone used their thumb, index, and pointer fingers to hold the end of the pen," I said.

"So, in other words, N-O to the T-H-I-N-G," Alyson clarified politely. "For a change. Whereas everything Tiger's * Eye and I have tried has worked."

Luckily I was wearing my Ignoring Ears so I couldn't hear this.

The rest of the conversation had pretty much the same result, though. I would hand Roxy something and say: "What about [insert object from box]? Could it be used to kill someone?"

And she'd say: "I could make a [nonlethal device], [other nonlethal device], [musical instrument], [bud vase], but nothing that would kill anyone through their hand."

And I'd say: "Okay, so we still have [insert word for nothing]."

And then Alyson and Veronique would take the object and start chanting over it. And I would [insert word for wanting to cry].

"If you could figure out how to get someone into the room with him, I'd have a lot more ideas," Roxy said.

"Like what?"

"You could poke someone in the brain through the eye with the screwdriver and cause a heart attack. I could come up with tons more," Roxy added. "But they'd all only work if there was someone with him."

"So we need to figure out how someone could have broken into his office," I said.

"I've got it," Veronique said from Planet Hench. She dropped the silk thread she'd been "ommmmmmmmmmm"ing over.

"What?"

"Behind the Music," she said proudly.

"The killer got in through music?"

"No. We have to find out what Arabella's *Behind the Music* moment was."

"Her what?" I asked.

"Duh, the moment in her life that changed everything," Alyson explained. "It's usually a horrible-slash-heartrending tragedy. Everyone has one. It defines them. God, Jas, you are so gignorant."

"What's that? I'm gignoring you."

We put the conversation on pause at this interesting point for a moment of awed silence as the waiter delivered our pizzas to the table.[23] I swear Roxy had tears of bliss in her eyes as she looked at her artichoke heart and prosciutto pizza, and even Polly looked a bit starstruck contemplating her pizza with arugula and walnuts on it. Tom had gone with the MangiaFuoco—fire eater—so his was covered with spicy sausages, peppers, and hot sauce, and I'd stuck with my favorite, pesto with pepperoni. Together they were glorious to behold and even the salads the Evil Henches had ordered instead of pizza (yes! They forewent pizza! If that is a word!) did not take away from the beauty of the table. Speechless with wonder is how I suppose you could describe us.

It's hard to be depressed in the face of such Wonder but I felt a little sad, anyway. Despite the new clues, I was still clueless

---

[23] BadJas: Excuse me, I thought we were having lunch with Max.

Jas: We said "maybe." Plus, this is important. This is part of the investigation.

BadJas: Ah. You're not just avoiding him because you kissed him and you're jealous of whatever Jack is doing so you are Torn Between Two Lovers.

Jas: YOU kissed him.

BadJas: But YOU liked it.

Jas: I HAVE A BOYFRIEND.

BadJas: Who you're not calling. Have you ever asked yourself why you do this? Get involved in these investigations? Could it be that you'd rather sort out other people's problems than your own?

Jas: No. Why are you torturing me this way?

BadJas: Because it's fun. Also because it's important for you to understand your own motives so they don't color your investigation. Right now, for example, you're missing a crucial clue.

Jas: What clue?

BadJas: I can't tell you.

Jas: What do you mean you can't tell me? You ARE me.

BadJas: But I'm that part of your brain that is tricky. The part that tells you that you're missing something but doesn't tell you what.

Jas: You're going to be the part of my brain that gets strangled in a second.

BadJas: You're just hurting yourself here!

Roxy: Jas, sweetie, your pizza's getting cold. Who are you growling at?

Jas: It's a long story.

about what had happened and why. Not to mention who did it. Or what Arabella's *Behind the Music* moment was. And I couldn't get away from the nagging feeling that I was missing something.

As we ate, I pulled the newspaper articles toward me and skimmed them. They were more than twenty years old, and the Italian was kind of old-fashioned and hard for me to understand. They were all written by the same reporter, Carlotta Longhi, and the more I got into them, I realized that they were all connected.

"These are all about Arabella's dad's house. Ca'Dario, better known as La Casa che Uccide. It's a five-part history of the place."

"What does La Casa che Uccide mean?" Tom asked.

"Oh, nothing," I said.

"Jas, what does it mean?" Polly repeated in the voice she will use in later life to frighten her children.

I said, "It means The House that Kills."

Chapter Nineteen

———— ❧ ————

Okay, I might have mumbled it. And whispered. From behind a napkin.

Polly frowned. "What was that? I could have sworn you said 'The House that Kills.'"

"I could have," I mumble-whisper-napkined now with added coughing action.

"That would be a good song title," Roxy pointed out.

"It would also make a good place to avoid," Polly said. "But I suppose that's too much to hope for. Anyway, the articles are all old. Mr. Neal didn't own it back then."

"No, but maybe Arabella found something in them that gave her a clue about how her dad was murdered."

"What do they say?" Roxy asked. "Is it morbid?"

I started reading out parts to my pals and the Henches, translating as I went.

"*'One palace on the Grand Canal always makes ooh and aah spurt out of tourists for its very beautiful face,'*" I translated.

"*And always they are electrocuted when they learn the truth of it.*'"

"Wow, Jas, your Italian is really good," Polly said. "I am electrocuted listening to you."

"'*When an ancient Venetian decided to make the most beautiful house as a wedding gift, never once does he think that instead of a glad house, he has made the house of tears, the house of stopped-breathing, the house of tortures. In different words: the house that kills.*'"

"Now I am electrocuted," Roxy said.

"I am stopped-breathing," Polly said.

"We didn't order the director's-cut box set, Calamity. Can you just skip to the good parts?" Alyson said.

"Fine. The next article talks about how the girl it was built for became dead, and then the two after that are about the house's other victims." I flipped through them, then stopped. "Hang on, Arabella underlined this part."

"What does it say?"

"'*The power endures—as recently as last month the house tries to claim another victim, a boy artist making the restoration. He is working alone in the studio when a beam falls on him from above, but he succeeds to escape with only a broken shrimp.*'"

Tom looked at me skeptically. "Are you sure the word is *shrimp*?"

"Not really. Anyway, a broken something. Then blah blah blah. Okay, here's a good part: '*When you pass the big door of the house you will sense that special feeling. As though digits are creeping up your spine and your hair is dancing up-ended.'*"

"Your hair does that all the time, anyway," Alyson chimed in.

"Thank you for enriching the conversation. Then it says that the palace is being restored from the foundation and wonders if the new owner will also become dead. The end." I looked up at my pals. "We have to get in there."

"Yeah, I can't wait to get that special feeling," Polly said.

Roxy seconded that emotion. "I love it when digits crawl on me."

"Your support warms le cockles of my heart," I told them. "Come on, aren't you even a little curious? How else are we going to figure out a way that someone could have gotten into Ned Neal's office?"

Tom said, "I'm curious about who would buy a house like that."

"Many of the owners didn't die there, they just died while they owned it. And it's really beautiful. And one of the articles said that guests hardly ever met a bad end. So see, it will be perfectly safe."

"I think it's an excellent idea," Veronique said. "Sapphyre and I will be able to pick up a lot of helpful vibrations there."

There was a pause then as I saved Polly and Roxy from choking to death. When they were better, Tom asked, "Are you planning to just walk up and ring the doorbell and ask to see where Ned Neal died?"

"No, we'll have to be clever about it."

"I hope you are using 'be clever' as code for 'eat some

gelato and then go to the hotel for a nap,'" Roxy said. "Menudo was fighting all the time so I didn't get much sleep on our flight."

Since I couldn't immediately come up with any clever ideas, and since at least if we went back to the hotel, Alyson and Veronique might change their outfits, and since I hadn't gotten much sleep the night before either, and really since wearing water wings is sort of uncomfortable and Polly had promised to let me take them off in my hotel room, I agreed.

We paid our bill, gathered up the crazy puzzle of Arabella's clues, and headed down a narrow *calle* back to the Grissini Palace. We passed by sixteen glass stores on our way, where by "passed" I mean "lingered endlessly at" as the Evil Henches stood inside sensing for a sign that Arabella had bought the cat there. The fact that every store had at least a dozen cats with goldfishes in their stomachs (as well as clowns plus fish, roosters plus fish, clear globs plus fish and [insert horrifying-to-think-of object here] plus fish), which made finding Arabella's store very unlikely, did not daunt them. It did suggest a Little Life Lesson to me:

Little Life Lesson 35: Many people lose their minds on vacation.

As we waited for the Evil Ones outside a particularly jam-packed-with-hideousness shop, Roxy said, "Why do they make glass candies? They are taunting me."

I groaned. "I told you not to use that word."

"According to St. Willy Wonka, candy is mixed with love

and makes the world taste good," Roxy said. "What's your problem with it?"

"Nothing."

Polly looked me over with her special Best-Friend-O-Vision. "Does this have something to do with Jack?"

"No," I lied.

"Ah, well, since we're speaking opposite-intention language, then I will say that does not surprise me at all since he has not been spending a lot of time with them," she said.

"Them?"

"Yes *them.* Candy. As in, the band."

"Candy is a band?"

The Evil Henches had rejoined us then. "Ooh, I love Candy," Veronique said. "All those girls are so hot. They're opening for the NASCAR Dads on tour, aren't they?"

Candy was a band. CANDY WAS A BAND!!!! A totally hot girl band, but still. I was so excited I wrote a haiku on the spot:

> *What does not melt in*
> *Your mouth or your hands? A band!*
> *I love you, Candy!*

"Who did you think Candy was, precious?" Polly asked.

"A sooty-lashed, fair-haired, tantric sex goddess who could stop a rhino from charging with a look," I explained.

"Oh, well, that makes sense. I could see how you would

leap immediately like an antelope to that conclusion."

"It fit all the evidence," I said.

"Which was?"

"He was meeting someone named Candy."

Polly got all matter-of-facty. "On that logic we can assume that Ned Neal was killed by a phantom who doesn't really exist. That fits all the evidence, right?"

"You're right," I agreed. And as we would find out in less than forty-eight hours, it was true.

Chapter Twenty

At the time, though, all I knew was that my friends Happy and Go-Lucky had rejoined me then. Life was all sunny-side up, don't hold the bacon.

I turned to Polly as we continued our walk back to the hotel. "Can I borrow your phone? I want to call Jack."

"I'm not sure that's such a good idea, Jas," Tom said.

My heart rate picked up. "Why? Is he with someone besides Candy? Tell me."

"It's nothing like that, just that it's only four thirty A.M. in LA. You might want to wait like, five hours. You know, if you want him to be awake."

Tom was right, of course. But a love like mine chafes at restraint. I would have to find something to do for five hours, something—

I don't know if it was because DJs Happy and G-Luck were again in da house or what, but at right that second I had a dazzling flash of brilliance.

"I've just had a dazzling flash of brilliance," I announced.

"I've just felt my hair dance up-ended," Polly said.

"I am spurting Oh Nos," Roxy added.

"My silly pals, there's no need for concern. I figured out a way to learn more about what Arabella was thinking."

"Does that mean you have a plan?" Roxy asked.

"Not exactly, but—"

Embracing her role as president of the Up-with-Jas booster club, Alyson said, "I bet it's something stupid-slash-boring that is going to get us shot at."

"These pep talks of yours are really uplifting," I said. "Look, why don't you all traipse back to the Grissini Palace and I'll meet you there in a little while."

"Of course. We will definitely be leaving you to make your own way in the world. You've only been hit over the head once today," Polly said.

"Is this your sweet way of saying you can't get enough of my company?"

"Yes, and that we want you to stay alive longer, precious, so we can enjoy it. Where are we going?"

I suddenly saw the fly in my brilliant ointment. "Oh, just this place," I said in a casual tone.

Polly stopped. "Tell me," she said in a not-at-all-casual tone.

I coughed. "Prada," cough.

Polly looked like I'd hit her. "Why do you want to go there? Don't tell me they have a secret new line of push-up bras."

"They do?" Veronique said. "I haven't even heard of them!"

"It's the last place Arabella mentioned going. I want to know who she talked to. No shopping, just asking questions."

Polly snorted.[24] "Ha. You'll have to buy some hideous logo-encrusted thing if you want them to tell you anything."

"Your positive attitude is like a rainbow in my humdrum day," I told her. "Come on."

When we got to Prada, Polly did her best imitation of a Balkanese puppy, putting its foot down and saying it will Go No Further[25] but I pacified her by promising to be out in three minutes. "You'll see," I said. "No mayhem or anything. You can wait here and observeo through the window."

Polly looked at her watch, crossed her arms, and said, "Go."

The Evil Henches accompanied me inside, if you can accompany someone at whom you hiss, "Stay away from us, Jas. You are totally tainting our Tabasco." Nice nice nice. La la la. But even their charms did not harm my sunshiny demeanor. I beamed on everyone.

---

[24] Polly: By which, of course, you mean that I made a delightful sound of derision.
  Jas: Of course. Just like an adorable piglet troubled by allergies.

[25] Polly: There is no such animal as a Balkanese puppy.
  Jas: Yes, it's a combination of Balky and a Pekingese. It means you were cute but willful.
  Polly: It means I have a smashed-in face.
  Jas: All the better for snorting with!
  Polly: Okay, Crazelope. That is a combination of Crazy plus an antelope.
  Roxy: What's mine? I want it to be something like Snarlufflepagus. Snarly plus Snuffleupagus.
  Jas: But you aren't snarl—
  Roxy: Grrrrrrrrrrrrrrrrrrrr!
  Jas: Okay, Snarlufflepagus.

Apparently beaming doesn't make you look like a worth-
while customer, though. Either that, or I'd recently acquired
a new superpower in being invisible to high-end salespeople.
Each person I approached would say "I will be right back,
madam" and flit off to help another customer. This gave me
time to study the street life outside which consisted of:

Polly tapping her foot
A nun with a camera
A mime
Polly looking around in horror as a group of French
    schoolchildren swarmed around her
Tom doing some kind of Swedish exercise to contort
    himself so Polly wouldn't see him laughing
Roxy staring at the mime
An old man with a guidebook
Polly glaring at Tom
Roxy poking the mime
A—

"Yes, madam?" a saleswoman finally said. "How can I help
you?"

I pulled out the photo I'd taken from Arabella's apartment.
"This friend of mine was in here the other day. I'd like to
know who she spoke to and what she asked about."

The saleswoman looked at me like I'd just fed her lemon

slices pretending they were delicious gummi bears.

"I'm afraid we cannot help, madam," she said.

"It's really important," I told her. "I only want to know what she was talking about."

"It is not our process to give out information about clients."

This was not going well. I decided to pull out the big guns. "It's a matter of life and death."

"Still, I cannot—"

"There you are, Princess," Polly's voice said behind me.

"Yes, we've been looking all over for you, Your Highness," Tom said.

I turned to stare at them, which wasn't hard since they were both wearing BluBlocker glasses.

Roxy, who'd been pretending not to be with them, came over and said, "Ohmygod, Princess! Ohmygod, I loved your last music video! Can I have a picture with you too?" She crowded next to me and took out her phone. "Smile," she said as the flash went off. "Ohmygod, my friends at home in Utah are never going to believe this!"

Suddenly it was like global warming inside Prada, and all the cold shoulders I'd been getting thawed like polar ice caps. One of the saleswomen pulled Polly aside, and I just heard the words "superfamous," "disco queen," and "father's a total despot."

Well, at least one of those was true.

The saleswoman I'd been talking to tapped me on the

shoulder. "I beg Your Highness's pardon. What did you wish to learn?"

I showed her the picture again. "Who my friend talked to and what about."

She put on a pair of reading glasses to study the picture, then said, "May I?" and walked off with it.

"Utah?" I asked Roxy.

"They are crazy about royalty there."

Even if that made no sense, I had to admit that my friends were le superfantastic with the superfantastico icing. Because the saleswoman came back a minute later overflowing with information. "Your friend is inquiring about a former employee here, a girl called Maria Longhi. She was wishing to ask her some questions about her mother. But Maria has not worked with us for more than a year and no one knew her well. We told your friend to come back yesterday because one of our more experienced salesgirls, who did know Maria, is working that day, but your friend, she never returns."

Unless she spelled it some faerie way, Maria began with an M. As in Arabella's note: FIND M. I tried not to let my excitement show. "Is the other salesgirl here now? Could I talk to her?"

"I'm afraid she has left for vacation, Your Highness. How much longer will you be here? If you come back tomorrow, I might be able to know more. And perhaps we could arrange a private showing of our collection?"

"Why don't we just give you our number?" Polly said,

pulling out a notebook and writing down her digits. "The Princess is horrified by the idea of visiting the same store twice."

"Of course," the saleswoman said, like that made sense. "Then please accept this gift bag in thanks for your having visited our store. And my apologies for the wait. You know, we get all kinds in here." She nodded toward Alyson and Veronique, who were fighting over a pair of shoes. "And one never knows who is a serious person."

I was liking Prada more and more. "I understand," I told her regally, taking the gift bag. "Thank you for your help."

When we were on the street and had walked a little way from the store, Polly grabbed the gift bag from me. "Well, at least that's over," she said as though we'd just been saving orphans from a burning carny ride. She was holding the gift bag in front of her like closer contact might give her mites. "Let's get out of here before—"

That's when three things struck my brain at once:

1) Arabella had been trying to find Maria's mother.
2) Maria's last name was Longhi, the same as the woman who had written the old articles about The House that Kills.
3) The Prada gift bag.

But only the last one knocked me to my knees when Polly hit me over the head with it.

Chapter Twenty-one

———— ❧ ————

Little Life Lesson 36: If you are thinking to yourself, "What can I do to spice up my day?" do not choose the Get Whacked Over the Head Twice option.

For one thing, it hurts a lot. For another, it makes you kind of goofy. So that when the mists of pain clear and you hear your best friend saying, "Tom, did you see which way the shot came from?" you will say, "What shot?"

And everyone will look at you with pity and concern.

Except Polly, who will say in a voice that was a combination of terror and fury, "The one that went right by there," while pointing to a place dangerously near your scalp.

Hypothetically, I mean.

When I reached up to touch the place she'd pointed to, I could feel it was warm. "What happened?"

"I saw something whizzing toward you so I knocked you out of the way," Polly said. She turned to speak to someone behind her. "Tom and I are going after the shooter. You get her to cover," and suddenly there were hands hauling me up and carrying me to an archway.

Being hit over the head twice apparently also makes you delusional because when I looked up I could have sworn that Bobby Neal was carrying me on one side, and Max on the other. I smiled at them and the Delusions smiled back. On second thought, maybe being knocked out wasn't so bad at all.

As they set me down in a sheltered archway, DelusionMax bent down and said with a smile, "Really, Jasmine, you do not need to take such dramatic measures to get my attention."

Which, for some reason, caused me to start laughing uncontrollably. Everything that happened next just made me laugh harder. First, the warring looks of confusion-slash-concern for my well-being on Bobby's face. Then him trying to shoot a ferocious glare at Max while demanding to know who the hell he was. Max smiling at him blandly and asking if he wished him to start with a list of his ancestors who had fought in the Crusades or no, perhaps it would be better to jump forward to the eighteenth century when—

Bobby interrupted him. "That's not what I meant." Squinting, he added, "Do I know you?"

"I have no way to say what is the width of your knowledge, Mr. Neal. But can any of us know anyone? Truthfully?"

"You think you're funny," Bobby said.

"Miss Callihan does," Max pointed out.

I'd moved from laughing to hiccupping, but I managed to pull myself together enough to realize that something else suspect had just occurred. "How did you know his name?" I hiccupped at Max.

"Mr. Neal is very famous in the gossip magazines, no?" he answered.

Not to be left out, Bobby pointed at Max and demanded, "How do you know this guy? Do you want me to tell him to get lost?"

"It pains me but I must deny you this pleasure," Max told Bobby. Then said to me, "I return to work. My gondola stand is right there if you need me." He pointed to a bunch of gondolas kitty-corner from the arch I'd been planted in. "I am there always, and always at your disposal. You are certain that there is no dangerous injury?"

"Thanks," I said, "I'm certain."

"Very good. And while you are still deciding about whether you will allow me to take you out, please consider that in addition to juggling, I can also tie balloon animals. *Ciao.*"

I was N.O.T. tempted to watch him go until I could no longer see his broad-shouldered back and perfectly sculpted arms. Instead I said to Bobby, "What are you doing here?"

"I was looking for you. You said you were going to Prada. I called the hotel and they told me you were out, so . . ." His voice trailed off. "I wanted to apologize for what happened before. At Arabella's. You're right, I'm—not handling this well. I just have a lot on my plate."

"I understand."

"Thanks. Also, I talked to Beatrice. She was really upset,

but when I told her you didn't think Arabella killed herself, it kind of perked her up. She asked if you would come to the house tonight. After what just happened, though, I'm guessing the answer is no."

"Come to the house? You mean your father's house? The House that Kills?"

Bobby winced. "Nice. Thank you for that. But, yeah, that's what I meant. There was supposed to be a big reception for this foundation my father funded but we canceled it. So it would just be us. And Lucien. Lucien Wilder." He did that thing again where he paused like I was supposed to know who he was talking about.

It sounded like something I might have once known before getting hit over the head twice, INCLUDING ONE TIME BY MY BEST FRIEND THANK YOU POLLY.

I must have looked perplexed because he added, "Lucien Wilder, the designer. He was my father's oldest friend. They used to chase girls together or something. He's the one executing the will."

But what I was really hearing was: blah blah Arabella thought there was something about the history of the house or how it was constructed that explained how her father was killed, YES OF COURSE I WANT TO GO THERE.

There was one tiny blot on the horizon of my excitement and it wasn't having just been shot at. Mr. T scoffs at shooting. "I'd love to come," I told Bobby, "but I have some friends visiting from California. There are six of us," I said, realizing it would be futile not to include the Evil Henches since they seemed intent on forever polluting my immediate environment with themselves. "I don't really want to leave them alone."

"No problem." He pulled out his phone. "Let me call Beatrice and tell her." He dialed, waited, then spoke into the phone. "Hi, Bea. Listen, Jasmine can make it tonight but— what? . . . No, I said she *can* make it. But she's got a few friends with her . . . Five." Not that I was listening. I just happened to be standing there.

At that point, my pals rallied around me to show their Concern and Consideration, which interrupted my not-eavesdropping.[26]

---

26   Polly: Just so you know, I will personally kill you if you let anything like this happen to you
               again. You do realize that someone shot at you.

      Jas: I didn't hear any shot and no one else seems to have noticed. Are you le positive?

      Tom: I found this.

      Jas: What is it?

      Tom: I'm pretty sure it's a BB pellet from a BB air gun. Which is why there was no sound.

      Jas: Could you tell what direction it came from? Or get any idea who shot it?

      Tom: After you, uh, went down, I watched for anyone taking off extra fast like you told me to
               when we were looking for that Robin Hood of the Circus guy last year, but no one did. In
               fact, like you said, no one seemed to notice, so no one budged.

      Jas: Clever.

      Tom: Yeah. The only people in the square were—

      Jas: A mime, a nun, an old man, and some schoolchildren.

     Roxy: We can rule out the mime because I was talking to him. His name is Davos.

      Jas: I so hope this doesn't mean what I think it means.

     Roxy: Davos ♥ is Greek. I like Greek food. He says his mother is a very good cook.

      Tom: Did you see the heart?

      Jas: I'm hoping if we ignore it they will go away.

Tom: Good plan. Ignoring.

Jas: Roxy, I thought mimes weren't supposed to talk.

Roxy: ♥Davos♥ made an exception for me. He has a lovely voice.

Tom: Ignoring really, really hard.

Polly: Hello? Team? Can we get back to how someone tried to kill our Jas?

Jas: BB guns don't kill people, P. People with real guns kill people. If it was only a BB, then they were just trying to scare me.

Polly: That makes me feel much better.

Jas: It makes me pissed. Mr. T wouldn't stand for this. They're toying with me. Like a cat toy!

Polly: I just thought of a Little Life Lesson! Polly's Little Life Lesson: If you find yourself mad that you were not shot at with a real gun, seek professional help.

Jas: On the other hand, there would be no reason to scare me if I hadn't gotten close to something. And since I was shot at near Prada, I could assume it was something I had—or could have—learned there. So actually, it's a good thing.

Polly: Polly's Little Life Lesson 2: Also, if anything about being shot at makes you happy.

Jas: Ho ho and also ho. Um, Roxy, what are you doing?

Roxy: Practicing my mime moves. Guess what I'm saying.

Tom: "You promised me a gelato but I have seen neither hide nor hair of it as of yet"?

Roxy: Exactly! ♥♥Davos♥♥ said I might be a natural.

Tom: Not. Working.

Jas: "You promised me a gelato but I have seen neither hide nor hair of it as of yet" would make a great song title.

Polly: Not to introduce a trivial note, but I don't suppose after being shot at you're ready to turn over everything Arabella gave you to the police and forget all about the investigation?

Jas: Sure, okay.

Polly: Sure, okay? Just like that? No arguing?

Jas: No. By the way, who is Lucien Wilder?

Polly: Don't try to change the—wait, did you say Lucien Wilder?

Jas: Yeah. He's someone famous, right?

Polly: He's only a fashion legend and my idol. You know that, Jas.

Jas: Oh. Well, we were just invited to have dinner with him tonight.

Polly: What?!?

Jas: Just us and a few other people. Is it healthy for your eyes to pop out like that?

Polly: We were invited to an intimate dinner with Lucien Wilder? We have to go!

Jas: I'm glad you think so.

Polly: Why?

Jas: I just like to make you happy. Hey, what is Roxy doing now?

Polly: I believe that is "Doesn't Jas's Behavior Seem Suspicious?"

Roxy: No, it was—

Jas: Love to chat but Bobby's off the phone. Excuse me.

Bobby hung up and turned back to me. "All set. Bea will send the launch to pick you up at seven o'clock. Does that work?"

"Totally."

"Great. Beatrice is really looking forward to meeting you. Well, see you later."

He'd only taken two steps when light was blotted out of the sky, the air was rent by a sound like the screaming of the souls of the damned, and the Evil Henches appeared from nowhere to throw themselves on him while screeching, "Reggie!"

Well, okay, maybe only the last part really happened.

"Reggie, you're so naughty!" Alyson said, tapping him on the nose. "We've been waiting for you to text all day!"

"You're Reggie?" I said.

"They started calling me that," he told me through a cloud of Evil Hench hair. Then he said, "If it isn't Gorgeous One and Gorgeous Two. What are you doing here?"

"Hi, cuz," I said.

"You two know each other?" Bobby-slash-Reggie asked.

Alyson said: "Barely."

I said, "She's my cousin."

He said, "Outstanding. Then you'll be at dinner tonight, too."

I was pretty sure the "too" in that sentence was Alyson, but she said, "Why does Jas have to come? Don't you want us all to yourself?"

I was totally interested in his reply but I didn't get to find out. His phone rang and after the Hench Genies helped him get it out of his pocket (E to the WWWWWWWWWWW-WWWWWWWWWW), he answered it. "Hi, Bea. What? No, I'm still . . . Okay, I get it, I have to go now. Bye."

"Do you have to Gulf Stream?" Alyson asked with a pout.

"'Fraid so," he told the Evil Ones. "See you tonight at seven." Then he said to me, "Bye, Jas."

"Bye, Bobby."

Veronique turned to ask me, "Why did you call him Bobby?"

"Because that's his name. Don't you know who he is?"

"Reggie," Alyson said. "The guy we met at the airport."

"No, that's Bobby Neal, Arabella's brother."

"He told us his name was Reggie," Veronique said.

"Are you sure?" I asked.

Alyson pretended to find something interesting in her cuticles. "Why would we forget?"

"We sort of forgot," Veronique reminded her. "You're the one who said the Ouija board spelled out 'Reggie.'"

"Ouija board?" I asked, but of course was ignored.

Alyson pointed a nail tip at Veronique. "You agreed."

"Not at first. I said, 'Are you sure? It looks like "Ralph"' and you said, 'Yes, I'm positive.'"

"If you weren't sure, you didn't have to go along with it."

"But you—"

Veronique had been nice to me recently, and it looked like she was in danger of losing an eye so I took Evasive Action. "If you didn't know who he was, how did you know he was rich?" I asked.

"We can just tell," Alyson said.

"And he had first-class tags on his luggage," Veronique added.

Alyson got a meditative expression on her face. "But you know, we were wrong. He's not two commas, he's three."

"You're right! Everyone at school is going to go R-I-P when we tell them. And you-know-who is going to be so jeal—" Veronique stopped because Alyson had apparently discovered the patented Strangle with a Look technique so popular with the Evil Genius set and was using it on her.

Then she turned Look-O-Death™ on me and said, "That was low-slash-lame even for you, Calamity."

"What? What did I do?"

"We saw Bobby Neal first. I wish you'd get a life and stop trying to lead mine."

I gaped at her. Maybe not literally, but I was totally brain-gaping. Which is probably why I could not think of any of the 999,000 superdeluxe responses to what she said that I should have.

Not that it would have mattered, because Polly appeared at my side then and said, "We have to get back to the hotel.

We only have five hours until dinner and I have to do wardrobe."

As we marched back to the hotel, I couldn't shake the idea that something about the way the Evil Henches had met Bobby didn't add up, but I had no idea what it was.

Chapter Twenty-two

———— ❧ ————

Camilla the concierge stopped us as we were going through the lobby to tell me that Dadzilla and Sherri! and my aunt and uncle had gone to Padua, a town on the mainland, for dinner with a world-famous soapologist, and wouldn't be back until late, leaving specific instructions I was to stay with my friends and cousin *at all times*, and did we need dinner reservations because she could recommend—

"No," I said, "we have plans."

"Where are you going? Maybe it is not a good place. There are many places that are not good in Venice. Once I was on a date with—"

"We're having dinner at Ca'Dario."

"We are?" Polly said. "Wait, isn't that—"

Camilla's eyes got huge and her voice got low. "The House that Kills. You must not go there."

"We'll be fine. Guests never get hurt there."

There was a long pause, the longest silence I'd ever heard from Camilla. Then she said, "I have enjoyed knowing you, Jasmine. Also, if you do not return, may I have your dress with the cherries on it? I am very fond."

I assured her she could and we headed for the elevators. My bed, when we finally got to my room, looked like a slice of linen meringue pie and I dove right into it. Polly had adjusted to the news that we were going to The House that Kills for dinner remarkably well—she only said, "I should have guessed" and "We'll need weapons"—and got busy with her scissors, BeDazzler, and campaign against my Wonderbras. Roxy and Tom were Assisting, and I was Fingerprinting the Glass I'd Taken from Arabella's with My iPod On.[27] And finally, Being Alerted to the Startling Fact that My Leather Pants Were Now a Jaunty Cropped Jacket.

[27] Roxy: I've been thinking. Maybe instead of trying to figure out who killed Mr. Neal or how, we should be looking at why.

Polly: What do you mean "why"?

Roxy: Well, you know how in movies a group of adventurous people will band together to try to steal a huge gem from the eye socket of an Incan idol? And then one of them makes off with it, leaving the others there to die? But one of the others always lives and comes back in disguise to exact a bloody revenge? That seems like a good idea to explore.

Tom: I'm not clear on that use of the phrase "good idea." Or how you're going to explore it.

Roxy: I'm going to ask probing yet subtle questions.

Tom: Ah. Of course.

Polly: What are some of your other ideas, Rox? And Tom, try to hold the pants straight while I'm cutting.

Roxy: What if his butler has a really beautiful daughter, and Mr. Neal had his way with her and got her pregnant and there's an illegitimate child and now the butler has decided to exact a bloody revenge?

Tom: If he has a butler. Also his death wasn't bloody. Polly, are you sure cutting the legs off Jas's leather pants is a good idea?

Polly: One hundred percent le positive.

Roxy: Bloody revenge is just a figure of speech. Okay, what if Mr. Neal was part of an ancient blood cult and had decided to spill its secrets so they —

Tom: Exacted a bloody revenge?

Roxy: Now you're cooking with gas! And of course there's the Russian Mafia angle.

Tom: Of course. They are famous for their figurative bloody revenge exacting.

Roxy: Or maybe someone stood to make a lot of money on the stock market if he died.

Polly: Those are all really great ideas, Rox, and I will be aflutter to see what your subtle probing reveals. But truthfully, I'm more worried about Bobby Neal.

Roxy: What do you mean?

Polly: He could have been the shooter today. Like maybe instead of running away, he ran toward Jas, covering his tracks in reverse.

Tom: He doesn't exactly seem like the type to think of that.

Roxy: That's EXACTLY the type!

Polly: He could also have been the one who hit Jas over the head.

Tom: You mean the first time.

Roxy: Ha!

Polly: Pretend I am laughing. But he could have been. He was in the right place to follow Jas when she left Arabella's. It all fits.

Tom: What do you want to do?

Polly: I say we should Be On Our Guard. Also Watchful. But I don't think we should tell Jas. She has enough to worry about.

Jas: What are you guys talking about?

Roxy: Nothing, sweetie. Were you able to get Arabella's prints?

Jas: Yeah, I've got two good ones. I did her phone too. Unfortunately, they all match the ones we found on the pen.

Roxy: Great!

Jas: No, le bad. It means the prints on the pen are Arabella's. Which means we don't have anything on the killer. What are you hiding behind your back?

Roxy: Ha ha, me hiding anything. You are such a funny joker.

Tom: Rox, is that thing you're making supposed to smoke and hiss and have purple sparks like that?

Roxy: The purple sparks are an unexpected bonus. I wonder what they put in that stuff.

Jas: What stuff?

Roxy: Nothing. Evidenceland, Jas. That is your desired destination.

Jas: Seriously, what are you — oh my God, are those my leather pants?

Tom: I think the verb you're looking for is "Were."

I sniffed the air. It was a little smoky. "Have you been burning something in here?"

"No," Polly, Tom, and Roxy said in suspicious unison.

By then it was 9:15 A.M. Los Angeles time, and Tom said I could try calling Jack, so I didn't pursue the odor. My heart was all poundy and my fingers shook a little as I dialed and waited for him to pick up. I was so nervous that when a voice answered and said, "Hey, it's Jack," I started talking before I realized it was only his voice mail.

But that was okay! Totally! I was not disappointed at all! Much! In the least! Nor did I feel like I'd been punched in the stomach by Disappointment and his best bully friend Thwarted Hope! Or wonder where he could be at 9:15 on a Sunday morning!

I had no idea what to say but luckily the monkeys weren't nearly as tongue-tied. They said, "Hi, Jack, it's me. Jas. Jasmine. I'm sorry I missed you on IM yesterday but I got arrested for murder. I mean, I didn't do it, but I accidentally told the police I did, so it was confusing. Now we're going for dinner at The House that Kills, but that is only a nickname because a lot of people have died there, but it's completely safe. Anyway, I hope you're having a very nice morning and not melting in anyone's mouth or hands—" No, monkeys! Bad, monkeys! "Sorry, I mean molting. On anyone. Ha ha. Because molting is bad. Unless you're a wee creature of the forest but—um, never mind, I've got to go, bye." After which, of course, I wanted to die.

But One cannot be a burden to One's pals. Even when One is worried that One's boyfriend—who One is pretty sure One is in love with, and One would give her right arm to get just an email from—is out with other girls causing One's heart to feel like the Incredible Hulk is holding it in a vise grip, One must set aside Le Wallowing in Misery and instead Wear Le Masko.

Plus, One's boyfriend could call back at any moment.

Yes, One is a jolly dreamer.

Anyway, determined not to let anyone know that I wasn't Jas but rather the hollow shell of Jas, I put on the new outfit Polly had made. It consisted of a modified-to-be-more-form-fitting version of a navy blue jersey dress I'd had, and my new pant-jacket which, I had to admit, was quite cute. The waist of the pants was now the neck of the jacket, and one of the pockets went across the front with a button. Polly was just explaining the safety features of the ensemble—"The button on the front can be used as a cutting device, the hem of the dress detaches for restraining your hair or bad guys, the pocket can be ripped off and has been reinforced with your Wonderbra underwires to function as a throwing star, the cuff has a two-way radio built in, and we added a Skittles-based tracking device to your boots"—when her phone rang.

She picked it up, listened for a second, and held it out to me. Jack! It had to be Jack! To laugh with me in light mirthful amusement at my message! My heart did a double axel combo that would have gotten tens across the board from the judges at the Olympics.

"Hello?" I said.

The voice on the other end said, "Hello, Your Highness?"

I don't know if it was the fact that it was a woman or that she called me Your Highness, but I caught on pretty fast that it wasn't Jack. Yes, tacks could take notes about how sharp I am. Also, the voice went on: "I work at Prada? I hear you asking about the girl in the picture today?" She was speaking the same nasal English as the saleswoman who had helped me earlier that day, but she sounded younger.

I pushed aside the le massivo disappointment that had washed over me and used my princess voice to say, "Yes. Do you know something about her?"

"Maybe. You will not tell that I call you? I will be fired."

"I won't tell. What's your name?"

"I tell you later. I am not sure how to say this, but your friend, the one who was here, is she perhaps a little crazy? Wrong in the head?"

I didn't have to think about that, but I was curious how she knew. I mean, it wasn't *that* obvious. "She might have seemed that way. Why?"

"Does this mean that there is no reward?"

"Reward?"

"Your friend says that there will be a lot of money if

she can find Maria Longhi."

"Oh, that reward," I said in my Why-Certainly-I-Know-Just-What-You're-Talking-About-Ha-Ha voice. "I'm sure that's real. Do you know Maria?"

"I never work with her, but she comes in to visit others from time to time in the past. I might be able to help you meet her."

"That would be great. Any information you can give me will lead to a reward," I assured her. I did not mention that the reward might be my *How 2 Break-dance Like Da Pros* DVD.

"Where can I find you if I learn things?"

"The Grissini Palace Hotel, room 549. Or call me on this number."

"Very good. Also if you see your friend's boyfriend can you please say I am sorry I cannot help him?"

"Her boyfriend?"

"*Sì*. He comes in later that day and wants to know what she'd been looking at so he could buy it for her as a present. He was *triste* when we explained that she is only asking questions so I tell him that when she comes back the next day to talk to Cristina I will make sure to see what she likes. But she does not come back."

Arabella had never mentioned having a boyfriend in Venice and her apartment was totally Single Use Only. "Can you describe what he looked like?"

"You do not know?"

"She had a lot of boyfriends," I said quickly. "I just want to tell the right one."

"This one speaks Italian and I think he is maybe—" She broke off, said, "I must go. *Arrivederci,*" and hung up.

I stared at the phone for a second. Reward? Mystery boyfriend? These were deep waters. I still had two impossible murders on my hands (and no call from Jack) but at least this was something New-n-Fresh. I'd known that Arabella was keen like a hungry dog sniffing a bone to find Maria, but the reward showed just how keen. Big dog keen. FIND M wasn't just an idea for her, it was the Idea of Her Heart.

And the "boyfriend" was a sensation. Because it proved without any shadow of doubts or shadows of doubt that she was being spied on. By a sinister, Italian-speaking man. *Alias* Number-One Suspect.

(I wished Jack were following me around.)

Him traipsing after her and wanting to know what she'd said—I was sure asking about purses was just a clever cover to get the information he wanted—confirmed that her death had something to do with the questions she'd been asking. And since those questions seemed to have been focused on learning more about her father's death—

"Well?" Polly said.

"Sorry, I was musing."

"Less musing, more explaining."

I told my pals about the call, concluding by saying, "See,

Polly, good things can come of going to Prada."

"Yes, precious," she said. "Now come here and put on your water wings. Roxy fitted each of them with several excellent devices, including mini smoke bombs in case you need to create a diversion. Just touch the two wires together. She made the fuel from the stuffing of your Wonderbras."

"And I used the cups of your Wonderbra to make snack holders for my water wings," Roxy chimed in.

Little Life Lesson 37: There should be a law against any sentence that combines the phrases "snack holders" and "Wonderbra."

"What part of my bra collection are you wearing, Tom?" I asked, and I meant it to bite.

But he just gave a hollow laugh. Which made me more nervous.

Just then the Evil Henches came crowding into my room, bringing on a moment of silence. They were dressed in the latest Nymphs of the Wooded Glen style, which appeared to involve diaphanous gowns in green (Alyson) and lavender (Veronique), flowered crowns, and platform boots. They each had a gem glued in the middle of their foreheads, and they were carrying a Ouija board.

"What are you staring at, Jas?" NymphAlyson asked.

"You look—"

"I know," Veronique squealed. "We're totally the Sauce."[28]

---

[28] Roxy: What kind of sauce do you think she means? Worstdressedshire sauce?
Tom: Steak-through-the-eye sauce?
Polly: Ho'llandaise? Gawk-amole?
Jas: Actually, I bet it's just cheese sauce.
Roxy: Ha. Hey, is anyone besides me hungry?

Fortunately, Camilla called on the hotel phone then to say that the launch from The House that Kills had arrived to pick us up and reiterate that she hoped nothing happened but, if for some reason I didn't come back, could she also have the boots I wore with the cherry dress because she'd found a shoemaker who could adjust them to fit her.

With that nice sentiment ringing in my ears and floaties locked and loaded (and no word from Jack), we set out for The House that Kills.

Chapter Twenty-three

⸺ ❧ ⸺

The launch was piloted by an 800-year-old man with a peg leg, who thought Polly was totally Jordache and insisted on turning around and smiling at her a lot, which was understandable but disconcerting because it was foggy on the water and it would have been nice for him to watch where he was going and also because he only had three teeth, one of which was a strange gray color.

We were all lost in our own thoughts so our conversation—

Me: I hope we don't crash.
Polly: We should have gone with poison darts.
Tom: This is a really cool boat.
Roxy: I wonder what we'll have for dinner.
Veronique: I hear dead people.
Forensic Files Voice-over Man: As they approached the house, our investigators were in for a chilling surprise.

Alyson: Is the moisture ruining my hair? How does
my hair look?

—sounded more like a game of word association than
anything else.

And, okay, maybe the *Forensic Files* Voice-over Man wasn't
there. But that's what he would have said if life came with the
Forensic Files Voice-over Man (like it should).

As we approached the dock, I composed this haiku prayer:

House that Kills please do
Not smite me I'm not ready
To go R-I-P

(Not before I kiss Jack again.)

At first it seemed like my prayer was answered. Pulling up,
everything looked hunky with a side of dory. The boat tied up
to a small wooden platform covered by a rubber mat with a
huge NN printed on it in gold in the same pattern that the pen
from Arabella's box had on it. The large planters with trees in
them that flanked the mat on either side were also emblazoned with golden Ns.

The door on the dock, with a double N door pull, was
glass, and beyond it we could see a marble hall lit with mel-
low butter-colored light. So cozy! So welcoming! Tom pulled
open the door.

Cut to: CHILLING SURPRISE.

It was like walking into a beating heart. *Buh-bump buh-bump* echoed off the walls, floor, and ceiling of the room, surrounding us and putting the EEEEEP! in CREEEEEEPY! Digits began scaling my spine with wild abandon.

Alyson stopped on the threshold and, taking a page from the Encyclopedia Drammatica, put her hand to her chest, saying, "I know none of you can feel them, but the vibrations, they're so strong-slash-powerful here."

"I feel them," Veronique said. "It's like they're—"

"From the three hundred clocks upstairs," a booming male voice said from in front of us. I was startled when I looked up and saw him. He was a massive man with a close-cropped, pointed white beard, wearing a royal blue cape over a dark blue-gray pin-striped suit, and a Three Musketeers–Style Hat Complete with White Feather, carrying a gold-headed walking stick, but he seemed to have materialized from nowhere, like a ghost. "They are supposed to calm the spirits. Welcome to Ca'Dario. I'm—"

"Lucien Wilder," Polly breathed, and I swear she almost threw herself at his feet.

He bowed to her. "Indeed. I'm afraid Beatrice and young Robert are busy upstairs so they sent me to escort you in. Please, follow me."

When I looked at him more closely I saw that he wasn't really massive, he just gave the impression of massivity (if that's a word). He had presence. As he gestured us toward a doorway with the gold head of his stick—which I now saw was a naked lady with blue sapphire eyes (classy!)—his expression glittered with something between humor and mischievousness, like he knew a joke but he wasn't going to tell us.

"Do you see the tailoring on his cuffs?" Polly leaned over to whisper to me. "He invented that."

"Wow. Are you sure your phone is on?"

"Yes, Jas. Remember how you checked four times during the six minutes we were on the boat?"

We followed the Cuff Inventor up a wide staircase with NN patterned carpeting into a long, high-ceilinged room with a stone floor and three tall windows that overlooked the Grand Canal. The light came from two enormous glass chandeliers blown to look like they were flowering bouquets that hung from the ceiling of the room, and a series of tall candles in the corners. There were couches with NN embroidered throw pillows on them grouped on top of a Turkish rug near the windows, and he gestured to them, throwing off his cape and settling himself in a large leather chair. He kept his left leg straight out in front of him.

"You children have the advantage over me," he boomed. "You know my name but I don't know yours. Which of you is Jasmine?"

"That's me," I said, sitting forward. I felt like I should curtsy or prostrate myself on the ground or something.

He used the naked lady stick to point at me. "What are

those contraptions on your arms, dear?"

"Water wings. For safety. You know, with the boats and all that."

He laughed a huge billowing laugh. "Take them off. They ruin the line of that otherwise scrumptious jacket. Who makes it?"

Polly turned a color I'd only ever seen her turn when she was caught in public kissing Tom. "I did, sir. But I'd rather Jas kept them on."

"Artistic integrity. Interesting. And you are?"

"Polly Prentis. I made it out of a pair of pants."

"You have talent, Polly Prentis."

"We made our outfits too," Alyson said, standing up and pulling Veronique with her.

Maybe that was wishful thinking, but I could have sworn Lucien winced. "Yes, you did. And you are?"

"Sapphyre with a Y and Tiger's*Eye with a star, but the star is silent."

"Ah. Bobby's little pets. Charming, charming. And you two? You are twins?"

"Yes, I'm Tom, and this is my sister, Roxy." Polly had coached Tom that afternoon, and he now launched into his speech. "It's a pleasure to meet you, sir. Polly has spoken so highly—"

"I like the way your jacket hangs, young man. Your handiwork?" he asked, pointing the stick at Polly.

"Yes."

"Bravo, young lady. You have a very good eye."

The only thing that kept Polly from fainting at that moment was the arrival of our hosts. Bobby, in a blue button-down shirt, a navy-and-white pin-striped blazer, and jeans, looked slightly disheveled, although that might just have been because he was standing next to the most put-together woman I'd ever seen. She was one of those women who make trench coats look chic and make you feel like a total mess even when you were dressed by Polly mere minutes ago and had miraculously avoided a hairtastrophe on the boat ride over.

From her perfectly tailored pencil skirt to the turned-back cuffs of her crisp white blouse and the carefully knotted scarf at her throat, there wasn't a single thing out of place. If I were a betting girl, which, of course, I'm not because it is illegal for people my age to bet and also because I am, according to Dadzilla, already irresponsible enough with money, I would completely have put cash on the fact that her underwear was ironed and matched her outfit. I recognized her as the other woman in the picture I'd lifted from Arabella's, only now her dark hair hung down her back.

She came forward and held out a perfectly-manicured-with-dark-polished-nails hand to me. "I am Beatrice," she said in a voice with a faint Italian accent I recognized from Arabella's phone. "You must be Jasmine. Thank you for coming."

The Evil Hench Nymphs cleaved themselves to Bobby (if that means glued themselves to his arms like they had suction cups for hands), and the rest of us followed them into the dining room. Beatrice said something about a simple, informal dinner, but there were three forks, two knives, three spoons, and two glasses at every place.

We were seated. We ate. We talked. Or at least, everyone else did. There was no I in DINNER for me that night. I don't know if it was the one-two punch to the head I'd had, or the vibrations in the atmosphere, but my mind seemed to be tuned to RadioJas, where the programming bounced between repeating my conversation with my mystery Prada caller,[29] wondering what seemed fishy about Bobby's meeting the Henches,[30] asking how I was going to convince Beatrice to show me Ned Neal's office,[31] and other topics of general interest. Pertaining to the investigation. Exclusively.

I was NOT, for example, wondering about Jack or why he hadn't called back or where he was or what he was eating for brunch or with whom or hoping that it was either Costume Sunday or freezing cold in Los Angeles so they would be wearing a lot of clothing, for example those wool face masks popular with bank robbers and kidnappers, unsightly wax lips, and gorilla suits.

(ATTENTION ALL TOTALLY HOT GIRL–BAND MEMBERS: This would be a very fetching outfit to wear to brunch.)

(Also, fake scars.)

(FYI.)

[29] BadJas: Who can take a sunrise, sprinkle it in dew, cover it in chocolate and a miracle or two?

[30] BadJas: The candyman can! The candyman can because he mixes it with love and makes the world taste good.

[31] BadJas: Who can take a rainbow, wrap it in a sigh, soak it in the sun and make a—
Jas: THAT IS LE NUFF!

(Love, your friend Jas.)

In between RadioJas broadcasts, I picked up snippets from the general conversation:

LUCIEN: It was four years before I reintroduced the boat neck that Ned Neal and I met. That must be—my God, twenty-six years go. And it was right in this house.

ALYSON: I look good in boat necks.

VERONIQUE: You look better in halters.

ROXY: Did Mr. Neal ever participate in any secret missions to pillage priceless gems from sacred temples, for example, the large ruby eye from an Incan idol?

BEATRICE: No.

VERONIQUE: Is Incan Idol like *American Idol* for Incans?

TOM: Yes, it is.

LUCIEN: The place was being restored for a foundation and they ran a scholarship program—more like a chain gang for starving young artists yearning to breathe. They impressed us into service cleaning the old frescos and things in the house.

ALYSON: I look good in both halters and boat necks.

ROXY: Did Mr. Neal ever have a butler? Perhaps one with a nubile young daughter?

BEATRICE: There was a housekeeper, Mrs. Lyons, but she had two sons. Why?

LUCIEN: I've never spent so many dreary days in my life. Couldn't stand the house from the start, personally—hated it almost as much as that stirrup pant trend—but Ned was crazy for the place.

ALYSON: I have a pair of stirrup pants! They're totally Visa with my ankle boots.

ROXY: Did you ever notice Mr. Neal engaging in surreptitious robe-wearing?

BEATRICE: I'm not sure I understand. Surreptitious? If he was sick he would sometimes wear his robe at breakfast.

ROXY: No, I mean like if he was sneaking out to attend meetings of a blood cult? Or villainous secret brotherhood?

BEATRICE: Absolutely not.

LUCIEN: Ned swore he'd live in this house someday. I don't believe he meant to die here, though. And thus, to paraphrase the poet Burns, the best-laid plans of mice and men go oft awry.

VERONIQUE: I read about that book. *Of Mice and Men*. There was a quote from it in *Rabbits for Dummies*.

ROXY: What about the Russian Mafia? Did he

have any dealings with—
BEATRICE: No.

Things kind of picked up for me after dinner. That's when Literary Critic Veronique and Fashion Jet-setter Alyson convinced Bobby to take them on a tour of the house and Polly, Tom, and Roxy got confidential with Lucien. I was just trying to figure out the best approach to get into NN's office when Beatrice leaned over and, as though she'd been reading my mind, asked if I'd like to see it.

To say I leaped like a leapfrog from my seat would be to understate things. I leaped so much that I bashed into Beatrice and knocked over a chair. And some small (piece of china, crystal goblet) items from the table.

But we had it cleaned up in no time, and then we were off.[32]

We went up a flight of stairs that had entwined Ns cut into the railing and down a stone corridor to a large wood door set into a marble frame. It had a huge old-fashioned round handle right in the center, but the lock on the side was modern, one of those electric, plastic key kinds.

"This registers whenever anyone goes in or out," Beatrice explained. "That's how we know no one entered the night Mr. Neal died. Although"—she pointed at nicks in the wood around it—"this isn't the one that was here that night because we had to break it off to get in. It took

---

[32] Jas: So, Polly—
    Polly: My phone is on, I have a good signal, and I will come get you if you get any calls.
    Jas: That's not what I was going to say!
    Polly: What were you going to say?
    Jas: Well, okay, it was. But I was going to say if I should *happen* to get any calls. Stop rolling
          your eyes at me!

Signore Pagano, the handyman, fifteen hits with the sledge-hammer to smash it."

I mentally checked the NO box next to "someone could have picked the lock."

Beatrice used a key card and there was a click and the door opened.

Chapter Twenty-four

———— ❦ ————

I'd sort of imagined billionaires did Big Important Things at Big Important Desks in Big Offices Filled with Important Furniture. But the room I walked into was small and spare, like something on a boat. There was dark wood paneling three-quarters of the way up each wall and a thick rug on the floor. In the middle of the rug stood a desk with four spindly legs. A leather desk chair stood behind it. Along one wall were three small file cabinets and back by the window was a globe that was actually a bar. That was it.

Which meant a NO for the "someone could have been concealed in the office amongst the furnishings to hide in wait for his prey and gotten in that way" check box as well.

The one large window overlooked the Grand Canal and had massive bars on it; definitive NO to "someone snuck in through the window."

The desk had a (monogrammed) leather blotter on it and a (monogrammed) leather-covered pencil cup with a bunch of pens identical to the one Arabella had left in the ballerina box. I rifled through them to see if any of them looked weaponized, but they didn't. In a (monogrammed) frame there was a photo of Arabella, Bobby, Beatrice, and Mr. Neal all wearing wetsuits in front of a blue sky and palm trees.

Beatrice stood on the threshold with her hand on the big knob as I explored, like she was afraid to enter or it was some kind of sacred space. She was staring at the rug between the desk and the door.

"That's where we found him," she told me. "Lying there. Nothing's been moved since then."

There was no sign now that there had ever been a body there now, but from the expression on her face and the way her knuckles on the knob went white, she was still seeing it.

"He'd gotten up from his desk and was trying to get to the door when he died. If only—" she said, and half stifled a sob. Between her reaction and the photo on the desk I realized that her relationship with Ned Neal wasn't a simple employer–employee one. He'd been old enough to be her father but my father was old enough to be Sherri!'s father (if he'd had her at a very young age) and I had to wonder if maybe—

Little Life Lesson 38: Some things are better left in NotWonderland.

I said, "I'm sorry, I didn't want to make this harder for you."

She waved my apology away. "No. I wanted you to see for yourself that there was no way he could have been murdered. It's impossible."

"Or maybe we're dealing with an exceptionally brilliant and cunning killer," I said.

She looked at me for a long time. "You're still not convinced."

"No. I think Arabella was murdered for getting too close to the truth about her father's death. If her father wasn't murdered, then no one would have had a reason to kill her for what she found out. And that would mean she committed suicide. And she didn't. I know all the evidence seems conclusive, but it just doesn't make sense."

"I agree," she said.

I was so startled I dropped the (monogrammed) pen I'd inadvertently taken out of the pen cup. "You do?" She was the first person to agree with me.

She stared down at the floor for a long time and I thought maybe that was the end of it but then she said, "I do. I don't know if it's just because I want to, but you're right, it doesn't make sense. Not now. There was a time when it wouldn't have surprised me. Arabella had been engaged but she and her fiancé parted ways and she was very low."

"Here you are, we've been looking for you," Bobby said, suddenly among us. I hadn't heard him approach but he pushed past Beatrice through the door with his Evil Hench

Posse. "And that's a laugh about parting ways. Dad broke the engagement off and you know it." His voice was loud and slightly slurred, like he'd had a few drinks.

Beatrice had jumped and turned a color I'd seen on a lipstick called "Pink Morn" when Bobby appeared. Her voice was higher as she started to say, "Bobby, that's not—" but he interrupted her.

"Don't let Beatrice fool you with all her Saint Ned Neal talk. My father didn't want anyone else having what he had. Look at this place, covered with his initials. Even the damn toilet paper has his monogram on it. Had to have custom-made clothes, custom water to drink, custom ink in his pens, custom cologne to douse himself in. Not exactly a big sharer, my pops. And the one thing he really didn't want to share was his little girl. He didn't like Arabella being in love with anyone but him, and he would do anything he could to prevent it."

"It's true that your father had very particular tastes, but you're wrong about Arabella," Beatrice told him in a tight voice. "It was just that she was only eighteen and he had strong opinions on the advisability of falling in love when one was too young."

I looked from one to the other of them. "Why?"

"I always figured he got caught up with some floozie when he was younger," Bobby said. I glanced over at Beatrice who had gone from "Pink Morn" to "Deep Rose."

Bobby, however, was O to the BLIVIOUS and went right on: "Got his heart broken, never recovered. Made us pay for his mistakes, decreeing that no one could know what they wanted before they were at least thirty just because he didn't. You won't break my heart, will you, girls?" he asked the Evil Henches, all man-about-town now. They giggled and I felt like I was watching a really bad sitcom. The kind that should come with a weapon you could aim at the TV that would make annoying characters' heads go *Splat!* in a satisfying manner. Maybe Roxy could invent one.

The way the vein was pulsing in her throat, Beatrice looked like she might be a good customer. She ripped her gaze from the Bobby–Hench combine and said to me, "Mr. Neal felt that Arabella was too young to be engaged, and that it would be better if she broke it off, so he—"

"Offered George a hundred grand to go away. He should have taken it."

"He didn't?" I asked.

"Nope," Bobby said, tickling Alyson's ear. *SPLAT!* "I think he was holding out for more. Didn't work, Arabella broke the thing off, anyway, to please Daddy Dearest."

"Bobby, I really don't think—"

"Oh, get stuffed, Beatrice. They're both dead and I'm in charge now and I say we start telling the truth. Dad was a sneak, Arabella was a pushover. I haven't figured out what you are yet."

He didn't use his Nice Voice to say it and Beatrice quickly ran through a spectrum of other shades from "Deep Rose" to "Xtreme Red." She swallowed. "In any event, Arabella was very depressed after it happened. She was still in the London apartment she and George shared, and I went over that night to make sure she was okay—I didn't like how she was talking. While I was there, George came by. He was as distraught as she was and they started fighting. I pretty much locked myself in the kitchen. But after an hour Arabella came in and told me everything was fine, that I could go. She was calling a taxi for George when I left."

"Didn't go, though, did he?" Bobby interjected.

"No, he didn't." Beatrice stopped then, like that was the last thing she was going to say, and suddenly got very interested in a blue string on the floor near her toe.

"What happened?" I asked. "Did they keep fighting?"

Beatrice shook her head. "Arabella told me afterward that they'd decided to get back together and elope. They went to bed together and she got up early and ran out to get things to make him pancakes. She thought they'd never been happier. When she got back, he was dead."

"Dumped an entire bottle of sleeping pills in his orange juice, gulped it, sat down at the dining room table, and died. That's the one thing that gets me, him letting her walk in and find him. If I ever see him again, I'll kill him for that," Bobby snarled.

"Yes, well, the chances of that are remote, aren't they?" Beatrice said. Her color was back to normal but her voice was still pinched. She moved her eyes to me. "Arabella was devastated by his death. That's what makes this so strange to me. Because she knew firsthand how hard it was to have someone you care about take their own life. How you are always looking for answers. I still sometimes get calls from George's brother—"

"That crazy bastard?" Bobby interjected. "The one who harassed Arabella and Dad? Said he wanted to make them pay? Heavy stuff, right? Not that I can blame him. He was right, it was Dad's fault his brother croaked."

"He just wanted to know what George's last days were like," she said patiently. "Arabella couldn't talk to him anymore because she felt so awful. That's why I just can't—I just don't want—to imagine she would have chosen the same thing."

"It was her *Behind the Music* moment," Veronique said solemnly. And since that was kind of a conversation stopper, we all got really silent and stared at our nails like we were trying to be best friends with them. Hello, tiny pals! Look at you putting the CUTE in CUTICLE!

Even that kind of delirious fun can only hold you so long. Bobby gave a big yawn and said, "Now that story time is over, we're going up to the roof to look at the stars. Want to join us, Jasmine?"

"She doesn't," Alyson assured him, assuring me at the same time by hitting me with a blast of HaterGaze.

"Too bad, we'll miss you," Bobby told me, and for a second he looked like he might mean it. "Very well, come along, baggage," he said, pulling an Evil Hench on each side, "I guess it's just us."

Beatrice and I watched them go in silence. "He didn't hate his father," she said softly. "He's just upset and wants attention. He's not really like that." And the hint of desperation under her words showed me I'd been wrong. She hadn't been in love with Ned Neal.

She was in love with Bobby.

And she was in agony about it, having to stand by and watch while he had brunch—or in this case, sexy good times—with other girls.

It was like we were sisters under the skin! Brothers from another mother! Only not brothers! Or really in any way related. Except for the very-possibly-having-our-hearts-broken way.

She'd been really nice to me and I knew just how she felt, so I wanted to try to make her feel better.

"Of course he's not. This is a hard time for everyone," I assured her. That didn't seem to do much so I tried changing the subject. I pointed to the photo on the desk. "It seems like you were really part of the family. Bobby told me you've been the glue holding them together for the past year."

"And look what a good job I've done," she said with a brittle smile.

"You can't blame yourself for what happened."

"Perhaps."

"You can't. Someone did this. Someone artful and clever and ingenious."

She smiled at me now, almost for real. "Thank you, Jasmine. I appreciate what you are trying to do. Is there anything else you wanted to see?"

I took that as a cue that my Cheer Up People Skills were not fully functioning so I fell back on my Trying to Find a Killer Skills. "Did the police give you a list of the things they found on Arabella's body? I'd like to take a look at that."

"Certainly. I've got it in my office down the corridor."

Her office opened with a plain, old-fashioned key. I checked out the room from the corridor when she went in. It was smaller than Mr. Neal's office with a smaller window that overlooked the side of the house, not the main canal, and a lot more filing cabinets and equipment. But it was also homier, with a mirror on one wall and a poster of Belize on the other.

As I waited, Bobby and the Evil Henches came back. "Beatrice is really showing you all the sights," he said too close to my ear. He had his shirt unbuttoned and seemed to have had a few more drinks. He was gripping my arm a little too hard, and I tried to pull away but couldn't.

That's how we were standing when Beatrice came out of the office. She flinched slightly but had herself under control and said, "It's getting rather late, isn't it?"

Bobby patted her on the shoulder. "Speak for yourself, Bea. I'm just getting started. Jasmine, do you play poker? The goddesses and I were just about to go into the game room to deal a few—"

"Are you sure that's a good idea?" Beatrice said, her tone icy.

"Man, Bea, you sound just like Dad when you say that. Even look like him. You'll have to work on that if you want to get anywhere with me."

"You're drunk. You should go to bed."

"So says you." He let go of me and took a step forward, staggering slightly. "I know what you want, Bea. But you're going to have to do some pretty fancy stuff to get it."

She said, "Bobby, you're disgracing yourself."

"Now, I wouldn't want to do that. Disgrace the fine Neal name. Such a joke." His expression flashed from bitter to jovial. "Oh come on, don't look so glum, Bea. You're right, as always, and I'm being an oaf. I should go to bed. Good night, Jasmine. Good night, kittens." He planted sloppy kisses on the cheeks of each of the Evil Henches. Then he turned to Beatrice and with a sweet smile said, "Good night, Dad."

She slapped him.

He laughed.

I decided that was our cue to leave. It's totally fun to watch these happy family moments, but you don't want to overdose.

I corralled Polly, Roxy, and Tom from the dining room where Polly and Lucien were talking and Roxy and Tom were playing Scary Monster Charades, declined the offer of going back on the boat, took the envelope with the police list from Beatrice, thanked her, and followed her to the street door. Lucien Wilder came with us. As we were leaving, I remembered the one thing I'd forgotten to ask.

"Do the names Maria or Carlotta Longhi mean anything to you?"

Beatrice frowned and shook her head like she was trying to recall something. "Carlotta Longhi. It sounds vaguely—"

"No, why?" Lucien said. It was the shortest sentence he'd uttered since he told Veronique books were not for reading *about*, just for reading.

"Those names came up today. They're a mother and daughter. Carlotta wrote some articles about this house and, um, the issues of its history." That wasn't what I had been going to say, but something about Lucien Wilder's expression stopped me. A gleam in his eye that suggested I "hold it right there, buster" if I liked breathing.

"Sorry we cannot enlighten and enliven," he said, one hand on the gold head of his cane and the other on Beatrice's shoulder. He was jolly again but it seemed forced. "If we think of anything, of course we shall impart it to you with all haste."

On the walk home the Evil Henches were very quiet, Polly was ebullient, Tom was listening, Roxy pretended to be a Smurfotaur, and I was plunged in Deep Thought. Because Lucien Wilder was lying. He knew the name Carlotta Longhi. And if the digits suddenly crawling up my spine were anything to go by, he didn't like that I did, too.[33]

I didn't want to, but I couldn't help wondering if the shiny object that hit me over the head could have been a gold naked lady with sapphire eyes.

[33] Jas: Hey, P—

Polly: No, there were no calls for you.

Jas: I totally wasn't going to ask that. I was going to ask you a very interesting question.

Polly: Such as?

Jas: Um. Such as. Um. Oh, now I remember. I was going to ask, does Lucien Wilder need his walking stick, or is it an accessory? You shouldn't snort like that, P, you could suck your brain out.

Polly: He had an accident when he was younger. And if you don't stop saying I'm snorting, I'll turn my phone off. Ditto on snoring.

Jas: Polly breathes so quietly and melodiously it's like the sound faeries make when they snort.

Polly: I've got my finger on the power button and I'm not afraid to use it.

Jas: I mean sleep.

Roxy: "I've got my finger on the power button" would make a sweet song title.

Chapter Twenty-five

The very best way in the world to be roused from a dream about you and your boyfriend is Not to Be. The second-best way is by a phone call from him, especially if you've been dying for one. So when the hotel phone jolted me out of a particularly excellent part of my dream, which for some reason involved Jack serenading me with "M-I-C, C you real soon, K-E-Y, Y, because we like you!" and I opened one eye and saw it was seven A.M. which meant ten P.M. in Los Angeles, le perfecto hour for calling, I held no malice. In fact, I smiled at it.

"I like you too," I answered, still half asleep.

"Jasmine, is that you? I've told you to identify yourself and the phone exchange when you answer the phone."

The trazillion-gillionth best way to be woken from a dream about your boyfriend serenading you in a gondola is by a call from your father.

"Yes, Dad, you have told me that, and in a spirit of sharing I've told you that since we no longer live in 1954, no one answers the phone that way, and also they're not called exchanges, they are called phone numbers. You'll enjoy being more up-to-date in your lingo. You'll find people stare at you less."

"Don't be cheeky."

I don't know why I bother. I put on my best operator voice to say, "Hello, this is Jasmine Callihan at room 549. Hold the wire please," and dragged the phone into the bathroom so I wouldn't bother Polly, where she was not-snoring in the bed next to mine, with my witty banter.

"To what do I owe the pleasure of this early-morning wake-up call?" I asked.

"I wanted to remind you that you have Italian class this morning. Just because your friends are here doesn't mean you should neglect your education."

Perish le thoughto! "You know, Dad, I'm really not feeling that great and I was—"

"If you're too tired from staying up last night, that's your fault. You should know better."

"It wasn't last night," the monkeys said. "It was the night before that, which I partially spent arrested for murder, and then the fact that I got knocked out twice yesterday."

THANK YOU MONKEYS FOR RUINING MY LIFE.

There was a long, LONG pause after that. And then my father (pick one):

a) roared in fury.

b) roared in disappointment.

c) roared with an unnamed BodingNoGoodForJas^{TM} passion.

d) started to laugh the way he only does while watching Donald Duck cartoons, which, according to him, are brilliant high art.

D! The correct answer is D! And not only did he give himself a laugh-cramp, he said, "I think I'm beginning to understand your sense of humor, Jasmine. Arrested for murder. Ha ha."

There was another pause, no doubt while he was drying his eyes, and when he started talking again his tone was kind of confidential. "Incidentally, don't let your cousin Alyson near any machines."

I wasn't sure I heard him right. "Machines? What kind of machines? Like gumball machines?"

"This is not a joking matter," he said, and hung up.

Of course. "I was arrested and knocked out twice" gets a sidesplitting HA HA HA. But a simple request for information elicits a stern THAT IS NOT A JOKING MATTER. The fact that I'm not in an asylum is truly remarkable.

But there was no time to pride myself on my sanity, or wonder at these machines he so cavalierly spoke of. I carefully dressed in a Polly-approved outfit, made sure that Polly's phone had not been abducted by aliens in the night and that the battery was charged and it was in a safe dry place and in no danger of falling or being crushed by meteors and that there were no missed calls, and with the Mickey Mouse Club theme song still playing in my head, flitted out the door, pausing just to grab the list of things the police had found on Arabella's body. I hadn't had time to look it over the night before due to Polly going on and on about the importance of tailoring, and my head going on and on about the importance of sleeping, and I figured Italian class was as good a place as any to study it.

Being there was sadder than I'd thought it would be. Although technically I'd spent the past thirty-six hours thinking about nothing but Arabella, her death—the fact that she was gone forever—somehow hadn't sunk in. But looking at the empty chair next to me and having no one with whom to comment on the state of Professore Rossi's (perplexing) hairo brought it home. I'd really liked her. And now I'd never see her again.

As Professore Rossi assigned parts for our daily dose of *diversità è ricchezza* in dialogue form—

DIVER 1: The shark is coming closer. He has locked on us with the laser.

DIVER 2: We will be undone by our own experiments!

DIVER 3: Oh, the irony.

DIVER 4: Oh, the tragedy.

DIVER 1: But wait, what is that ahead?

DIVER 2: The submarine. They have found us. We

         are sav—(dies)

—I opened up the list Beatrice had given me. Not only had she Xeroxed the official police report, she'd written up a translation of it for me so I didn't have to bother Professore Rossi with questions like what does *"mutadine"* mean and have him tell me "underwear." I could see why she'd been such an important part of the family.

Arabella had been found in black pants, a black sweater, black socks, black boots, black underwear. I guess Arabella was the match-your-undies-to-your-outfit type too. In her pocket was a wallet with her photo ID and seven euros.

And that was it.

But that couldn't be it. Something was missing.

Little Life Lesson 39: It's a lot easier to notice Something that is there but shouldn't be than Something that isn't there but should be.[34]

I closed my eyes and tried to picture Arabella sitting next to me—

"Signorina Callihan? Do we interrupt your nap?"

My eyes snapped open. Her brooch. Her brooch was

---

[34] BadJas: Unless that Something is a call from your boyfriend.

    Jas: I WAS JUST STARTING TO FORGET ABOUT THAT.

    BadJas: As ifo.

missing. I distinctly remember the police saying that when she'd been seen on the bridge, one of the things people identified was the brooch. And now it was gone.

It could have fallen off in the water, but I doubted it. The currents weren't that strong. Which meant that someone had taken it off of her. The killer. As a memento.

I was so excited that I stood up without realizing it.

I said, "I've got to go. I have to do something."

"Class is not over for another fifteen minutes yet."

"I'm sorry, I'm sick." I gripped my stomach for effect. "Really, I have to leave." And I, as the Evil Henches would have said, Gulf Streamed it out of there.

I made a list of What to Do Next in my head as I walked back to the hotel. Step one was to call Beatrice and find out more about the history of the brooch, where Arabella had gotten it, and when. The fact that the killer had taken it meant it was as important to him as it was to her. So if I could figure out who the brooch meant something to, I'd know who killed Arabella.

As it turned out, I was right, but not in exactly the way I thought. At the time, though, all I knew was that the brooch was the key to unlock the mystery. I simply had to figure out what the lock was.

Little Life Lesson 40: Never use the word "simply." The Fates don't like it.

Of course I had no idea where to start looking. But at least

I was one step closer to getting the solution into the desired Colonel Mustard in the Library with the Candlestick form. The form that led to And They All Lived Happily Ever After (except the dead person).[35]

Step two was—well, I wasn't sure what step two was. But I knew it had to do with getting back to the hotel and finding my pals ASA and also P.

I hadn't really noticed it on my way to class, but suddenly I was aware that it was a really awesome day. Everything seemed more beautiful and crisp, and my mind was filled with self-actualization. I saw how I was being ridiculous about Jack. He was just a busy rock star. His silence didn't mean anything. He'd said he was working on the video of the song he wrote for me. That meant he liked me—boys didn't write songs for girls they didn't like. (Well, except maybe those songs about how much they hated those girls and wished they had crabs. But my song wasn't that kind of song.) How could I expect him to have time to pick up the phone even for a second or send one small email even if he always had his BlackBerry with him, so really how hard could it be? I wasn't one of those girlfriends who needed constant attention. We were two modern individuals with

---

[35] BadJas: That's your problem, you know.

Jas: I thought my problem was three letters starting with Y, ending in U, and rhyming with POO.

BadJas: No, it's that you believe in Happily Ever After. But life doesn't work like that. That, my friend, is the path to Heartache & Ruin.

Jas: You're so uplifting and cheery, I wish we had these chats more often.

BadJas: You see, you need to learn to be happy with reality. By practicing Expectation Management.

Jas: Okay, right now I am expecting you to shut up. How will that conform to reality?

BadJas: I'm not sure—

Jas: Or I could start singing selections from *Annie*.

BadJas: Ack! Not *Annie*! I think you will find your expectations met.

modern lives. We were wild and independent and free! And yet together!

Filled with modernity, I jetted to the Grissini Palace and waved breezily at Camilla as I went by.

"Jasmine, wait," she called as I breezed past. "I know you are anxious to get upstairs to your big box, but someone leaves another object for you."

I had no idea what big box she was talking about, but since Camilla was prone to these sorts of riddles I decided to let it go. I backtracked to her desk to take the large brown paper envelope she was holding out to me.

It had my name and room number written on it. "Who left this?" I asked. Because I am Always the Investigator.

"I cannot tell you. It is crazy here this morning with everyone getting ready for the ball tonight, and I am rushing around like the headless chickens, and when I come back it is sitting here. I do not even have time for my break!"

"I'msorrythenIwon'tkeepyouCyourealsoon," I said fast before she could launch into an inescapable story, and headed for the elevator. I was so excited to see what was in the envelope—I figured it had to come from my Secret Prada Informant—that I ripped it open as I rode up and slid the object out of it.

I stared.

The doors opened on my floor.

The doors closed on my floor.

The doors opened again.

Still I didn't get out. I couldn't. My legs refused to move and I had to steady myself against the back wall. Because what I held in my hands stunned me.

It was a glossy gossip magazine, and the cover was half taken up with a photo. A photo of Jack.

Passionately making out with a girl who was definitely not me.

Chapter Twenty-six

Jack[36] hadn't been kidding about having something to tell me.

I felt like I'd been kicked in the stomach and run over by five ice-cream trucks at the same time. And then mauled by a bear. Who had been modified in a lab to have poisoned razor claws.

It was like all of me ached, not from the outside, but from the inside. And it would never stop.

In Times of Torment™ it is good to have a mentor, someone to look up to for guidance. So I asked myself WWMrTD and suddenly all was clear: Mr. T would shove the magazine into the bottom of his bag and, pretending nothing was wrong, go see his pals. Yes, this was UNBELIEVABLY PAINFUL AND I WANTED TO DIE but Mr. T would

---

[36] BadJas: I told you not to get too hung up on him.
Jas: Please, be quiet.
BadJas: I knew something was wrong.
Jas: I do not require your services at this time.
BadJas: I warned you not to—
Jas: You're not helping. You're making me feel like a moron.
BadJas: Takes one to know one. Ha ha ha.
Jas: Okay, now I do feel a bit better, thank you.
BadJas: Wait a sec, that's not what I meant!

want me to hold it together. And as long as no one said the word "Jack"—or "how" "are" "you" "is" "everything" "okay" "what's" "wrong"—or, better yet, as long as no one spoke to me at all, I'd be fine.

I opened the door of my room, stepped in, stepped out to check from the number that I had the right place, then stepped back in.

It didn't look like my room anymore. It looked like Control Central for a special ops mission to Nutsembourg. Roxy was surrounded by wires and circuit boards. Next to the window, Tom was wearing BluBlockers and soldering things with one of those handheld blowtorches people use to make crème brûlée. A guy I didn't recognize was using an Xacto knife and glue gun on my beige cowboy boots with the nuts embroidered on them. Alyson and Veronique were huddled around my computer. And Polly was busy sewing something that looked like she'd skinned it off a retired character from the Bear Country Jamboree.

All of which led me to conclude that something was Le Up.

Mr. T is a quick study.

"What's going on?" I asked Polly.

And she said, not answering my question, "Jack just called!"

"Oh, did he?" I said with dead lips. Yes, lips can too be dead. But I smiled when I said it.

"He said to call whenever you got in. That he had something to tell you."

"I bet." They were maybe even more like zombie lips. Lips that were totally unconnected to my brain.

"What was that?"

"I said, I'm beat.[37] By the way, who is the man mauling my cowboy boots?"

"That's Davos and he's not mauling them, he's modifying them."

"For what?"

"Go look on the bed."

Roxy said, "But first give me your water wings. I need to test the device."

"What device?" I asked.

Little Life Lesson 41: You might think "I need to test the device" when coupled with "water wings" are the scariest words in the English language, but you would be wrong.

"BED!" Polly ordered.

I handed my water wings to Roxy and reported to the bed. I'd thought Polly, sensing my delicate condition, had been ordering me to rest, but when I got there I began to suspect

---

[37] Polly: Are you okay?
  Jas: Me? I'm great. I figured out something important about the investigation.
  Polly: Can you try saying that again, this time with all the feeling in the right place?
      Are you sure something isn't wrong? Your expression says something is wrong.
  Jas: Can't you recognize a zesty smile of joy?
  Roxy: It looks like you're having cramps.
  Jas: Oh, my funny friend. I can't thank you enough for making me laugh.
  Polly: You're not laughing.
  Jas: I am. On the inside. Now can we get back up to the story?
  Polly: Don't you want to call Jack?
  Jas: What's that? The story can't tell itself? How right you are. Up up up.

that was not the case. There was a huge red box sitting in the middle of my bed. It had to be two feet tall and three feet long. The top was off of it and it was billowing tissue paper everywhere. I reached inside and pulled out a white curled wig like they wore in the eighteenth century, the kind of satin mask that goes over your eyes, a small peaked hat, and then the most gorgeous dress I'd ever seen in my life. It had a dark green bodice that laced up the front, a huge dark green skirt, and a delicate petticoat embroidered with dragonflies to wear under it.

"Wow," I said.

"Don't look at the dress, look at the note," Polly told me.

It was written on plain white paper folded in thirds. I opened it and read:

Meet me at the third pillar from the organ at 10:15 if you want to know more about Arabella.

An admirer

And there was an engraved ticket to the Save Venice Four Seasons Masquerade Ball at the Vivaldi Church that night.

I should have been excited, right? A message from an admirer? Along with a totally rad dress?

And this is how dead inside I was. All I did was say: "Hmm."

And then, "Who opened the box?"

"I did," Alyson said. "I thought it might be for me."

"But the envelope has my name and room number on it," I pointed out.

"It says Miss Callihan," A-Hench said. "That's my name, too. So the dress could be for me."

"It doesn't matter," Polly put in. "I think it's better if you don't wear the dress anyway, Jas. It could be from the killer. In which case it's a T-R-A-P."

I got more interested. "You're right."

Alyson stood with her hand on her hip. "I'm not a puppy."

"I thought you weren't dominos."

"I mean I can spell."

I clapped my hands together in girlish wonder. "Someone please give Alyson a smiley-face scratch-and-sniff sticker."

"It's Sapphyre. And I don't think it's a trap. Besides, who would want to kill me?"

Sadly, this was a rhetorical question.

I turned back to Polly. "Even if it's a trap, I have to go. We'll just have to take precautions."

"We've got it all planned," Polly said. "Roxy's on weapons, and Sapphyre and Tiger's*Eye are working on security."

Little Life Lesson 42: You might think that "Sapphyre and Tiger's*Eye are working on security" are the most frightening words in the English language, but you would also be wrong.

"What do you mean, Sapphyre and Tiger's*Eye? And security?" That's when I remembered my conversation with

Dadzilla that morning. I pointed at Alyson. "You're not supposed to be near machines."

"Who told you that?" she hissed.

"My father. Are you in trouble? What did you do?"

"It wasn't anything bad," Veronique assured me, "Sapphyre
just hacked into—"

"Need to Know Basis, Tiger's＊Eye," Sapphyre said, shutting
her down.

"Wait, you're a hacker?" I couldn't believe it.

Alyson turned around from my computer. "Do you want
the security cameras in the church routed to your laptop
tonight or not?"

I looked at Polly. She nodded. I said, "Yes."

"Then stop talking to me. And Polly, tell her about the
agreement."

"Sapphyre gets full custody of the contents of the box,
as well as immunity from any of us ever telling anyone that
she knows anything about computers, in exchange for her
assistance. And you have to call her Sapphyre and not make
a face when you do it."

"Okay. But if, um, Sapphyre is wearing the dress, what am
I going to wear?"

Polly's eyes lit up. "Don't worry, Jas, I'm working on a
brilliant costume for you. You just go call Jack and leave
everything to us."

Of course, I had no intention of calling TRAITORLIPS
McSNEAKYSON but her saying that reminded me that I'd

wanted to call Beatrice. I didn't have her number, so I started looking around, and that's when I thought of Arabella's phone. Beatrice had called on it the morning of Arabella's death.

Fishing it out of the pocket of the jacket I'd been wearing, I remembered the other call. The one that had come in when I was on the phone with Arabella before she died. Possibly the last person to talk to her.

I couldn't believe I hadn't thought of it before. I scrolled quickly through the call log, finding Beatrice's call (three minutes five seconds), Arabella's call to me (six minutes thirty-one seconds), and the call that had interrupted it (twenty-eight seconds). That one came from an Italian cell phone with no name attached, but if she had friends in the city, maybe they could tell me more about her. I dialed, let it ring ten times, got no answer, and hung up. Then I tried Beatrice's number, with the same result.

Basically, I had no boyfriend, no new leads, and was about to walk into a trap set by a cunning killer. I was in grave danger of bungee-jumping headfirst into the Pit of Self-pity when something zipped by my cheek and planted itself in the wall.

"It works," Roxy said.

"What was that?"

"My new dart gun. I made it out of the pen and some of the other stuff in Arabella's box. It couldn't have been used on Ned Neal because it would only work if you were up close to him, but it'll come in handy tonight. I'll put one in your boot with the, um, other thing."

"What other thing?"

Polly said, "Nothing. Now come here and try on your costume."

"I'm not wearing that," I said when I saw what Polly was holding. "No. And also Way."

"It was the only thing that came in your size and was roomy enough for all the weapons systems. And the head is reinforced with your dad's bike helmet."

Little Life Lesson 43: *Those* are the most frightening words in the English language.

Polly went on. "What's wrong with it? It's completely fetching."

"Does fetching mean moldy?"

"And it's filled with my latest technological advances," Roxy said.

"Mr. T wouldn't wear this."

"Oh, yes, he would."

Little Life Lesson 44: Never think that just because your day started with a dialogue about laser sharks and segued into you learning your boyfriend was seeing someone else by having a photo of it flaunted in your face (and who would do that, incidentally?), it cannot get worse. It can always get worse.

Chapter Twenty-seven

———— ❦ ————

Here's how we went to the masquerade ball:

ALYSON: In the green velvet part of magical
   princess dress. Beautiful.

VERONIQUE: In the petticoat of magical
   princess dress. Also beautiful.

ROXY: As human version of Operation game.
   Attractive in its own way.

DAVOS: As a mime. Elegant.

POLLY AND TOM: As twin harlequins, one
   of which had Sir Lightning emblazoned
   up the arm. Adorable.

JAS: As a SIX-FOOT-TALL FULLY WEAPONIZED
   SQUIRREL WITH MANGE WEARING
   COWBOY BOOTS AND WATER WINGS.
   May Cause Retinal Scarring.

I am surprised people's eyes didn't fall out and roll around on the ground with all the staring they were doing. Right from the beginning it was clear that being a GIANT MOLTING SQUIRREL COMPLETE WITH SQUIRREL HELMET was going to be a challenge.[38] For example:

Little Life Lesson 45: Walking in a six-foot-tall molting squirrel costume is completely out of the question due to the presence of a four-foot-long tail. Aka the Magical Tripping Machine.

Little Life Lesson 46: Also, dancing.

Little Life Lesson 47: Also eating, drinking, or going to the bathroom.

Other than that, the ball went great. The time passed pleasantly,[39] and before I knew it (by which I mean, before I lost consciousness from breathing through the tiny holes), it was 10:15.

My pals assured me they'd planned for every possible scenario. Polly and Tom went outside to man the computer, which they'd somehow synched to the closed-circuit camera system of the church, and Roxy and Davos were at strategic points inside the church keeping an eye on me. Alyson's job was to circulate and see if anyone shot at her or tried to knock her out (le not).

But we weren't ready for what actually happened. I was

---

[38]Polly: By which you mean growth experience.

Jas: No, I don't.

Roxy: Just think of all the Little Life Lessons you'll be able to collect.

Jas: Somehow that does not make me feel better.

Roxy: "Life through the eyes of a squirrel." That wouldn't just make a good song title, it would make a great *album* title.

Jas: Still. Not. Feeling. Better. Perhaps because I can't breathe.

[39]Jas: For all those not dressed as squirrels.

subtly standing by the pillar but probably not doing a very good job of it[40] when I heard a voice. It said in English, "I'm disappointed you didn't wear my present."

At first I thought it was in my head,[41] but then I realized it was outside. And yet, despite my limited range of vision,[42] I could tell there was no one near me.

"Where are you?" I said. Or rather mumbled.[43]

"That doesn't matter," the Voice said.

That's when I remembered an episode of *Commissario Rex* where a cop and an informant conducted clandestine meetings in a church that had secret whispering corners so that people could stand on opposite sides of it and chat without anyone in the middle hearing anything.

Which, I had to admit, was le super cool–slash–smarto.

"You've done a very nice job, Jasmine," the Voice went on. "It's been a pleasure to watch you work. Surprising even."

"Who are you?"

The Voice laughed. "You can't guess?"

That's when I realized I was talking to the killer. I scanned all the pillars around the church but they had people near them, most of whom were wearing masks that covered their mouths, and since I couldn't tell whether the voice belonged to a man or woman, I had no way to narrow the field. The squirrel costume acoustics being what

[40] Jas: Little Life Lesson 48: Squirrel costumes are not good for subtle standing.

[41] Jas: Little Life Lesson 49: Squirrel costumes are not good for hearing.

[42] Jas: Little Life Lesson 50: If being able to see is your desire, do not sport squirrel attire.

[43] Jas: Little Life Lesson 51: If you wish to have a chat, do not wear a squirrel hat.

they were, I also couldn't tell if it had an accent.[44]

"Have you figured out how I murdered Ned yet?" the Voice asked.

For some reason,[45] my brain chose that minute to both conjure up an image of the invisible note Arabella had left me and replay the Mickey Mouse Club song that had been running through it the night before. Which was distracting. Until I realized it was a clue.

C you real soon.

C—Arabella's box at the Bauer was 34C. But the C hadn't appeared on the invisible note. Arabella hadn't left off the last part of her box number at the Bauer, it had been covered by the tape along the side. And she hadn't written FTHR POSND THRU HAND. It was HANDLE.

I got really excited. "I do know. You unscrewed the handle from the door of his office in the corridor and took it off, which made an opening. A small opening, but big enough for the dart gun you made out of one of his own pens. Those wouldn't work at any distance, but you didn't need distance. I bet you stood at the door and whispered to get him to come close to you so you'd be sure to hit him. That's why he died between the door and his desk. And you tied a piece of blue thread to the end of the dart, so you could pluck it back after it had struck him. After that, all you had to do was screw the knob back on and the room seemed locked and impenetrable again."

There was a laugh. I kept watch on the pillars across from

---

[44] Jas: Little Life Lesson 52: Trying to conduct a murder investigation? A squirrel costume will only cause consternation!

[45] Jas: POSSIBLY BECAUSE I WAS DRESSED AS A SQUIRREL AND THEREFORE NUTS.

me, but I didn't see anyone laughing. "Marvelous, Miss Callihan. It's a thrill to hear your reconstruction. I'm very impressed. Now, what about the other murder?"

"You mean Arabella?"

"I see," the killer said, chuckling again. "You still haven't pieced that together. You will soon. In the meantime, someone you care about is going to die tomorrow. Would you like to suggest a method? Or would you rather I surprise you?"

"Which person I care about?"

"You can't figure it out? Try to keep up, won't you? This is only fun if it's a real competition."

"Well, then you should tell me. What kind of a challenge is it if you keep hiding yourself?"

"Amusing. But a fair point. I won't tell you who, but I will tell you when. Tomorrow at four fifteen P.M. Unless you stop me first."

"Where?"

"Greedy. I don't want you to get bored. I'll let you ask one more question. Make it a good one."

"Why did you take the brooch?"

"That *is* a good question. When you answer that, you'll know everything. More or less."

"Where are you?"

"Closer than you think," the voice said. And at that moment I felt fingers circle my paw.

Bobby was standing in front of me. He had his mask in

his hand and was wearing a blue cape with a black lining. He said, "Hey, Jas. Feeling nutty?" and gave me a big smile.

I have to admit, I was slightly discombobulated. Could Bobby really be the killer? He was certainly killing me with his humor. I said, "Will you do me a favor?"

"Sure thing, Squirrel. What?"

"Stand here and wave when you hear me."

"What? Where are you going? Is this because of my joke?"

Despite the best efforts of my tail I made it across the room without falling down and stood at each pillar saying "Hi, Bobby" until I saw him wave.

"Hey, this is cool," he said. "I didn't know—"

I didn't hear the rest because I went tripping outside to where Polly and Tom had set up their communication center.

"What happened?" Polly asked when I came up. "On the monitor it looked like you were all alone."

"Even killers stand Jas up," Alyson said. "Especially in that outfit."

"Yes, I am deeply, almost pathologically uncool, and therefore you should stay far away from me," I told her.

"What?" she asked.[46]

Veronique, under her three layers of eyelashes, looked concerned. "Don't be so hard on yourself, Jas. You're kind of adorable. You know, like a cute dork. Or a cooser. Like a cool loser. Or—"

"Thank you, Tiger's∗Eye," I said with a meaningful look.

---

[46] Jas: Little Life Lesson 53: Squirrel costumes are not recommended for the Making of Barbed Insults.

But, of course, no one saw it.[47]

I turned to Polly. "Can you show me video on the other side of the church when I was talking?"

They cued it up and played it. At first, I didn't notice anything, but then I saw a figure in a dark cape with a huge beaked nose standing by the communicating pillar.

"That's him."

"Who?"

"The killer. He talked to me from there."

"That's across the church."

"I know, but it has one of those whispering effects."

"What did he say?" Polly asked.

For once I was glad I was wearing the squirrel helmet. "That unless we stop him, someone I care about will die tomorrow at four fifteen."

There was silence until Roxy said, "Then we'd better figure out who's under the mask."

Polly frowned. "How? It's a traditional Venetian costume, so there are at least a dozen people dressed that way."

"We could go inside and bump into people dressed like that and see if any of them are people we know," Tom suggested.

"Or we could just follow that guy," Roxy said, pointing at the hooded figure who had just come out of the church, looked stealthily in both directions, and plunged into the heart of Venice.

---

[47] Jas: Little Life Lesson 54: Four out of five doctors surveyed did not recommend
           squirrel costumes for their patients who wanted to give meaningful looks.

Polly: What is that, Jas? Are you upset about something?

Jas: Grr.

Polly: I don't think squirrels growl, precious.

Chapter Twenty-eight

———— ❧ ————

Tom had his BlackBerry out, with a map of Venice on the screen. "Up ahead he can go in one of four directions. We should break into teams and communicate via our walkie-talkies."

We all set out—Polly with Tom, Hench with Hench, and Roxy with Davos—and me with tail. But I didn't mind. Army of one! Go squirrels!

Sigh.

Little Life Lesson 55: Although probably not an ideal date activity, it's kind of lonely to chase after a murderer by yourself.

I'd gone about fifteen steps when a voice near my squirrel ear said, "We are going on an adventure?" and I looked over and saw Max.

"Where did you come from?" I asked.

"I am rowing gondolas for the party and I see you and

your friends come out, but before I can come and talk to you, you have scattered. Where do we go?"

"We're following someone." I looked at him suspiciously. Not that he could tell through the Demented Squirrel costume. "How did you know it was me?"

"Only you can pull this costume off with such style. Also I can tell because you are taller than all your friends."

It was a good point.

"But we should be wagging a leg, no?" he said. "Or, in your case, a tail. We do not want the someone to get away."

I agreed and we hurried (him) tripped (me) on.

When we'd gone halfway down the *calle* he said, "I do not mean to be the stickler, but I do not see anyone. Is our prey perhaps invisible?"

"No, we're just not sure which way he went."

"And he looks like what?"

"Black cape with a black hood."

"Ah, the someone is from the ball. You have neglected to mention why exactly do we follow this someone?"

"I think he's a murderer."

I expected him to stop walking or lecture me or something, but instead he said, "You have really the most interesting hobbies. I am wondering, if you do not mind me asking, is it always like this when you are around?"

"Like what?"

"Not boring?"

"If that's what you want to call it."

"I think it is. You are a most fascinating woman, Jasmine Noelle."

Little Life Lesson 56: One good thing about being dressed as a giant squirrel is no one can see you blush.

"Thank you," I said. I think my voice might have cracked a little.

He grabbed my paw. "And now I think it is time that we end the dillying because I believe I see a black cape up ahead."

We rushed on, rounding a corner, and I thought I saw the tip of a cape, too. We were closing on him.

Max leaned close to say, "Your killer makes a mistake. This *calle* ends dead at a canal."

My heart started to beat fast. BUT ONLY BECAUSE WE HAD THE KILLER. NOT BECAUSE MAX'S FACE WAS NEXT TO MY, um, squirrel head.

I gulped, looked at the street name, and pushed the button on my wrist walkie-talkie. "Calle Terrazzera. It's a dead end, the killer's trapped," I whispered into it, then looked at Max. "Let's go."

We hugged the wall of the *calle* as we went, staying in the shadows. It made a sharp left in front of us, and Max put up his hand to stop me.

"I go first in case there is shooting."

"No, I go first in case there is shooting," I told him.

"I do not like to introduce the note of disagreement between us but really, it must be me."

"Why?"

"Your costume is rented, no? If something were to happen to it, this would cost a lot of money."

"If something were to happen to you, you wouldn't be able to row the gondola."

"Nothing will happen to me. I am trained for six months in the army special forces to do evasive maneuvers."

"I am trained for six weeks in break dancing."

"Really? What can you do?"

"Moonwalk, the worm. I'm working on the windmill."

"You must show me sometime. But not now. Now I proceed."

"I'm armed and dangerous," I informed him. "You don't have any weapons."

"Weapons? What kind of weapons?"

"Weapons to cover our approach," I said, smushing together the wires on one of Roxy's smoke bombs the way she'd shown me, and throwing it into the mouth of the *calle*.

It made a hissing noise, a popping noise, and a fizzing noise. Then nothing.

"That was very thrilling," Max said. "Follow me."

He gave an impressive demonstration of Evasive Maneuvering, which mostly made him look like a turtle doing the hustle, then when he'd decided it was safe, beckoned to me.

We ran down, around another corner, and stopped.

We were standing at the edge of a canal. A dead end. There was nowhere for the killer to go.

But we were alone.

I peered out over the water, hoping to see a boat or something in the distance, but there wasn't anything. And yet we couldn't have missed him.

"You are sure this killer, he is of flesh and blood. Not invisible?"

"I am. I was. I guess—"

This was too much. First Jack making out. Then having to go to a ball dressed as a giant mangy squirrel. And now losing the murderer who had threatened my friends when we'd been so close. The weight of it all hit me and I sort of crumpled.

"Jasmine Noelle, you are cold."

"No," I sniffled.

"But you are trembling."

"I'm just upset."

"Here," Max said, and put his arms around me. "You are very woolly."

That made me laugh.

"Perhaps you will be happier if you lose your head?"

"I feel like I've already lost it."

"I refer, of course, to your costume."

"Oh, right," I said. "Yes."

I reached up and pulled the squirrel head off.

"But you are crying!" He pulled a handkerchief from his pocket and very gently dried my cheeks. "Is this because you miss your friend?"

"Partially."

"Max cannot stand to see *le bellissime donne* cry," he told me. "It is not good form. Did I mention that in addition to juggling and balloon dogs, I also make pancakes in amusing shapes? It is a family talent. Perhaps you would like me to show you?"

"Maybe sometime. I guess we should go find my friends."

"Yes."

But neither of us moved. We stood there, staring at each other. He smelled like pizza and the ocean all rolled together.

"You are not like anyone I have ever met before, Jasmine," he told me. "And I do not just mean because you can do the moonwalking."

"You're not like anyone I've ever met before, either."

"*Bene*, then we have something in common!"

I laughed.

He reached out with the hand that had been drying my tears and touched the side of my face. "You are very lovely."

His thumb grazed my lips.

My heart started to pound.

His eyes went to my mouth.

I bit my lower lip.

He bent closer. I bent closer. Jack had kissed another girl.

Our mouths hovered over each other.

There were footsteps in the *calle* behind us and my pals arrived.

We jumped apart like we had super-magnets repelling us. "Oh, hello," I said, trying for the casual, light tone as I disentangled myself from my tail.

"Where is he?" Polly asked.

"He? Who?"

She frowned at me. "The killer."

Right. That's what we'd been doing. Trying to catch a killer. Not trying to make out with gondoliers we'd just met two days earlier because we'd seen compromising photos of our boyfriends.

"He disappeared," I said. I'm not sure I said it with the right amount of gravity, though, because Polly looked suspicious. "We were just—"

"Looking for the clues," Max said. "But we find nothing. There is no evidence of a murderer. He has gone poof."

We spent a few more minutes scouring the ground for any sign of the murderer, but found nothing.

"He must have gone another way," Tom said.

"Unless he's a ghost," Veronique interrupted her chanting (!!!!) to say. "There are a lot of vibrations here."

"These two are sane, you are sure?" Davos asked Roxy, pointing at Alyson and Veronique. "I do not see it."

Finally, we all gave up and headed back toward the ball to pick up our equipment. As we walked, Max reached out and held my paw. It felt nice. Different from being with Jack, but nice, and for a moment I felt like maybe I wasn't doomed to a life of living atop Misery Mountain.

"I will see you tomorrow, perhaps?" Max asked as we got to his gondola.

"Yeah. Okay."

He took his notebook out and wrote on it. "Here is my number. I work on the gondola until four, but you may call anytime if Max can be of service."

"Thanks."

I turned to go.

"He's very lucky."

"Who?" I asked, turning back.

"This man you love."

"What? How did you—"

"Max knows. How else could you be immune to my charms?" He said it in the regular Max way, joking, but there was something else under it.

"I'm not completely immune," the monkeys told him. THANK YOU SO MUCH FOR THAT, MONKEYS!

He smiled at me, but it was a little sad. "Have golden dreams, Jasmine Noelle."

"I will," I said. But as I walked back to the hotel, reality seeped back through my costume. We'd been within inches of catching the killer and he'd vanished. And every minute that ticked by was a minute of the life of one of my friends.

Stepping into my room, I found a phone message that had been slid under the door. It was in Camilla's writing, and the time stamp said eleven minutes earlier.

FROM: A friend
TO: Jasmine Callihan, room 549
MESSAGE: Better luck next time.
Remember, tomorrow at 4:15. Don't be late.
I won't be.

Chapter Twenty-nine

———— ❦ ————

I stayed up most of the night arranging and rearranging clues, and not getting anywhere. I must have drifted off at some point, though, because the next thing I knew it was ten thirty in the morning and I'd missed Italian, and Polly was standing in front of me holding the magazine with Jack's kissy face picture on it. Only now it was open to the story inside. I hadn't even known there was a story (Yes, okay, I never opened the magazine. I didn't need to see more.) but apparently there was. With the title "NASCAR Dad Revs His Engine?" And the same picture as on the cover only now in a larger Hungry-Man-dinner-sized portion.

"Is this why you were so weird yesterday?" she demanded.

"Where did you find it?"

"Under your laundry where you hid it. I was looking for something."

"You're confiscating my last Wonderbra too? Is nothing sacred? Can't you see this is a difficult time for me?"

"No. You're not seriously upset about this, are you?"

"That old thing? Why, what would possibly upset me about a HALF PAGE PHOTO OF MY BOYFRIEND SUCKING LIPS WITH ANOTHER GIRL? I am not upset at all."

"Jack would never wear Seven jeans."

"Yes, that is clearly the crime in this photo." It is so sad when Good Friends Go Mad.

"Don't you see, Jas? Jack would never wear these jeans and he isn't wearing them."

"Of course he's not, lovie. He's actually naked. Those jeans are just a figment—hey, why are you pointing the BeDazzler at me?"

"To make you stop talking. Look at this photo," she said, holding the magazine open and standing right in front of my face so I got a good long whiff of My-Boyfriend-Is-Making-Out-with-Another-Girl Poofume. "It's not Jack."

"Really? Has he been cloned? It has his unbelievably cute scar next to his lip that I used to, in happier times, so enjoy kissing."

"The head is him, but it's been Photoshopped onto someone else's body. It must be a promo thing their label's PR department did."

I was suddenly interested. "I am suddenly interested," I told her.

"I thought you might be. It's actually easier to see at a distance. Step back and look at how the color of his neck changes where it meets the shir—"

"Oh. My. God."

"I know, it's actually amazing they're allowed to do it. It should be illegal. Anyway, I hope—"

"No," I said. "That's not what I'm looking at." I pointed at the page facing the Jack page.

Polly leaned her head over it, then looked more closely. "Isn't that Arabella in the photo?" she asked.

I nodded mutely.

"And isn't that—is that Max with her?"

I knew why she thought that, because I'd thought it, too. It looked a lot like him. Then I saw the caption. It read, ARABELLA NEAL LAST YEAR WITH FIANCÉ GEORGE MANZONI. MANZONI WAS FOUND DEAD IN HER DINING ROOM TWO MONTHS LATER.

I couldn't take my eyes off of it. The first thing I thought was, *Max hadn't been lying when he said his uncle was the chief of police.* And that was the last happy thought I had. Because suddenly my brain went to BoNkErToWn.

Max was Arabella's fiancé's brother. The brother who had harassed and threatened the Neals after George's death. The brother who still harbored enough hatred to kill them?

No. It wasn't possible. I didn't want to believe it was possible.

But it was. The more I thought about it, the more possible it became. Little things started to click into place. Him talking about how hard it was to accept the suicide of someone you cared about. And—

"He recognized Bobby Neal."

"So?"

"He made it sound like it was from gossip magazines or something. But the Evil Henches, who we know are certified experts on the men of Gossipshire, didn't know who Bobby was. They had to consult their Ouija board to figure out his name, remember?"

"Yeah. So you're thinking—"

"It shows Max was lying. He didn't know Bobby from photos, but because he'd been studying the Neals."

"Your Prada mystery caller said that Arabella's 'boyfriend' spoke Italian. That could totally be Max."

"And he was on the spot both times I was attacked. Only he came toward me rather than running away."

Like he was daring me to make the connection. Bold. Clever. Like the killer the night before.

The killer he'd claimed to see run into a dead end. The killer who had disappeared.

And yet, even as the puzzle began to fill out, fill out perfectly, part of me didn't want to believe it.

"This is all circumstantial," I told Polly.[48] "We need to test this before we do anything."

"How?"

I looked around at all the evidence we had. Fingerprints, the pen, the invitation from the night before—

[48] Polly: I didn't know "circumstantial" meant "I don't want to believe the guy I was kissing last night is a killer."

Jas: I didn't know "best friend" meant "one who makes up things." We weren't kissing. Stop raising your eyebrow at me!

Polly: Whatever you say, HotLips Callihan.

"Do you have nail polish remover and a pair of nail scissors?"

Polly looked at me like I was crazy. "Of course I do."

"We need those, and a glass from the bathroom."

"What are we going to do?"

"We can assume that the killer sent the invitation to the ball, right?" Polly nodded. "We're going to see if it was written by Max."

"Like, match the handwriting? Do you have a note from him?"

"Only his phone number, no words. But that would just tell us that someone wanted it to look like it was from Max. We're going to do better. We're going to match the ink."

Roxy and Tom came in then. "We wanted to see if— ooh, what's going on?"

"Max is the killer, Jas is in denial, and we're doing science."

"I'm not in denial." I carefully cut a thin strip of paper with writing on it off of the invitation from the killer, and another the same size, with the same amount of writing on it, from the note with Max's phone number. On each piece, I left a little bit of blank paper on the bottom, which I trimmed into a point. Then I poured about a pinkie's width of nail polish remover into the bottom of the glass, and stood the two strips in it.

"What happens now?" Roxy asked.

"We wait. The nail polish remover separates out the different chemicals in the ink. This will tell us if they were written with the same pen." I set the timer on Polly's phone fifteen minutes.

Which was just enough time for me to call Jack, say something absurd about how I hoped he was having a nice bath-I-meant-night, hang up, explore the far corners of the Continent of Self-Loathing, and get dressed.

"So if Max's phone number doesn't match the ink on the note the murderer sent, what does it mean?" Roxy asked right before the timer went off.

"It means they weren't written with the same pen. So it's inconclusive, but we've still got circumstantial evidence."

"And if they do match?"

"It means Max is the killer."

It matched. Both inks separated exactly the same way, with a golden hue below, bleeding up into a darker gray. Both notes had been written by the same pen. I stood there staring at them, not wanting to believe it. Looking from the part of the killer's note that read, "at 10:15," to the strip of paper with Max's phone number—

I grabbed Arabella's phone and scrolled through the call log. My heart fell. I could have maybe come up with some explanation of how Max could have accidentally used the killer's pen if I'd tried really hard. But there was no way around the fact that Max's number was the other Venice number that had called Arabella. The one I'd tried and gotten no answer on. After all, what killer would take a call from his victim's phone?

I dialed it again, this time from the hotel phone. He answered on the second ring.

I hung up and dialed Beatrice's number.

"Beatrice? It's Jasmine. I was wondering, can you tell me the name of Arabella's fiancé's brother? The one who threatened the Neals?"

"George's brother? Let me think. It was something that began with an M. Maybe Max. Why?"

"I think he might be the killer."

"What? Do you have proof?"

"Yes."

I looked at the last line of the note Arabella had written in lemon juice. FIND M.

I had.

"We need to go to the police," I said.

Chapter Thirty

Little Life Lesson 57: If you have once run into the police, announcing that a gondolier is an assassin, and another time saying you yourself are a killer, returning to the first theme is not the best way to gain their trust and admiration.

I guess I should have known based on the way Officer Allegrini put his hands on his head and groaned when I walked into the police station. Still, I was sure that he'd see things clearly once I'd laid my facts before him in Italian.

I said: "But, man, this is a real, live serious killer."

He said: "Get out of here."

Me: "For truth, man. It's heavy. And he threatens my friends."

Him: "Out."

Me: "He did in both Ned Neal and his little girl."

That got his attention. He went, "You want me to reopen two closed cases?" and when he said it he looked like someone had lit a firecracker under him. And not in a good way.

If there is a good way to look like that.

"I have proof. Look at the ink on these notes."

"Get out or I will have you removed."

After ten minutes like this I hadn't managed to convince him that there really was a killer, but he'd convinced me—largely by rattling his handcuffs—that I had two choices: leave, or get thrown in jail. Since I couldn't catch a murderer in jail, I left.

"That went well," Polly said when we were outside. "What does '*rompicoglioni*' mean, anyway? He kept muttering it."

"You don't want to know."

"What do we do now?" Roxy asked. "It's twelve thirty. That gives us less than four hours until the deadline."

"Tom, did you bring your tools?" I asked.

"Always."

"No," Polly said. "We are not breaking into the house of a murderer."

"He's at work until four," I told her. "Besides, what choice do we have? We're going to have to drag solid pieces of evidence—and possibly a dead body—back here before the police will do anything. It's the only chance we have of saving one of our lives."

"How are we going to find out where he lives?"

"We could ask the Ouija board," Veronique offered.

"We could look in the phone book," Tom suggested.

We went with Tom's idea. There were two M. Manzonis in

the phone book, so in the interest of time we decided to split up. Roxy and I took the farther one, along with Polly's manicure kit, and Tom and Polly the closer one. I tried not to cry salty tears when the Evil Henches announced they were going with Tom and Polly because that was the address that the spirits told Alyson was right.

Although Tom is the actual pro lock-picker in the family, Roxy isn't bad at it. Still, breaking and entering a house, especially if you don't know it's the right house, is not without its nervous moments. There were two sets of doors, an outer lock, which Roxy got through in forty-three seconds, and then one on the door of M. Manzoni's apartment. That one took her almost three minutes, three of the longest minutes of my life.

Finally the door opened and we stepped inside. And gaped.

"I think this is the place," I said.

One whole wall was covered with magazine photos, articles, and Xeroxes. Some of the photos had the faces scratched out. But even like that it was clear that all of them, every one, was about the Neal family.

"This should be enough to convince the police," Roxy said.

I nodded. "Do you remember the way back to the station?" It was a stupid question; Roxy has a perfect sense of direction. "I want to stay here and look around, but you should go get Officer Allegrini."

"Polly will kill me if I leave you here alone."

"Max is at work for another three hours. I'll be perfectly safe."

Little Life Lesson 58: Never say "I'll be perfectly safe" unless you're prepared to lose a limb. Or your life.

"The place could be booby-trapped."

"Then it's a good thing I have my weaponized water wings."

"Take these too." She handed me a pair of tweezers with a battery pack connected to them. "It's like a Taser. Just hold it against his neck and push the button on the battery pack. It'll take him totally by surprise because he'll think you just want to do some grooming."

"Ingenious."

"It works great too. I made the whole left side of my body numb yesterday when I sat on them."

I slipped the Taser-Tweezers into my back pocket and made a mental note not to sit down. "Thanks. Go. The sooner you go, the sooner we can get this finished."

Roxy gave me a last, concerned look from the door and took off. Alone, I started studying the wall. The first thing I noticed was that many of the photos had small holes in the faces, like they'd been used for dart practice. Cozy!

I was peering closer at one article that had a picture of a young Ned Neal and a young Lucien Wilder on crutches standing on either side of a dark-haired woman on the dock of The House that Kills, when the door opened behind me.

"Roxy, that was fast. Does this woman remind you of anyo—" I said without taking my eyes off of it.

"You," a voice said from the door, and my hair danced up-ended on my neck. It wasn't Roxy at all. It was Max. "What are you doing here, Jasmine?"

His tone was like ice and so sharp you could have cut pizza with it.

"I was looking for you," I said. I turned to face him. He was standing in a tense pose, like he was ready to leap. I suddenly wondered how much he'd learned in his six months of special forces training. Like, did they teach you to kill with a single blow? Or merely to disable?

"I see," he said, moving carefully into the room. He shut the door behind him and locked it. "And you come looking for me why?"

I decided to keep things light and breezy. "To say hello!"

"You cannot call?" He stayed close to the wall, circling toward me. I circled away from him.

"I tried but you didn't answer," I said. "From Arabella's phone. The one you'd called the night she died."

"That was you. I should have guessed." He was approaching me with his hands out, like he was trying to show that he was just a good guy, nothing to be afraid of.

His hands were big. And strong. Like they could circle my neck easily and crush the air out of—

"So, your apartment is cozy," I said to distract myself.

"I do not wish to talk about my apartment."

"Do you want to talk about the art on the walls? The Neals?"

He stopped, as if noticing the display for the first time. "That is old."

"Why did you do it?"

"I am angry. I blame them for George's death. I want it to make sense. Now, of course, I see that is not possible, but before . . ." His voice trailed off. Then he snapped abruptly, "Please keep your hands where I can see them."

I stopped reaching into my back pocket for Roxy's Taser-Tweezers.

"Thank you," he said. "I had hoped—I did not want this to be the ending."

I didn't like that word, *ending*. I gulped. "It doesn't have to be. You have a choice."

"No, Jasmine, I am afraid I do not. I admire you, but I cannot let you—"

There was a thud from the other room. We both stopped moving and goggled at each other.

"What have you done?" he asked me.

Which seemed like a strange question, but before I could comment he bolted toward the room and went in. I followed but he was blocking the door. Over his shoulder I saw what he was staring at.

Beatrice was lying on the floor. She was gagged with her scarf, her legs and hands duct-taped together. The roll of tape was still attached to her hands and when she saw Max her eyes looked terrified. Imploring. Above her was an open window. Roxy and I must have interrupted Max while he was binding her hands and he'd gone out the window and come back up when Roxy left, not realizing I was still in the house. I should have guessed that Beatrice would be next on his revenge list. The woman who had stood between him and the Neals. The one who had carefully filed his threats, filtered his phone calls.

This was the moment for le hightailing it out of there to get help, but I couldn't leave Beatrice alone with him. I was trying for the Taser-Tweezers again when he whirled around and grabbed me in a headlock that immobilized me.

Little Life Lesson 59: The first six months of Italian army special ops training is pretty thorough.

Little Life Lesson 60: Your back pocket is not an ideal place for your weapon.

It all happened so fast it was a blur, but I still had time to see that his eyes burned with a mixture of rage-slash-fury. Like he'd had the Big Gulp–sized Haterade for breakfast. His grip on my arm made my hand numb and the Taser-Tweezers fell from my fingers and hit the floor, sparking.

Twisting my head, I saw him look at them with a demented smile. He brought his foot down hard on the battery pack and crushed it. Then he moved the smile to me. I struggled, and his hold on my neck got firmer. "I do this for your own good, Jasmine. You wish to meet a killer. *Bene.* You meet a killer."

He shifted his body, like he was getting ready to slam me onto the floor, and then all of a sudden we were both falling. A glance beyond him showed me that Beatrice had managed to wiggle toward the door and kick him with her bound legs. It looked like she'd got him in the calf with a stiletto.

For a second his grip on me loosened and I wrenched my arm free. I clawed at his face to get away but he pinned my wrists to the ground. "You must stop. It goes better if you do not struggle."

I asked myself WWMrTD and the answer came to me in a brilliant flash. Mr. T would remember there's only one thing to do when you're doing battle on your back on the ground with your wrists pinned.

The Windmill.

I sliced my legs into the air and brought them down on top of Max. I'd been aiming for his kidneys but I think the heel of my boot caught his head instead. There was a thump and a weird scattering noise and something that I could have sworn was a Skittle hit me in the eye.

Max groaned and flipped onto his back, so I was on his chest, and I decided this was a good time to pull out another break-dance move.

Which is when the door crashed open.

Little Life Lesson 61: Being caught doing a one-handed up-rock handstand on the chest of a killer, even if you are just doing it to get enough momentum to pull away from him, does not make you look like a serious citizen in the eyes of the law.

And yet, something in Officer Allegrini's attitude had changed toward me. He moved quickly past sneering, and after helping me off, slapped some cuffs on Max. Roxy had a profound effect on most men, and I'd noticed her calling him "Arnoldo," but this was pretty strong even for her.

She'd managed to find Polly, Tom, and the Henches too, so we all worked together to free Beatrice. She had tears running down her face, and as I untied the Hermès scarf around her mouth she said, "Thank God, Jasmine. I thought he was going to kill me."

She explained that after she'd hung up with me, she'd gotten a call from Bobby saying he had something important to show her at Arabella's but as soon as she stepped outside The House that Kills someone had knocked her out.

"Seems like a theme for our killer," I said.

"Yes. I woke up here with the gag in my mouth and my feet taped and he was taping my hands when you came in. You—you saved my life."

Roxy had been looking around the room while Beatrice spoke and now she said, "I think I found something." She was standing at Max's bureau. On the top of it was a metal trophy awarded to George Manzoni for Archery by a summer camp in Virginia years earlier. Like a kid would have. Inside the top drawer were Arabella's brooch and a BB gun. Like a killer would have.

Tom pointed to a hair looped around the base of the trophy and it took me a second to realize it looked familiar because it was my hair. "I think he used this to knock you out that first day. There's no shortage of evidence," Tom said.

"No," I agreed. "There's almost too much."

"Whatever it takes to put him away," Beatrice said. "Thank you, Jas. Thank you for catching him."

There was a lot of giving statements and fingerprinting and evidence collection after that. "What did you do to Officer Allegrini?" I asked Roxy in between interviews. "He seems practically human."

"Arnoldo? I fluttered my eyelashes. Also they were bringing in some man when I got there, and I had the impression that his arrest had something to do with you. He was wearing an old trench coat and had a limp and was carrying a teapot. Does that make any sense?"

I remembered the case file I'd seen on Officer Allegrini's desk the morning of Arabella's non-suicide and laughed. "Yeah."

Finally, although it's hard to imagine, the police decided they'd had enough of us and packed us onto an official boat to take us home. Another boat had been provided for Max, who glared at everyone and said what I thought was, "This is not over," as they hustled him, handcuffed, inside. As we pulled up at the Grissini Palace dock I looked down at my watch. It was 4:13. Game over, with two minutes to spare.

I looked up and saw Dadzilla standing there. Boy, was he happy to see us. He was shifting from one leg to the other, and I could have sworn there were wisps of smoke coming out of his nostrils. It's not easy to talk when your jaw is firmly clenched in the closed position but he managed to pry out, "Jasmine, go to your room this instant. I'll join you there shortly."

Little Life Lesson 62: There are worse things than being attacked by a murderer and their name is Dadzilla.

Chapter Thirty-one

While I waited for Dadzilla's not-at-all-setting-my-knees-atremble arrival, I entertained myself by making up jokes such as:

Knock knock.
Who's there?
Life.
Oh, I won't be needing one of those.

I also decided, since it was pretty clear I was about to be locked in a dungeon for period ever period, to check my email. Not that I was looking for anything in particular (message from Jack). I just wanted to see what had come in (and if it was a message from Jack).

There was only one email.

(Not from Jack.)

To: Jasmine Callihan <Drumgrrrl@hotmail.com>
From: J.R. <JR_211@hotmail.com>
Subject: Ask your father

About Smokey LeBraun

Oh, goodie! More mysteries! Now new and improved with Creepy-sounding Names!

This would undoubtedly come in very handy in the case of awkward pauses during the upcoming Once Upon a Time There Lived a Girl Named Jas Who Was a Massive Disappointment to Her Father and Was to Be Locked in Her Room Forever story time.

As if Dadzilla was going to be letting me get le word in edgewiseo.

But my way is not Abandon All Hope Avenue. I prefer to travel on Making the Best of It Boulevard. So when Dadzilla pounded on my door like he meant to pulverize it, I put in a sad-yet-winsome smile and let him in.

Little Life Lesson 63: Apparently to a father, there is no difference between his daughter being escorted home by police because she *is* a murderer, or his daughter being escorted home by police because she helped them *catch* a murderer.

Things started off well. He said, "Get that drippy smile off your face. You have nothing to smile about."

Exit: One smile, pursued by a bear.

Then he moved from Anger to Grave Disappointment. He shook his head. "That's it, Jasmine," he said. "No more."

"No more what?" I felt it was important to be clear on that. Food? Shelter? Breathing?

But I don't think he was really listening to me because he said, "Seventeen-year-old girls are not supposed to be meddling with death. They are supposed to be playing with dolls. And tea sets."

Yes. That is what most seniors in high school are doing. When they're not making bonnets for their stuffed animals and chasing rainbows. But since such nuances are lost on the man who made me keep training wheels on my bike until I was fifteen, I simply said, "I don't have a tea set."

I thought it was relevant and to the point, but he ignored it. "This ends now, Jasmine. The deception. The lies."

"I didn't lie to you. I told you what was happening. The other morning. You laughed."

"I did no such thing."

That made me mad. "You did too. And I don't see why I am in trouble. I didn't do anything except avenge someone's death. Besides, how am I supposed to behave honestly when I don't have a good role model for it?"

"What are you talking about?"

I actually had no idea what I was talking about, so I said the first thing that came to mind. "Smokey LeBraun."

It was like I'd dusted him with magical lose-all-the-blood-in-your-face powder. He went totally white and stared at me.

"What do you know about Smokey LeBraun?"

"Enough," I lied. I wasn't sure how long I'd be able to keep this up, but it seemed worth it. Especially if it delayed the "you are being sent to a reformatorium-slash-place-where-they-make-sausage-out-of-naughty-little-girls" portion of our discussion.

Dadzilla ran his hand through his hair and it looked like he'd started to sweat. "How on earth did you find out about him?"

"On the Internet," I said. Which was not strictly untrue.

"This isn't how I wanted you to find out about your mother."

BUH-BOING!

That is the sound my eyeballs made popping out of my head. Who had said anything about my mother?

Dadzilla kept talking. "I've tried so hard to protect you. I didn't think you needed to know the truth."

EYEBALLS. STILL. POPPING.

"Lying is never the answer, Dad. You should have told me."

"That's enough, Jasmine. Go to your room."

"Um, we are in my room."

We stared at each other, him with Dadzilla Expression number five: Scowling Menace; and me with Jas Expression number one: Blank Innocence (Because I Have No Idea What I'm Talking About and Also My Eyeballs Are Stuck Somewhere on the Far Wall). And then he did the last thing that in eighteen million six hundred ninety-five thousand and two years I would have imagined. He said, "You might be right."

I almost fainted. In fact, I think I did faint, but it was like a mini-faint, so I was back in time to hear him saying, "I should have told you about your mother. I will tell you."

"When?"

"When we get back to Los Angeles. We leave next week."

More almost-fainting now with heart rate picking up with joy. "We do?"

"Yes. I got word yesterday that Smokey is back in jail."

Back in jail? Is what I wanted to ask. Instead I said, "What about your book on soap?"

He smiled. And not in his dangerous Dadzilla way. In this far-off oh-the-times-we-had way. "I did the research for that twenty-one years ago. That's how I met your mother."

"You and she met here?"

"In this hotel. She loved Venice."

"Is that why we came here now?"

"That, and I knew you'd be safe. Thought you'd be safe. I never would have guessed what kind of mess you'd end up in."

"What mess? Nothing bad happened! In fact, the police—"

"Pfui."

We were back to our old selves.

"Don't forget that you have Italian class tomorrow."

"Golly, no. I so enjoy it."

He made a stern face. But at the door he stopped and turned back and looked at me. "You're just like her, Jasmine. In every good way."

And suddenly I found it a little hard to breathe. Or see. Or swallow.

When Polly came back she said, "You've been crying! Was it awful?"

"No, it was fine. I think I just have allergies. Late-onset."

"Late-onset allergies. Got it."

And because she puts the RAD in BEST FRIEND EVA, she didn't ask any more questions. Not that I would have known the answers. But I would have made stuff up. Anyway, after everything that happened, my head was spinning so much as we went to bed that I barely even thought about the fact that Jack still hadn't called back. Or emailed. Or probably even thought about me one half a time.[49]

Venice looked different to me the next day as I walked to Italian class in the outfit Polly had laid out for me (dark green sweater, denim skirt, beige cowboy boots with the nuts on them, floaties). Maybe it was because I knew it was my mother's favorite city. Or because I knew there was one less killer on the streets. Or maybe it was because I knew we'd be going home soon. But somehow even the prospect of whatever dialogue Professore Rossi had in store for me seemed appealing. The birds—even the pigeons—were

---

[49] BadJas: What's that smell?
    Jas: What are you talking about?
    BadJas: Like smoke.
    Jas: I don't smell any smoke.
    BadJas: Look out! Your pants are on fire!
    Jas: Careful you don't choke on your tongue when you chortle like that.
        It would be such a pity.

adorable and the tourists were charming and the croissant I had for breakfast was extra flaky and delicious.

As I walked, my brain kept wandering to the hole in my life where the call from Jack should have been, so I tried to keep it reined in by thinking back over the investigation. There were still a ton of unanswered questions. I thought back to all the evidence, the prints on the glass and the pen and the phone.

The phone. My brain hiccupped. Why had Max left the phone when he knocked me out the first time? He had plenty of opportunities to take it. He had to know that his call would be on the call log, like a neon arrow in the night pointing toward a connection between him and Arabella.

Oh. My. God.

The last pieces fell into their places like checkers in a Connect Four game. The ruffles in her bathroom being wet, the ones on the couch all pointing in the same direction. The missing curtain rope and dust on the window. The fact that the killer had left the phone when I was knocked out. Beatrice being the next victim. Arabella asking Professor Rossi how to say "birth certificate." I knew why the brooch had been taken. I knew how Arabella had been killed.

The killer had been scattering evidence around like birdseed for me to find. Laying a trap I'd walked right into.

The killer had said, "This is only fun if it's a real competition."

There was only one person who could have done all of it.

One person who would have said that. And it wasn't Max. Max never used contractions.

I wanted to hit myself over my own head when I thought of it. It was so obvious, staring me in the face, and I'd missed it like a train to Bologna.

I had to get to the police. I turned around to run to the station and saw a shadow loom up over my shoulder. Even before I felt the searing pain, I knew what it meant. I hugged my arms around myself to minimize the chances of broken ribs as I fell and was out cold before I'd even hit the pavement.

——— ❧ ———

Chapter Thirty-two

When I woke up, Bobby was hovering over me with a knife. I thought my eyes were blurry because he seemed kind of out of focus, but then I realized it was because his eyes were doing this weird rolling around thing, and he was sort of weaving back and forth. My wrists were taped together over my chest and he kept jabbing toward them with the knife. My feet, I discovered when I tried to move, were also taped together.

"I'm sorry, Jas," he said. "I think you could have made a better man out of me."

He rose up, holding the knife over his head like he was going to stab me through the heart.

I said, "Bobby, you don't—" but stopped as he came plummeting toward me. I rolled out of the way. The knife blade sliced into the floor. And stayed there, quivering. Bobby was passed out cold.

That's when I saw the hypodermic needle in his arm. And the murderer standing behind him.

"How sweet that he was trying to free you," she said. "He really did have his moments."

"Hi, Maria."

"Hi, Jas."

"Or do you prefer Beatrice?"

"Beatrice doesn't exist. I borrowed that name from the woman Dante wrote his *Divine Comedy* for. She's just a phantom, a nom du murder, if you like."

"Oh, yeah. That's nice." I tried to keep it light, conversational. "What did you do to Bobby?"

"It's only a tranquilizer. He'll wake up just in time, don't worry."

"In time for what?" I asked, although I wasn't sure I wanted to know. All I was sure of was that the longer I kept her talking, the longer I stayed alive.

"You'll find out." She looked at me carefully. "You're not just asking questions to buy yourself time in the hopes that your precious pals will come looking for you, are you? Because that would be completely pointless. They all think you're in class for another hour."

"The thought hadn't crossed my mind," I lied.

"I'm glad. I've been so looking forward to having a chat with you. Tell me, how long have you known?"

"That you were Maria? Or the killer?"

"Both. I want to know what I did wrong." She leaned toward me like she was really interested.

"Nothing, your crimes were perfect. If I hadn't refused to believe in Arabella's suicide, you would have gotten away with everything. But even when I proved it was murder, you still had a suspect all lined up."

"Max was easy prey. I would probably have had to kill him anyway, but him getting arrested is just as good. And it holds up so beautifully."

"You mean because he was obsessed with the Neals?"

"Precisely. I just wish—well, I know it's picky of me, but it would have been nice if you could have waited a little longer. I had it all planned for four fifteen when Max got home from work."

"I'd been wondering about the time. That was quick thinking on your part yesterday. You went to his apartment to plant the brooch, the gun, and the trophy you'd knocked me out with, didn't you? I bet that trophy used to sit on the dressing table here. Probably Arabella liked it because it reminded her of George."

"God, I wish we'd talked before. This is so fun. You're right, of course. I was at Max's to leave all that stuff, but you walked in before I could get away, so I pretended to be tied up."

"I bet you could have gotten away. I think you wanted to hear what we would say about your crimes."

Maria gave a little minx-like smile. "Maybe."

"Max's brother didn't commit suicide, did he? He died from drinking orange juice with ice you poisoned, hoping to kill Arabella, right?"

"You understood that? We're such a good team! You know, I've never felt as close to anyone before as I do to you. I feel like you really get me. You feel it too, right?"

Hello not-so-fresh feeling. "Sure."

"You're right, George wasn't supposed to die that night in London, it was supposed to be Arabella's turn. It seemed like the perfect psychological moment for it. You have to get that, the right moment, it's what makes the whole thing work, you know? She was depressed after her breakup, so no one would question it if she committed suicide. While they were fighting that night I poisoned her ice. But then she had to go and decide to make him breakfast."

"People mess up even the best plans."

"They do. That's why you have to stay flexible."

"Like the other night, after the ball, when we followed you. You hid in the water, didn't you?"

"Yes, I'd left my scuba gear at the end of that dead-end *calle*. I didn't expect anyone to come after me, but it's always important to be prepared."

"That's how you got into The House that Kills the night you did in Ned Neal too, right? You swam up to the dock and hid behind the planters so the security cameras wouldn't see you."

"Exactly. Then I climbed up the side of the house into my own office window and went down the hall to his door. No one suspected a thing."

"What was the psychological moment for Mr. Neal? Why kill him when you did?"

"That was a pity. I'd really hoped to keep him alive until his other children were dead, let him suffer a bit, and then do him in. But he started getting suspicious of me, asking questions. Nosing around at Prada about Maria Longhi. So he had to go."

"Is that how Arabella got on your trail, too?"

"No, she found those old articles by my mother and started bothering people."

"Your mother and Ned had an affair when he was here working on the Ca'Dario as an art student, right? And your mother got pregnant with you."

"And Ned abandoned us. Bastard."

"Lucien knew."

"Yes. Funny thing, he's disappeared."

That sent a chill down my spine. "Did you have something to do with that?"

"No. I'll have to hunt him down and kill him, of course. But that's later. How did you figure out that I was Ned Neal's illegitimate daughter?"

"I should have seen it earlier. One of the saleswomen from Prada called and asked me if Arabella was crazy. At first

I thought it was just because she did seem kind of nuts, but I realized she meant something else. I'd shown them a photo of Arabella that also had you in it. And they were wondering why Arabella was asking about you if she already knew you. Especially because Arabella had said there was a lot of money if she could find Maria Longhi. The saleswoman thought that meant a reward, but Arabella really meant inheritance. Because she was looking for another Neal heir. So I knew that Maria Longhi was Ned's daughter. The piece I missed originally was that she was you." I paused. "You didn't have to kill Arabella, you know. She would have shared the money with you."

"Who says I killed her? All the evidence points to suicide. No other possible explanation. They're waiting for Max to explain it, but of course we all know how that will end."

"I know how you did it. It was really smart."

"Tell me." Her eyes were glowing.

"Arabella didn't die on the bridge. You just wanted everyone to think she had. I realized it when I remembered that she'd told me she would be in disguise when she came to meet me. There was a wig in her armoire that I bet she was planning to wear. But since she wasn't wearing it when her body was found, that meant she was killed before she could change. You drowned her here, in her own bathtub. That's why she had water in her lungs. If the medical examiner had taken a sample, he would have seen that it didn't match the canal water. You stripped off the outfit she was wearing and because it was soaking wet you had to get rid of it, which is why it wasn't in the laundry hamper. Then you dressed her in a simple black outfit that would be easy to match."

"Go on."

"You dragged her from the bathtub and, using the tie from the curtains, lowered her body into a boat through the window. All the ruffles on the couch were pointing toward it— one of her feet must have dragged."

"I didn't even notice that!" she said, and clapped her hands like a little girl. "But if Arabella was killed here, how did everyone see her on the bridge right before the body was discovered?"

"You were wearing a nearly identical outfit, except you put on the brooch because you knew it would be identifiable. You parked the boat under the bridge, got out, and walked up and down a few times wearing the brooch to make sure you were seen, then went back to the boat, dumped the body, and took off."

"It sounds complicated."

"It was. And brilliant. You fooled everyone."

"Except you. I realized it yesterday when you said that there was too much evidence. I knew you'd figure it out eventually. And I couldn't take that chance."

"Why did you do all this?"

"To get what is mine. The Neal money."

"That's not the only reason. I mean, you planned this for ages. You worked for Ned Neal for a year."

Maria smiled then, a mischievous girly smile. "You're right. It was also fun."

"That's why you went from trying to scare me to trying to fool me?" I remembered something else then. "You were surprised when Bobby called you from outside of Prada and said I still wanted to come to dinner. You thought shooting at me would have frightened me off."

"I admit, I underestimated you, Jasmine. But after that I worked with you. To lead you, not fool you. I fed you little drops of evidence. It was so gratifying to watch you digest them."

"You're the one who sent me the magazine, aren't you? Because you wanted me to see the picture of George with Arabella in the article about her death. So I'd make the connection to Max after you'd so skillfully steered the conversation we had in Mr. Neal's office. You didn't even know I'd be interested in any other pictures."

"Guilty as charged!" she said with a girlish shrug.

"But you got lucky, too. There's no way you could have planned for me to test the inks on the different notes I'd gotten, but you'd had Max meet you at The House that Kills once—how did you do that, by the way?"

"I promised to put him in touch with Arabella. Easy."

"Of course. Anyway, he must have taken one of the pens with the custom ink while he was there, so the ink of his note matched the ink on the one you sent with the invitation to the ball. Your luckiest moment, though, was with the phone. You left it the day you knocked me out because you wanted to make sure there was evidence of your call that morning to Arabella, establishing that you thought she was still alive. But you couldn't have known that Max had tried calling her too, right before she died."

"That was a good break. It added a little something extra."

"And then the way you taunted me. That night in Ned's office you purposely pointed out that blue thread in front of me. That must have given you such a thrill."

"It did."

"So, what happens to me now?"

"Oh, I have something special in mind for you." She started walking around, like a director setting a scene. "You see, you and Bobby were having an affair. Naughty! You asked him to meet you here and he showed up, drunk, and told you he didn't want to see you again. He'd been discussing it with me and realized I was the woman for him."

"But you're his sister."

"Neither of us knew it at the time. That was what was going to precipitate his hopeless suicide in a few months, but

I had to move the timetable up a bit."

"The psychological moment."

"Exactly. You were upset and hit him over the head, but he managed to stab you fatally first. Don't worry, I'll give you a mild sedative for the pain before I use the knife."

"Thank you."

"No, thank you. You're a really great collaborator. Or should I say partner in crime?" She giggled. "Anyway, after realizing what he'd done, he stabbed himself as well. It will make exciting reading, murder–suicide, the last casualties of The House that Kills."

"Why do it here rather than at the house?"

"I don't want to get the rugs dirty. Besides, have you met the landlady here? She's a bitch. It'll be a pleasure to watch her try to rent this hovel again after something like this."

It sounded like a lovely way to go, but I wasn't quite ready yet, so I made my move. I *had* been trying to buy myself time, but not for the reason she thought. As we'd been talking I'd been working my left floatie down. Now I could just grasp it with the fingers of my right hand. I felt around for the two wires, said a small prayer to the smoke-bomb gods, and smushed them.

The smoke-plus-purple-spark light show that erupted from my arm, startled both of us with its size and majesty.

Maria leaped away from me and I leaped to my feet.

My throat was burning and I was coughing and my eyes were watering but I tried to hop to where I thought the door would be. Only I missed and fell onto the couch.

Maria was back then, now holding a syringe pointed at my throat with her left hand. She used her right hand to tape my palms and fingers together.

So much for tactical planning.

She was coughing too. "Don't do that again. I admire the effort, but . . ." She dragged me with her to the window so she could open it and air the room out, pressing me against the wall so I was immobile.

I took stock of the situation:

I had no hands.

I had no defense.

I had Miss Crazy holding a syringe to my neck.

Every time she coughed I was in danger of being jabbed by the syringe. Things did not look good. But they looked worse when she shoved my head out the window and said, "Take a last glance at Venice. It's a lovely city to die in."

That might have been true, but it was so not how I wanted to die. *Please,* I prayed silently, *if I make it through this, I promise to be the best, most Model Daughter in the world. I'll never make anyone upset, never give Dadzilla a moment of worry, never even call him Dadzilla, never have my name in the papers, never—*

It hit me. I was never going to get to kiss Jack again.

Three things happened at once:

I started to cry.

She plunged the syringe into my neck.

The shiny black cat with the green eyes came out of nowhere and leaped through the open window onto Maria's chest.

Little Life Lesson 64: Sometimes being attractive to cats isn't such a sucky superpower after all.

She was flung back, away from me, tripped over Bobby's body, and went down. Whatever she'd injected me with was starting to work and I felt more like a Weeble than a girl. The knife skidded across the floor away from Maria and as she got on her hands and knees to reach for it, I Weeble-wobbled over to her and sat down on her back.

Okay, more like fell on her back. But either way, she was pinned under six feet of Jas.

Little Life Lesson 65: Sometimes being tall isn't so sucky for detective work either.

That's when the fourth thing happened, in the form of Arabella's door bursting open and Officer Allegrini pushing into the room. Behind him were the landlady, Polly, Roxy, Tom, Alyson, and Veronique.

Polly said something that sounded like, "Your alarm went off!"

Roxy said something that sounded like, "We followed your Skittles trail!"

I said something that was supposed to sound like, "I have no idea what you're talking about."

And passed out.

Chapter Thirty-three

—— ❧ ——

When I opened my eyes I was still a bit groggy from whatever Maria had injected me with. I had vague, delirious images of white-coated men and hospital boats and a conversation I must have hallucinated about the NASCAR Dads coming to Venice to play a concert in Menudo's place. In fact, I was still hallucinating because I was in my bed in the Grissini Palace. But I could have sworn that the person sitting next to it was Jack.

"Hi, hot stuff," I told the hallucination.

He seemed to have been asleep, which was weird because why would a figment of my imagination sleep, but after my experiences with BadJas I wouldn't put anything past my brain.

He said, "Hi, super girl."

Since he was just a hallucination, I decided I could say pretty much anything I wanted to him. "You're really handsome."

"Thank you."

"How long have I been asleep?"

"Twenty-six hours."

"What happened to everyone?"

"Maria was arrested, Bobby is out of the hospital, and your friend Max was released."

"I owe him an apology for getting him arrested."

"I don't think you have to worry. He has a big crush on you."

"BadJas wanted to believe that, but I doubt it. He's nice. Not as nice as you, though." I feasted my eyes on Hallucination Jack. "The first time I saw you, all I could think about was how I wished you'd take your shirt off."

"Is that so?"

"Yeah, and I thought you might be The One. I still think that."

"Really."

"That's one reason I'm glad I didn't die. So I could find out. How did Roxy and Polly find me?"

"Roxy said something about putting a stroke monitor in your floatie. That it kept track of when you changed altitude, like when you fell down, and set off an alarm. I guess after you got knocked out twice, they thought it would be safest. And they installed some kind of pressure-sensitive Skittles dispenser in your boot in case you got dragged somewhere."

"My friends are crazy."

"Yes, they are."

"That's probably good, though."

"Yes, it is."

Hallucinations are really agreeable listeners. "Sometimes I dream that you and I are eating Nutella together in our Underoos. Yours are Incredible Hulk."

"Nutella, huh? I'll have to make a note of that."

"Please do."

"What else happens in these dreams?"

"Kissing mostly. Sometimes we eat ice cream. And you laugh at my jokes. And sometimes I ask you why you're with me instead of girls who can save whole orphanages."

"Do I tell you it's because you are the most courageous, most loyal, most exciting person I've ever met? And that just hearing your voice makes me smile?"

"No. Mostly you say you're not sure."

"I think I need someone to write better lines for me."

"Okay, I'll work on that."

I dozed off again. When I woke up, Hallucination Jack was still there. Now he was reading a magazine. "What's she like?" I asked.

"Who?"

"The girl you're making out with in that photo?"

"Rachel Tiegs? She's beautiful."

"Yeah, I got that."

"Would you let me finish, please? She's also incredibly dull. She once talked about her nail beds for five straight hours on the bus. And just to be clear, I'm not making out with her. You can see they Photoshopped my head onto some other guy's body. I'd never wear those jeans."

"That's what Polly said."

"I'll have to remember to thank her."

"I thought it was you."

"Jas, why would I want someone else when I could have you?"

I think I started to cry then.

"What's wrong, super girl?"

"I wish you were real and not just a hallucination."

"Hmm. What if I told you I *am* real?"

"Ha ha ha. If you were real, I'd never be saying all these things to you."

He started to laugh and reached out and put his hand on my palm. "I have bad news for you, Jas."

But I barely heard that last part because my body was reeling from the sensation of his fingers entwined with mine. Real fingers. Which could only mean—

Oh.

My.

God.

Jack was here. Sitting by my bed.

AND I'D—

Oh. Oh, no.

He leaned toward me. "What's wrong now?"

"I told you I fantasized about you in Incredible Hulk Underoos," I said, mostly into my pillow.

He gave his amazing, makes-my-knees-melt laugh. "Yeah,

about that." He moved over to sit on the side of my bed and cupped my cheek in his hand. "I don't have any with me. But we could certainly work on the other part of your dream before your dad comes back to check on you."

"Which part?"

"This part," he said. And kissed me.

Little Life Lesson 66: Maybe there is no such thing as happily ever after. But there's definitely happy.[50]

<hr/>

[50] Jas: Agreed?
    BadJas: Agreed.

To: Jasmine Callihan <Jasmine.Callihan@westborough.edu>
From: Office of the College Counselor
<James.Lansdowne@westborough.edu>
Subject: Your latest

Dear Miss Callihan,

"My Friend Arabella" is a moving and lovely essay. The moral about learning to trust yourself and others is excellent, although perhaps somewhat undermined by the inclusion of the giant crime-fighting squirrel.

We are all very glad to have you backo. Ha ha.

Yours,
Dr. L

P.S. What do you mean by "Does being a consultant to a foreign police force count as an extracurricular activity or as work experience?"

To: Jasmine Callihan <Drumgrrrl@hotmail.com>
From: MaxAttack <MaxGondolier@hotmail.com>
Subject: Re: La Dolce Vita

Jasmine Noelle,

It is very nice to get your email. You must excuse the quality of my writing English, I perhaps should have studied more.

You are right that at my apartment at first I think you are the murderer. But then I see Beatrice and I know the truth. It is my wish to get you out of there but you were, if you will pardon me saying so, a big troublesome so I had to take fierce measures. I did not learn the move I performed on you from the Special Forces. It is something my brother and I practiced from watching the American show *World Wrestling Entertainment.* I am delighted it impressed you, however.

While on the topic of my brother, thank you very much for telling me about his death. Indeed, knowing he did not take his life does make it better. And knowing that the one who did is behind bars improves it even more. Everyone here thinks you are the TNT for catching her when the police could not.

I felt very honored to collect your honorary medal from the *carabinieri,* although I cannot agree with you that I deserve it more just because you kicked me on the head. Being hit on the head by lovely ladies is part of what Max does. Since you say your father will not let you have it I will be happy to keep it for you.

So yes, everything is fine now. Actually, I lie. Venice is much less robust without you in it.

I shall miss seeing your face but I am sending you all the best wishes.

Your friend,
Max

P.S. Should you ever be in Venice again I do not think I mentioned but I can also do many interesting card tricks.

To: Jasmine Callihan <Drumgrrrl@hotmail.com>
From: J.R. <JR_211@hotmail.com>
Subject: Welcome back

I'm glad the name Smokey LeBraun came in handy. I'll be interested to see what you do with what you learn about him.
Good luck. I'll be watching.

A friend